"You are the darnedest woman, Linnea Holmstrom."

He sounded angry; he sounded amused. "Is there a chance now that you'll invite me in for a cup of tea or something?"

"Not a chance on this earth." She left him standing in the yard, bathed in moonlight, looking as confused as she felt.

She'd been mean to him. It weighed on her conscience as she bolted the front door. Maybe that would stop him from coming back to the door and knocking. Trying to get the kiss she'd denied him tonight.

But she sat at the window and peered through the night shadows. She spotted him against the dark night. He walked home, his head bowed, his hat in his hands.

She'd hurt him. When she'd only meant to keep a proper distance between them. She'd done the right thing, but it didn't feel that way. Not one bit...

Praise for Jillian Hart's previous work

Montana Man
"…a great read!"
—*Rendezvous*

Cooper's Wife
"…a wonderfully written romance
full of love and laughter."
—*Rendezvous*

Last Chance Bride
"The warm and gentle humanity
of *Last Chance Bride* is a welcome dose of sunshine…"
—*Romantic Times Magazine*

Jillian Hart

Bluebonnet BRIDE

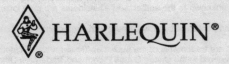

HARLEQUIN®

TORONTO • NEW YORK • LONDON
AMSTERDAM • PARIS • SYDNEY • HAMBURG
STOCKHOLM • ATHENS • TOKYO • MILAN • MADRID
PRAGUE • WARSAW • BUDAPEST • AUCKLAND

ISBN 0-373-29186-8

BLUEBONNET BRIDE

Copyright © 2001 by Jill Strickler

This edition published by arrangement with Harlequin Books S.A.

Visit us at www.eHarlequin.com

Printed in U.S.A.

Please address questions and book requests to:
Harlequin Reader Service
U.S.: 3010 Walden Ave., P.O. Box 1325, Buffalo, NY 14269
Canadian: P.O. Box 609, Fort Erie, Ont. L2A 5X3

Chapter One

Montana Territory, 1888

"*Dotter,* is that you?"

"Yes, Mama, I'm here." Linnea crossed through the dim splash of light from the crystal lamp, the tap of her shoes on the bare wood echoing in the dark corners of the room. "I thought you'd be fast asleep by now."

"Much troubles an old woman's dreams." Her mother stirred against her pillows, her sightless eyes fixed upon the ceiling overhead. "Come, tell me why you are not climbing in beside me."

"I'll be there soon enough."

"What? You are not ready for bed? You work too hard, my child."

"Mama, I do not work hard enough." Linnea knelt, and the handle of the trundle bed still tucked safely away nudged her in the knee. "Are you thirsty? Can I fetch you a glass of water?"

"No. I am only lonely on this cold winter's night."

Linnea brushed her hand across her mother's cool fingers. "Let me fetch another quilt."

"You should be taking care of your own husband and family instead of fussing after me."

Linnea's step faltered. An ache, so sharp it stole her breath, twisted in her chest. The brief images snapped to life, images of a little girl playing with toys before a crackling fire—only dreams. Only dreams a spinster like her had no right to cling to.

She tugged down the bundle of soft flannel and laid the warm log-cabin quilt gently over her mother's frail form. "This will keep you toasty."

"You're a good girl, Linnea." Bony fingers caught hers and squeezed with a lifetime of love.

"Not so good, Mama." She stepped away, her chest tight, and drew the door closed behind her.

The empty shanty echoed with each rustle of her skirts and sound of her shoe against the wood floor. Linnea closed her father's book and laid it on the small table next to her rocking chair.

Maybe it was the way the wind whispered at the eaves and the dying fire snapped and popped in protest, but tonight the cozy room felt forlorn and so very empty. She grabbed her wool shawl from the peg and slipped out the front door.

Frigid night air struck her face, icy and sharp, and knifed through her layers of flannel and wool. She dashed down the steps, shivering. Ice cracked beneath her shoes and frozen snow crunched, shattering the night's stillness.

The Montana high prairie lay wrapped in silence and the deepest shadows. No dusting of starlight sheened on the miles of black snow. Thick clouds gathered overhead, hiding the proud white moon, signaling a coming storm.

Yes, the air smelled like snow. Would it be enough to keep her from her trip to town in the morning? She'd looked forward to going all week. Maybe, *maybe,* the storm would hold off.

She'd been alone on the homestead for a fortnight now, with only her mother's company. *Best not to wish for too much, Linnea.* Unlike the stars hiding behind the clouds this night, wishes had a way of falling to the ground, broken and spent.

Frigid air burned in her chest as she knelt before the woodpile. Behind her, the slim crack of light from inside the shanty cast diffuse shadows, not enough to light her way. She stacked the wood in her left arm by feel. The split pine was rough against her fingers and a sliver bit into the pad of her thumb. The loneliness of the night enveloped her. The wind whipped with a keen sorrow, and there were no other sounds on the vast prairie that stretched unseen but not unfelt.

She straightened, taking her time, even though the cold breeze knifed through her clothes, chilling her from skin to bone. There was a beauty to the solitude, a reverence in the night. She breathed it in, glad for this private time before duty beckoned her once more.

Her teeth chattered and she turned toward the light and warmth of the house. The snow crunched beneath her shoes. Her toes had cleared the first ice-crusted porch step when she heard a faint drum on the horizon. Like thunder, it grew in volume as it approached, echoing sharply across the endless plains.

Was it them? It had to be. Linnea bent to let the bundle of wood roll from her arms to the swept-clean porch floor. She turned, heart hammering, running across the slick, frosted surface of the snow as fast as she dared.

The barn loomed like a great hulking beast in the night, and she dashed around the straw stacks, great humps covered with shadowed snow. She turned toward the east holding her breath. There was no sign of them, but they had to be close—she could hear them.

The night kept the wild horses cloaked, shrouded like a secret on this solemn midnight hour. The rumble of unshod hooves on the hard prairie reverberated with an off-rhythm music that lured her north, toward the darkest edge of the horizon where not even shadows lurked.

There they are. Like phantoms, they ran across the face of the night, dark manes and tails snapping behind them. Like unearthly creatures, they wheeled as a group, fluid as shadow, and thundered straight toward her.

Untamed power and grace, they sailed over the fence rails and ran again, like thunder and storm, shaking the ground beneath her feet. Then the stallion lifted his head high and trumpeted, and the herd of mares skidded to a halt.

The only sound Linnea could hear was her heart knocking in her ears. She stood trembling, spellbound, the cold and fatigue forgotten. The wild mustangs pawed through the thick mantle of frozen snow to the dry hay beneath.

She'd worked hard last summer to cut that hay, but her outrage was nothing compared to the privilege of watching them. Such beauty. What would it feel like to run free like that? As fast as you could across the untamed prairie?

The stallion lifted his head, magnificent as he scented the wind. Then he whinnied and the mares headed off across the barren fields. Immense, graceful, mesmerizing, the wild horses galloped closer.

Why, they hardly touched the ground. It stole her breath just watching as the mares soared by, a parade of raw power just barely earthbound. The stallion followed, ears pinned back and nostrils flaring, muscles and tendons straining.

The majestic sight left her breathless. She watched them fade back into the veil of darkness, becoming part of the night once more. Their thundering hooves grew faint until there was only the suggestion of it. She turned, straining her eyes and ears, but there was only silence.

And the *whoof* of surprise as a horse snorted behind her, steeled shoes sidestepping rapidly on the snow's frozen surface.

"Whoa, there," a molasses-smooth male voice rumbled, both soothing and powerful. "Ma'am, are you aware this is a road?"

She whirled out of the way, suddenly realizing how foolish she seemed, staring after a dream, a grown woman like her. No, not just a grown woman, but a spinster and no green, daydreaming girl.

She bowed her head, keeping to the shadows. "I'm sorry I startled your horse."

"Were you watching them?"

"The mustangs?" She took a step closer to the barn. She shouldn't be out alone in the night talking to a complete stranger. "Why, yes—"

"They're beautiful, aren't they? I've been following them all the way from the river. Been as close to them as a quarter mile. Takes my breath away just looking at them.''

His voice was rich and as smooth as a fine velveteen ribbon, fluid and graceful in a masculine way. A flicker of alarm twisted through her, and she stepped closer to the house. No matter how wonderful his voice, this man was a stranger, and she was alone with him and unprotected.

The beauty of the dreaming gone, the horses lost to her in the night and the vast Montana prairie, she turned, hurrying toward the house.

''You don't need to be afraid of me. Some say I'm harmless enough.'' Warmth laced his voice, and she couldn't help turning.

It was too dark to see anything but the faintest outline of a solid man. His shoulders were wide and his arms relaxed, the tip of his hat was high and proud, his profile ruggedly cut.

''I don't mean to be rude.'' She stopped in the middle of the yard, instead of scurrying for the house. Iron County was a safe, neighborly place, but it wasn't immune to trouble. ''I have to go—''

''The wild horses. Do they come here often?''

He asked the one question she could not turn her back on. She lingered in the shadows, safe enough for a few more words, and then she would leave. ''They feed on the hay and grain left for the cattle. They're regular visitors this time of year.''

''I'd wager the local ranchers don't take kindly to that.''

''No, they don't. But I don't mind. They're so grand I can't seem to summon up enough fury to chase them off.''

''You love horses, then.''

"I know little about them. I just know there's a majesty when they're racing across the horizon." Just like she wanted to do.

Heart yearning, she turned away, embarrassment gathering like shadows inside her. Who was she to have secret longings? Secret dreams? She'd wasted them once and had no right to more.

She headed toward the house before she could regret talking to a strange man in the road.

"That's how I feel, too." His words called her back, so genuine and sincere she nearly missed a step.

The man on the horse couldn't see her. Couldn't see she was nothing but ordinary, nothing but a plain woman with lines on her face and spent dreams. He probably thought he was talking with someone younger, which was why he lingered in the frigid shadows.

"Good night." She spoke the words so there would be no more conversation. No more quiet inquiries to lure her from the shadows.

Besides, she had wood to stack, the ashes to bank and water to draw for the morning's work. Inside, Mama waited, sleepless and alone.

Linnea retreated to the porch, where light poured in a slim line across the jumble of spilled wood. She knelt and filled her arms, working quickly, hearing the slow step of steeled horseshoes on the iced snow, then silence. Leather creaked. Was he watching her?

She peeked over her shoulder and her heart tumbled. Yes, he watched, straight and strong in his saddle, his hat at a dignified tilt, his presence more substantial than shadow.

The foolish part of her, the part that would not quit dreaming, wondered what he would look like by day.

Would he have black hair or brown? Blue eyes or hazel? Would his complexion be fair or bronzed?

But the sensible part of her, the one ruled by duty, did not wonder and did not wish. She reached for the last stick of wood and stood, skirts rustling, and hurried into the house.

When she shut the door and barred it tight, her heart was still beating, still thundering in her ears. Out of breath and trembling, she leaned against the stout wood walls and couldn't shake the feeling he was still watching and waiting.

She pulled back the edge of the curtain. The shadowed man and horse remained motionless in the middle of the road. She let the curtain fall and did not dream. Not even in the loneliest hour of the night as she banked the embers, each movement echoing in the empty rooms.

Not even when she finally lay down to sleep in the narrow trundle bed, tucked beneath the quilt she'd made long ago, stitched with love and a young woman's hope.

She closed her eyes and slept, and not even then did she dream.

Seth Gatlin gritted his teeth against the ache in his legs and back from riding all day and half the night in the bitter cold and stumbled up the porch steps.

His stepsister's house was in sad need of attention. He could tell this even in the dark. The eaves beneath the door were damaged, as if the roof had been leaking over time. The porch boards sagged beneath his weight.

The house was dark and quiet. The boy would be asleep. He lifted his hand and debated knocking.

As if in answer to his uncertainty, the door creaked open, the hinges in desperate need of oil.

"Ginny?" he asked. "Is that you standing in the dark?"

"I was listening for your horse in the driveway." She eased back into the shadows of a room, faintly lit by a new fire. Bright flames crackled greedily in the grate on the wall behind her. "I figured you'd be frozen clear through, what with that wind out there. I put some stew on to warm. Come, sit by the fire."

"You don't need to wait on me." He tried to keep the bristle from his voice as he stepped inside and shut the door.

"I don't mind. You came all the way from Fort Benton in this cold, just to help me." Her fingers brushed his jacket's collar as she tried to help him out of his coat.

Surprised, he let her take the garment, and she hung it with care by the mantel. His chest tightened with the gesture. Their family had been a fractured one, chaotic and filled with hurt. He'd taken off the first chance he had and never looked back. Maybe he'd been wrong not to keep better track of his stepsisters.

"Here, this is the warmest chair in the house. I know it isn't much. I miss the house I had in town." Ginny placed her hands on the back of an upholstered overstuffed chair next to the hearth. "You sit here and I'll bring your plate. Do you take coffee or tea?"

"I don't mind fixing my own."

"Nonsense. Sit right down there by the fire and let me make myself useful." Ginny's gaze met his and he saw the grief there and the shadows.

She looked like a ghost with hollowed eyes and gaunt cheeks sunken in beneath prominent cheekbones. Sadness made her once-beautiful face haggard, and worry had drawn lines around her once always-smiling mouth.

Stunned to see her this way, he didn't argue as she scurried away, her movements nothing more than a whisper in the dark recesses of the kitchen.

What had happened to her? She'd written only of her son in her obligatory Christmas letters and of the home she kept in town. He'd thought little of it— they'd never been close, and even that much contact, a yearly letter, was more than he received from his other stepsisters.

He thought of his mother, browbeaten and broken by a man—Ginny's father—who'd vowed to cherish her, and anger gathered like a hard fist in his abdomen.

"Here you are." Ginny swept back into the room, a tray prepared with everything he might need—flatware, honey, butter and jam, thick slices of fragrant bread and a big bowl of steaming stew. "I just put the coffee on. It should be ready in a moment."

She looked nervous, and he hated that. "I told you, you don't need to wait on me. Sit down and help me eat some of this bread. I swear, I haven't seen such good-looking food in a long time."

Not since he'd had his own home and a wife to cook for him.

"I'm a passable cook." Ginny slipped onto the edge of the horsehair sofa, biting her bottom lip anxiously. "Do you like the stew?"

"It's good and tasty." It was, but it troubled him she would worry about pleasing him. "We're family, Ginny, even though we're strangers. I gave you my word I would help you, and I mean it. I'm not going to change my mind if I don't like your cooking.''

"Thank you." She breathed the words, her relief bright in the dark room.

"Who lives down the way from you? The little ranch with the barn by the road?"

"Oh, the Holmstroms." Her voice became tight. "It's just the old woman and her daughter now. They're good enough tenants, quiet, keep to themselves. Although I'm not happy having them for neighbors."

There was dislike in Ginny's voice. He wondered at that. "It must have been the daughter I saw tonight. She was out watching the wild horses in the fields. They were a beautiful sight."

"A nuisance. I lost half my winter's feed to those creatures." Ginny sounded bitter and turned her face. "Linnea must have been doing chores."

"I suppose." He remembered the wood she'd gathered from the porch, lithe and graceful even performing a mundane chore. He was a man and couldn't help noticing a woman's beauty. "Then you know her."

"It's best to keep away from her." Ginny's mouth narrowed into a harsh line. "That woman has caused nothing but trouble in this family."

He didn't know what to think, but he remembered the woman's voice, dulcet and wistful, hesitant and wary. She did not seem like a troublemaker, but then Ginny's warning didn't matter. Not truly.

His heart had long been buried with three caskets in a graveyard outside of Miles City. His time for loving a woman was past and would never be again.

"I made up a room for you in the attic like you asked." Ginny broke quietly through his thoughts.

"I'm not sure if that's acceptable. I'll be happy to trade you—"

"The attic is fine." He tried to keep the anger from his voice and failed. He could see that by the way Ginny's shoulders hunched just a little.

"I don't need any special treatment," he told her, gentling his voice. "You don't have to be afraid of my temper, Ginny. I'm not your father and I'm not your husband."

"I know." She smiled up at him with tears in her eyes.

Need. It tugged at him, when he'd worked so hard to cut all ties to his heart. Like winter, he wanted a thick mantle of ice and snow to protect him from feelings too painful to face.

So he grabbed his saddlebags with one hand and carried the tray to the kitchen with the other, refusing Ginny's assistance. He bade her good-night and climbed the narrow ladder up into the dark. The bed was comfortable, the best he'd had in a long while.

He slept and dreamed of wild horses and the woman who watched them, her unbound hair waving in the wind.

Chapter Two

Snow fell from sky to earth in heavy, wet flakes. The wind shaking the cottonwoods and pines and creeping beneath the doors didn't feel quite as frigid, a sign that winter would soon be over. But that was little consolation as Linnea stood at the kitchen window, debating.

Did she want to break a path all the way to town? They had no horses, sold long ago to pay for her father's burial. Maybe, if the snow stopped falling, she could manage it.

"Linnea, wishful thinking will not alter the weather," Mama commented, voice warm with love and brittle with age. "I can feel the spring in the air, even though I know it is snowing."

"How do you know?"

"I can hear the hush. Now come here. You eat too little and work too hard. You are nothing but skin and bones. Finish your breakfast and tell me. Do you think you will get good wages for the shirts?"

"Mrs. McIntyre said she will always pay for men's shirts." Linnea tried not to let her weariness show.

She loved making beauty with fabric and thread,

but the mundane sewing of the same practical garments over the years had drained the joy from her art. Still, she needed the money to support them. Without it they would be destitute, with no way to pay for the roof over their heads. No, the practical sewing was necessary.

Maybe today she would gather enough courage to try to make a change.

"Those McIntyres. They do not pay you well enough for your work." Mama blew on her morning coffee to cool it. "They take advantage of you. How it angers me."

"They are the only ones in town who will pay." Since a dressmaker had moved to Bluebonnet last year, she'd had a harder time. The surrounding area was small and the demand for ready-made clothes even smaller. "Unless I wish to find work in town—"

"No girl of mine will wait on tables."

An old argument. She would make better money, but that would leave her mother alone all day, blind and in fragile health. "I never said that's what I intended."

She would put it off as long as she could, for Mama's sake.

"The snow is stopping." Turning her blind eyes toward the window, she set down her cup neat as a pin in the saucer. "Good. Now you can go. I know you've been hoping for a trip to town."

"Just to sell the shirts and to do a little shopping." She gathered the empty plates and stood. She would not think about what she planned to do today or her stomach would twist into knots. "Would you like anything from the mercantile?"

"You know I need for nothing as long as my

daughter is with me.'' A lifetime of love shone in her eyes, a beautiful bluebonnet blue. ''You go on ahead and leave me to do the dishes. I am not helpless.''

''But they're mine to do.'' Linnea emptied hot water from the reservoir and filled the washbasin. ''Let me pour you a second cup of coffee—''

''Do what your mother orders.'' Older hands covered hers and squeezed gently. ''Go to town, sell your shirts and buy some little luxury for yourself, dear *flicka*.''

''But I need for nothing, for I have you.''

''Ah, you are my heart. Now hurry and listen to your mother. Do not forget something nice for yourself. I wish to see it when you return.''

Linnea hurried to wrap the waiting shirts, neatly starched and folded, in an oiled canvas to keep out the snow as she'd done all winter and for many winters before.

Heart pounding, she laid the shirts over her most recent quilt, carefully hand-stitched with white on white in a rose design, the alternating blocks a bright splash of wild calico roses, appliquéd through long evenings before the warmth of the fire.

Maybe Mrs. McIntyre would like the quilt. Maybe she would place it on consignment in her store. What if she would buy it outright? It could lead to more work, something more interesting than the endless fitting of shirtsleeves and interfaced collars.

''There, now, are you dressed warmly enough?'' Mama's fingers fluttered over Linnea's ears and throat. ''Tie that scarf tight, dear. The last thing you need is to catch a touch of quinsy.''

''I'm not five years old.'' She almost laughed, that was how happy she felt. ''The wood bins are brimming full, and I've left a sandwich covered on the counter. You'll be all right while I'm gone?''

''I am able to care for myself, *dotter*.'' Mama's kiss brushed light and sweet on Linnea's cheek. ''Now go and have fun in town.''

She hated leaving her alone, but the walk through the snow was too difficult for the old woman. Maybe the snow wouldn't last much longer. Linnea tipped her head back to study the heavy charcoal clouds above. It was a warmer sky than it had been only yesterday.

That thought brought another touch of happiness to her heart. She didn't mind wading through the new foot of snow along the pristine road. Her boots squeaking and crunching seemed like the only sounds in the bright white world.

As she struggled along, she watched pine boughs laden with heavy snow shake tiny clods of white from their green needles. Split wood fences seemed to will the narrow stands of snow from their top rails. The river, frozen to all but the very center, sent a current of water to chip away at the encroaching ice. It was a beautiful morning.

Then she heard the squeak of a sleigh's runners on fresh snow and the muted clomp of steeled hooves on the road behind her. She tensed, going through a list of who might be passing by her. The Neilsons, the Hanssons, the Schwartzes, or Ginny McIntyre—all of whom she dreaded meeting on the road.

She straightened her spine and prepared to meet her neighbors, determined not to look down this time, not to be intimidated.

The clomp and squeak grew louder, closer. She saw the sheen of a beautiful black horse, far grander than any she'd seen before. None of her neighbors owned such a fine animal, not even Ginny McIntyre.

"Whoa, boy." A voice deep as midnight, rich as satin, more masculine than she'd ever known rumbled behind her.

And she knew it was the man from last night. The starch drained from her spine and a panic set her pulse to racing. Not only because he was a stranger, but also because she wasn't prepared for this.

Going to town took a certain kind of courage and had ever since her reputation had been ruined beyond repair, ever since her actions had been the cause of her dear father's death.

"Would you like a ride to town?" that wonderful deep voice asked.

"No, thank you," she said calmly, taking another step, refusing to look to her side, where he sat in a sleigh, holding the reins in broad, gloved hands.

She didn't dare look at his face. He was probably handsome and young and strong. He was no man for her, that was for sure. She eyed the embankment and wished the endless row of split rail fencing didn't hem her in.

To be seen unchaperoned with a man again... Her chest squeezed so tight she couldn't breathe. No, she could not go through that humiliation one more time.

But his horse and sleigh kept pace with her as she walked. She could feel his gaze, feel his questions.

She walked faster.

"My name is Seth Gatlin."

She couldn't resist the urge to turn and look. To see the man who belonged to that voice. She nearly stumbled.

Why, he wasn't a striking man, not handsome in a

traditional way. But he *was* pleasant-looking. No, more than that. He was impressive with a dark shock of hair tumbling over his brow and lines carved into a face browned by the sun, even in the last weeks of winter.

"Since I'm new to town, do me a favor and ride with me." He didn't quite grin, but there was a hint of sparkles in his eyes as he considered her. "I need to find the hardware store and don't know where to look. You could show me."

"Try Front Street. You'll recognize it by all the tall storefronts and the traffic."

"You're a big help." A hint of a grin touched his straight mouth.

"Bluebonnet is a small town. You won't need directions to find your way."

"I was using it as an excuse. Can't ride on and leave you here struggling through all this snow." He sounded kind in the reassuring masculine way that a woman dreamed of. "I try to be a gentleman when I can, so you don't need to worry about bad behavior on my part."

She kept walking. Just like last night when she shouldn't have said a single word, she wanted to answer. "You're telling me that you're not a scoundrel."

"That's right. Women in need of rides to town are always perfectly safe in my sleigh."

"I don't even know you."

"I don't know you, but I'm willing to risk offering you a ride."

"The risk is not the same for a man."

"True, but I'm a gentleman, remember?"

"You said you *tried* to be." Linnea felt his warm

steadiness and some of her uneasiness faded. He was new to the area, and he didn't know anything about her. That didn't mean she should even consider…

No, he was just being kind. Offering her a ride to town was a polite gesture. It spoke well of him, for she could name any number of her neighbors who would not do the same.

"That's quite a load you're carrying."

"And I'll carry it all the way to town." She kept glancing at him, her soft oval face framed by her gray hood.

She looked like a winter bird, dark and colorless against the snowbound world, fragile and easily startled.

"You're telling me that you won't accept a ride from a stranger, is that it? But I'm your neighbor."

She flashed him a warning look, like one a schoolteacher might give a misbehaving student. She was strong, he could see that in the firm cut of her jaw. But she was kind, too. It shone in her eyes deep and true, and he couldn't help looking twice.

She halted in the road, her heavy and bulky package held tight in both slim arms. "Are you the Hanssons' new hand?"

"No. Helping out my sister. Ginny McIntyre."

"Oh, I see." The bright gleam in her eyes faded. She took a step back, graceful as the breeze. "I really can't accept a ride. Good luck finding your way to town."

"I said the wrong thing."

"No. Good day to you."

She turned and kept walking. He didn't know what to do. He just might follow her to town, to make sure she arrived safely.

But then, she didn't appear to want his protection. She didn't turn to look at him as she waded through the wet snow, her bundle awkward in her arms.

She probably looked at him and saw a man worn of heart and too old for her. She was young and feminine, her face as soft-looking as white silk.

He didn't know why he kept watching her. She just reminded him of a time when he didn't feel so hopeless. When he lived for the sight of another woman's smile.

Just lonely, he supposed. And he couldn't help wondering at the stiff set of her spine. There was a reserve to her, as if she were far too used to protecting herself.

That was what drew him, he realized. He recognized a kindred soul when he saw one.

His sister's words came to mind, warning him away. A troublemaker, she'd called this woman with the curls of sunshine peeking beneath her dull gray hood and eyes the color of bluebonnets.

Trouble came in all different sorts, but Seth would bet good money Linnea Holmstrom had known trouble rather than caused it in her short life. And he knew that kind of burden, too.

He drove past her, slowly. If she so much as moved a finger he would stop, but she stared hard at the ground over her burdensome package.

He sensed pushing her any further would only upset her, so he rode on but didn't stop wondering about the woman he'd left behind.

Linnea recognized Seth Gatlin's horse and sleigh tethered in front of the hardware store. The back of the vehicle was already loaded with bright honey-gold lumber. She tried not to look, but her gaze kept sliding across the street. He'd been kind to her today, nothing more.

Still, a part of her kept hearing the rum-smooth tone of his voice and remembering the faint glimmer of his grin.

The sun broke through the clouds and it felt almost balmy as she crossed the slushy street to the mercantile.

McIntyre's was crowded with shoppers. The noise of conversations and the jangle of the bell on the door sounded unnaturally loud after her quiet walk to town.

As soon as she pushed through the door, she saw Mrs. McIntyre's nod and went to the back counter to wait. All the clerks were busy, including those at the yard goods counter where several women stood in line talking about the latest spring fashions in *Godey's* and did not make eye contact.

Linnea stood to the side and studied the colorful array of threads. The bundle in her arms no longer felt heavy as she hugged it tight.

What if Mrs. McIntyre liked her idea? That would mean the chance to start on her next project right away. Something in shades of blue, perhaps, with greens and yellows.

"Miss Holmstrom." Mrs. McIntyre nodded, terse as always. "Show me what you brought."

With trembling fingers, Linnea unwrapped the dozen shirts. They would only bring a few dollars apiece, but they were well made, she saw to that. She laid each work shirt on the counter, smoothing the wrinkles out of the cotton. New buttons gleamed in the lamplight.

"Fine work, as always." Her mouth pursed into a

hard line and she didn't make contact, although that she accepted the work was praise enough. The woman turned, already walking away. "I'll take all of them, and another dozen the first of next month."

"Mrs. McIntyre." Linnea took a deep breath. "I wanted to ask you to take a look at this."

She rolled back the canvas, exposing the snowy white cotton to the light. She could hear the women in line silence as a multihued appliquéd rose appeared.

Heart pounding, she caught the merchant's gaze. "This quilt drapes a double bed."

Mrs. McIntyre's heels rang on the floorboards as she approached. There was a sparkle of interest in her hard brown eyes, but her mouth remained an unforgiving narrow line. She paused at the counter's edge and ran a thumb over the precise stitching.

Seconds ticked by. Linnea endured the store owner's silence and the heat of the women's gazes. She tried not to notice, not to remember the past.

She watched a muscle jump in Mrs. McIntyre's throat. *She's going to say no.*

"This is fine work, Linnea."

"You like it?" Hope soared in her chest. "I would be willing to offer the quilt on consignment if you'd rather."

Seconds stretched forever. Linnea couldn't hear anything over the rush of her pulse in her ears. Mrs. McIntyre's gaze didn't stray from the quilt. Maybe she really was going to take it.

"I'm afraid I just can't." Those unforgiving eyes showed a brief, surprising gleam of apology. "Considering our past, be grateful I purchase what I do from you. Mrs. Johanson was in here just last week, swearing she could do better work and for cheaper, too.''

"I see." It took all her courage to face the woman now. "Thank you for your time, Mrs. McIntyre."

The woman's mouth drew tighter and she turned without a word. Linnea vowed not to remember the past, not to feel it heavy and condemning on her back as she wrapped the quilt. Her fingers shook, and she hated that her feelings showed so easily. The store remained silent, the women in line watching her.

The eldest McIntyre girl at the front, tallying up a purchase, slipped an envelope across the counter to her. The quiet measure in her eyes was one of sympathy. Once she and Shannon had been best friends in school, but their friendship had been broken long ago, even if the memories from better times remained.

"These are fine shirts, ma'am," a man's voice rumbled, not louder than the other voices in the store, but distinct and familiar. "I'll take a half dozen."

"You're Ginny's brother, the major."

"That's right, ma'am."

Linnea could see the impressive line of Seth Gatlin's shoulders above the shelves of canned goods. His hat was off, revealing dark-brown, almost black, hair that matched the intelligent blue intensity of his eyes.

"I'd like to buy more of those shirts, but I don't want to take all of your stock."

"I could always order more if you need them, Major." Mrs. McIntyre sounded eager to please.

"I'd appreciate that, ma'am. I just left the army and I don't have enough civilian clothes."

Over the gleaming tops of canned pears, his gaze caught Linnea's in a brief, snapping connection. The noises in the store faded, the lamplight dimmed and for that one second there was only the hint of his smile.

She *knew*. He'd heard how Mrs. McIntyre had treated her, and he was buying every one of her shirts.

Her chest warmed, for it felt good to have a champion. Not that she needed one or deserved one. Not that he was doing anything more than being polite. And she knew, in time, that politeness wouldn't last. She'd do better by not counting on it.

"I'll take another dozen shirts as soon as you can manage it." Mrs. McIntyre caught Linnea in the aisle. "But you and I will need to renegotiate the price."

It looked like the extra threads she'd been eyeing would have to wait. Linnea chose several skeins of fine blue wool as a treat for her mother.

Once, she caught sight of Seth Gatlin standing in line to pay for every last one of her shirts. Smiling to herself, she lingered at the yard goods counter to avoid standing behind him. She wanted to thank him but not here, where everyone might notice.

"Miss Holmstrom?" A handsome woman dressed in the latest fashion appeared quietly at her elbow, the town's dressmaker. "If you would like to bring your quilt by my shop today before you head home, I would be interested in seeing it."

Linnea thought of all the beautiful dresses and hats on display in the dressmaker's front window. "You make everything you sell, don't you? Why would you want to see my quilt?"

"Because I sew a lot of wedding dresses, and I believe any bride-to-be who sees a quilt like yours will want it for her wedding bed." The woman smiled and pressed a calling card into Linnea's cloak pocket. "If you can't come today, then come anytime."

Linnea opened her mouth, but no words of thanks emerged. She watched, disbelieving, as the woman turned away and bypassed Seth Gatlin at the counter. The bell rang, and the door closed.

Could it really be true? Linnea didn't dare hope, but a part of her couldn't help it. Across the store, Seth Gatlin gave her a nod, and his blue gaze flickered acknowledgment. Then he reached for his billfold, while the McIntyres' oldest daughter offered him a beaming smile.

An army major. Linnea should have known. There was a quiet dignity to him, of control and carefully leashed power. Not that she had the right to be looking and noticing.

She spun away, heart pounding, and considered the racks of colorful threads and flosses. Today she would take time and plan her next quilt. Later she would come back and buy some of those colors.

Maybe her luck was starting to turn.

Chapter Three

"**W**here's your quilt?" a voice—his voice—broke through her thoughts.

Linnea skidded to a stop in the melting snow, nearly dropping her packages. Seth Gatlin tipped his hat to her from the front seat of his sleigh.

Goodness, she'd been so lost in her plans she hadn't heard him approach. "It's on display in Mrs. Jance's shop. She thinks she can sell it."

"Congratulations."

"I can't count my pennies until it's sold." Linnea tried hard not to notice how pleasant-looking he was. The straight cut of his nose, the high, intelligent forehead and strong, chiseled chin. Or how solid and substantial he seemed, unlike a lot of men she'd come across. "Thank you for what you did in the mercantile today, buying the shirts I made."

"I need new clothes." He shrugged one wide shoulder. "Will you accept a ride now?"

"I don't mind walking."

"Yeah, but I'm not about to leave you in the road one more time." His mouth almost grinned. "Besides, you owe me now because I bought all twelve of those shirts.''

''I guess you're right.'' She didn't see the harm in just once accepting a ride from a man who didn't look at her with judging eyes. ''But if you're going to be my neighbor from now on, you'll have to let me walk.''

''It's a deal.'' He held out his hand with a masculine ease at the same time he slid over on the bench seat to make room for her.

She brushed her fingertips on his upturned palm, the lightest touch she could manage. Her heart skipped at the contact. Sensibly, she lowered her gaze and stepped into the sleigh, clutching both her packages and her skirts in her free hand.

She felt self-conscious of every movement she made as she settled onto the padded bench seat and arranged her packages. She could feel him watching her and it was making her nervous.

He didn't speak and the silence stretched between them. Was it up to her to break the silence? Linnea hadn't been on a drive with a man since she was sixteen. What should she say? She tried but couldn't think of a single word.

Seth whistled to his stallion and the beautiful creature shook his massive head before deigning to step forward. The horse lifted his nose to the wind, trotting straight into it, making his sleek mane and tail ripple like poetry.

''He's beautiful,'' Linnea breathed. ''Not even the wild mustangs are so breathtaking.''

''And he knows it, too. Look at him.''

The stallion's ears swiveled, and he pranced even more handsomely, the king of the road.

She couldn't help chuckling. "Why, he's listening to us. He's smart, too."

"He's no fool, that horse. He'll do nearly anything for a pretty woman's praise."

Linnea blushed. Seth was being polite, that was all. He radiated integrity and courtesy, and she felt plain and mousy on the seat beside him. "What's his name?"

"I call him General, because he thinks he's that important." Quiet humor and steady warmth brightened Seth's voice and drew her hesitant gaze. He looked straight ahead at the road and his horse, affection warm in his steady voice. "He's a good friend and saved my life more times than I can count."

"In the army?"

"Cavalry. I raised him from a foal." He gestured with one hand, his leather glove accentuating the width and length of his well-sculpted fingers. "Look, he's still listening. Probably hoping for more praise."

Anyone could see the fine breeding of the stallion, the straight lines and careful curves of flank and fetlock. The animal's healthy coat gleamed like ebony velvet in the gentle sunshine.

The silence pressed back over them, and Linnea stared down at her gloved hands. She couldn't think of anything to say. Maybe it was for the best. She was too old to dream, too old to start hoping for a man to come and change her life.

And besides, Seth Gatlin didn't look at her that way, like a man searching.

He cleared his throat. "I was sincere about the shirts. They could use some tailoring. I would pay."

"You want me to alter them?"

"Who better? You're the seamstress who made them and my neighbor."

His smile was kind and it warmed her all the way to her toes. "Then I accept."

"I could use some other clothes, too, and I know my sister doesn't like sewing."

Ginny McIntyre. Linnea had almost forgotten. "I'd be happy to make whatever you need."

To think she had extra work again. It had been a long time since anyone had requested her skills with a needle.

Surely by now someone must have whispered in Seth Gatlin's ear about her past, but while he kept a distinct curtain of politeness between them, he wasn't judging her. He'd actually hired her. Oh, to think what the extra income would mean.

The sleigh slid to a stop in front of her house. So suddenly it was there, and the stallion snorted with impatience as if eager to be off and running and looking so grand pulling the sleigh.

The door opened and Mama stood in the doorway, diminutive and frail, her sightless eyes bright, cocking her head to listen to the sounds in her yard.

"It's me, Mama," she said before the woman could worry. "Major Gatlin was courteous enough to give me a ride. He's Ginny's brother."

"Ah, come to help her." Mama smiled. "Pleased to meet you, Major. I am Elsa Holmstrom. Would you like a cup of tea?"

As Linnea climbed out of the sleigh, she caught Seth's quick glance at her, a simple question. Her heart pounded. Not everyone treated her mother well.

"I would like that, ma'am. Maybe I could come back in a few hours, after your daughter shares her good news. I know Ginny is your landlord and since I'm looking after her affairs, I'd like to come and look over the property.''

"Of course. Tell me, Major, do you have a sweet tooth?''

"A terrible one.''

"Then I'll whip up a treat to go with the tea. Thank you for looking after my girl.''

"No problem.'' Seth's gaze sparkled with merriment and understanding.

Linnea's throat closed, filled with so many confusing emotions. He lifted one gloved hand in farewell and the stallion trotted off, all majesty and grace.

Just like his owner. Linnea couldn't move, spellbound, watching the heavily loaded sleigh with its lumber and packages speed out of sight.

What kind of man was Seth Gatlin? He puzzled her. Even knowing her past, he'd spoken to her, offered her a ride, bought the shirts she'd made and treated a blind old woman speaking in a thick foreign accent with kindness and respect. He was like no other man she'd ever known, except for her father.

"Linnea, are you standing there in the cold wind? I hope you have your hood up.''

"*Mama.*'' Still she didn't move, even though Seth's sleigh was out of sight and there was nothing to look at but the sparkling white landscape. "It's not so cold. The wind is warmer.''

"What we need is a good chinook to blow all this snow out of here. This winter has been far too long. Come, and show me what treat you bought yourself today at McIntyre's. The major said you had good news.''

"Very good news." Linnea forced her feet forward, hugging her packages. "I bought a few extras."

"Coffee. I can smell it," Mama guessed as she backed away from the threshold.

Linnea knocked the snow from her boots before she stepped into the house. How good home looked, she thought as she shut the door tightly behind her.

Fire crackled merrily in the gray stone hearth. The polished wood floors shone like molasses. The spots of color in Mama's tapestries and samplers brightened the walls. And her own pillows, cushions, tablecloths and curtains added a special touch. Home. She'd always been safe here and loved, no matter how difficult the circumstances or what mistakes she'd made.

She set down her heavy purchases and shrugged off her wraps. "I bought some white sugar to sweeten the coffee."

"What a treat." Mama beamed. "You spoil me far too much, Linnea. Our budget is very tight."

"Yes, but I sold another dozen shirts, thanks to Major Gatlin." She would save her news about the quilt until it sold—if it did.

She flung her cloak and scarf on the nearby peg and scooped up the packages.

"My, he had a good-hearted voice." Mama sighed. "I hope this means we'll have no more problems with Ginny McIntyre."

"You never know." Linnea couldn't bear to think of their troubles, not on a day with so much good news in it. She had twice the shirts to make and right away, Seth Gatlin's shirts to alter and a new quilt to plan. So much good all at once, why, she couldn't believe it.

"Sit down, Mama, and let me pour." She carried

the package to the counter to unwrap it and plucked out the soft wool skeins.

"This is for you." Linnea laid the bundle in her mother's lap.

Sensitive fingers brushed over the fine wool. "Oh, child, you should not have bought this for me. What use does an old woman have for such finery?"

"You tell me. It's your yarn." Linnea pressed a kiss to her mother's papery cheek.

"But what treat did you buy yourself?"

"Well, it was something I couldn't buy. But believe me, Mama, I got something very special today." Linnea poured the tea and remembered the sight of her quilt on display in Mrs. Jance's front window with the exquisite gowns and striking dresses, the elegant hats and lace.

That wasn't all. She remembered Seth Gatlin's smile, quiet and deep, and tucked the memory into her heart for safekeeping.

When the Holmstrom shanty came into view, a neat, dark square of a house against the endless sparkling white of the plains, he pulled back on the reins. The horse questioned the bit and barely slowed.

Heaven knows he'd ridden the animal long and hard yesterday, and the stallion probably yearned to run out the kinks in his muscles. But Seth's hands remained firm on the thick leather. General accepted the command and slowed to a walk.

Keep your distance from her, Ginny's quiet warning, spoken as he left the house, troubled him now. Rumors and gossip—he knew what small towns were like. Good in some ways, not so good in others.

But he'd learned a lot from his years fighting for

the country. He'd traveled as far as Mexico and all
the way back to Virginia. He'd seen a lot and learned
even more leading men and being led. He was a man
able to judge for himself.

What about Linnea Holmstrom? He'd never forget
the look of happiness in her eyes, flower-blue and
dazzling, when he'd purchased her shirts. Like the
first blush of spring and, once, he'd known exactly
how happiness felt.

She made him remember, and he didn't like that.
But that wasn't her fault, and he had to admire her.
He'd seen how Mrs. McIntyre treated her—and she'd
handled herself with quiet dignity.

He knew something about that, too. That's why
he'd purchased those shirts. Why he'd asked her to
sew for him. Helping out Ginny's tenants would only
help him in the long run. He had to make sure his
sister wouldn't be left with an empty house in a de-
pressed economy.

Linnea. He saw her in the fields, a slim reed of a
woman against the endless white. Beneath her dark
cloak, the red hem of her dress was a bright splash
of color swirling in the wind. Her honey-gold hair
twisted out of its pins to flutter in careless abandon
as she turned to look out over the plains toward the
mountains tall in the distance. Then she spun away,
a water bucket in each hand, and waltzed from his
sight.

His heart punched. Yes, she made him remember.
He squeezed his eyes shut briefly, trying to blot out
those feelings. He'd worked hard to bury emotions
long spent and burned out, like a candle to a stub and
there was no more light to give.

When he opened his eyes, General had finagled his

way into a quick canter, and Seth had only time enough to slow the spirited stallion and guide him toward the shelter of the old barn. He tethered the animal in an empty stall next to a very friendly milk cow, grabbed the package of new shirts and headed out of the barn.

He noticed the water stains high in the rafters and the slow sag of the building to the right. The house needed work, too, he noticed. The porch floor had been fixed recently, but the roof would have to be replaced this summer, judging from the uneven lay of snow over the structure. And the Holmstroms were still hauling water from a well.

Maybe they could increase the rent, Ginny had hinted quietly. He hated having to tell her she was lucky to receive the income she did.

He lifted his hand to knock but the door swung open. Not Linnea, but Mrs. Holmstrom stood there, a frail reed of a lady gnarling with age, but her smile was that of a young woman, pretty and lively.

"Major, I am so glad to have you in my home." She held the door wider. "Goodness, we have never had an army major in our house before."

"I'm retired, ma'am." He wanted to tell her not to be impressed, that it was only a title and not who he was. "You have a nice home here."

"Why, thank you. My dear Olaf built this little house for me when Linnea was just a baby and we'd moved from our family in Oregon Territory. Such a long way to come, but with our new daughter, we wanted to build her a good life."

This tiny woman was so full of love, she radiated it like light from the sun. Seth had never seen the like. He could only stare.

"You may hang your jacket there, by the door." Mrs. Holmstrom covered the distance between the parlor and the dining room with confidence.

He shucked off his jacket and hung it on the peg. He couldn't help noticing the cheerful handmade touches that made a house a home. The old furniture gleamed like new. Books, their pages yellowed with age, marched across three shelves beside the fireplace.

The Holmstroms did not have much, but they cared for what they had, and it touched him. It reminded him of the home he'd once had, of a life he could never reclaim.

He wondered where Linnea was hiding in this small shanty. Or was she still outside, daydreaming on the plains?

"Did you come today to raise our rent?" Mrs. Holmstrom's question was gently spoken, with a tremor of worry. She turned from the counter, her sightless gaze finding his with eerie precision. "Or to ask us to leave? I ask this now because I do not wish to have Linnea surprised with such news, not today when there is so much good to be thankful for."

"I have no intentions toward either." Seth crossed the room, taking a steady breath. He realized he still held the package of shirts. He stared down at the brown paper. "It's my hope that you will stay here. I'll be overseeing my sister's property until she's able to manage for herself and gets used to living on the ranch."

"Terrible man, running out on her like that, leaving her near to bankrupt." Mrs. Holmstrom turned toward the counter, and the lid of the teapot clanked hard on the wood. "A terrible, horrible man."

A cold breeze tore through the kitchen, and Seth

saw Linnea in the open back doorway. The drop of her soft mouth and the open pain in her luminous eyes made his heart catch. He saw the wood she carried and he stood to take the burden from her.

But she saw what he intended and moved fast, shutting the door with her foot and barreling across the kitchen to the small cookstove at her mother's side. "Mama, I'll not have that man spoken of in this house."

"His name was not said."

Seth measured the sadness marking the old woman's face and the raw pain in the daughter's. He didn't know how their homesteaded land had come to be in his sister's possession, but he saw it was still a hard subject, full of pain. "I didn't come here to cause hurt feelings."

"No, of course not." Linnea stood, arms free of her burden, and bustled toward the back door, loosening her cloak's sash. "I see you brought the shirts."

"Just like I said." The package felt awkward now, and he set it on the edge of a small table, on top of a delicate lace cloth.

He looked up and Linnea's presence struck him hard like a blow to the abdomen. Hers was a quiet gentle beauty that didn't grab a man at first glance, but it grabbed him now. He froze, struggling for breath, and hoped no one noticed. He couldn't seem to get enough air into his lungs.

"Let me take a look at those shirts." Linnea breezed close, demure and shy.

Her fragrance of winter wind and lilacs made his heart kick. He couldn't help noticing the threads of gold that shone in her blond hair. Couldn't help listening to her rustling skirts, a thoroughly female sound that put him on edge.

She opened the package and shook out a blue muslin shirt. His skin prickled as she circled behind him, and the hair on his arms and the back of his neck stood on end. He felt the heat of her touch at each point of his shoulder seams where she held the shirt up to his.

"I can let out the seams here, and it should be roomy to work in." She sounded practical, sensible, like a woman comfortable with her singleness, like a woman not looking for a man.

And that knowledge helped him relax. The air whooshed from his lungs and he could breathe again. His skin stopped tingling. "The sleeves seem short."

"I can take care of that, too." She stepped away, eyes down, graceful and reserved and so beautiful it hurt to look at her. Her complexion was as smooth as cream, her nose slim and delicate cheekbones high. It was a wonder she hadn't married.

But when Mrs. Holmstrom carried the pie plate to the table, counting the steps from the counter, he knew the reason why.

"Mama, let me help you. Goodness." Linnea set down his shirt and rushed to her mother's side.

"I am not too frail to serve a handsome guest a slice of my blueberry-preserve pie." The old woman seemed undaunted by her handicap and flashed a smile that made her hidden beauty shine. "Come, Major, sit and enjoy. Maybe there is a chance I can charm you into fixing the leak near the chimney."

"Cut me two slices of that blueberry pie and we've got a deal."

He approached the table, and Linnea nearly

dropped the plates at the sight of him. He stalked toward her with an easy strength that left her stunned. Behind him, the windowpanes caught the playful rays of the sun, glinting and reflecting, casting light to halo him and burnish the breadth of his powerful shoulders.

He was so effortlessly masculine, she could not look away. He was like no man she'd ever met, broad and stalwart but not brash. Just looking at him made her heart kick and, feeling overwhelmed, Linnea broke away, using the excuse to fetch more water.

Mama, who knew there were two fresh bucketfuls, said nothing as she excused herself. Linnea grabbed her cloak and unlatched the door, hurrying out of his sight before she made a complete fool of herself.

Stabbing her arms through her cloak sleeves, she shut the door behind her. She tripped down the steps and sank ankle deep in the snow. The quietness of the landscape was gently welcoming and chased away the embarrassing mix of attraction and loneliness aching like a wound in her chest.

He isn't interested in you, Linnea. She'd spent ten long years with a shame so great on her shoulders no decent man would so much as speak to her.

Dreams. She felt that part of her heart ache and yearn. Made her wonder what it would feel like to be loved by a man like Major Seth Gatlin. His affection would be quiet and steady, just like he was. And his smile would be all for her.

She knelt in the cold snow and hauled the bucket up from deep in the earth. She heard the distant echoing sounds of water splashing as she pulled. Loneliness curled around her like the wind and it felt as vast as the prairie.

Hoping for love at her age. What was she thinking? And was she so foolish that she would feel this for Ginny McIntyre's brother? The wife of the man who'd broken every last one of her dreams?

Her gaze strayed to the far hillside, where two carved crosses marked two graves. Where two crosses marked the losses of a lifetime and more shame than she could endure.

There would be no love for her, no man with broad shoulders and a quiet smile to ease this lonely yearning from her heart.

Be sensible, Linnea. Be grateful for all that you have. She was. Truly. She had a wonderful life here with Mama. She woke up to the majestic hush of the morning prairie. She went to bed at night knowing her day had been filled with love.

She would go back inside, sit down at the table and eat pie with Mother and Major Gatlin, and not once think foolish thoughts, not once wish and yearn and dream.

He was a neighbor, a gentleman and their landlord. That was all.

She retrieved her bucket, dropped the rope back down the well and covered it tight. When she stood, a hard gust of wind nearly knocked her to her knees.

The chinook. It was late, but it had come. The long cold winter was over and the wonder of spring was about to begin.

Chapter Four

Seth sank into the carved wooden chair at the head of the table, the one Mrs. Holmstrom offered him.

He watched as she breezed to the counter and worked easily and quickly, running her fingers along the cupboard shelves until she located the small dessert plates. The chink of china and the ring of flatware knelled in the small room and the sound penetrated through the thick walls around his heart.

Maybe it was the warmth from the fire. Or the feminine scents of soap and flowers.

Whatever it was, he didn't like it. Memories long buried tugged at him like a rope at a stubborn mule. He fought but they came all the same. Long-lost flashes of happier times. The faint echo of children's laughter. The scent of apple crisp fresh from the oven.

And sunshine. Always sunshine.

No sense going back there, he told himself as he measured sugar into the steaming china cup Mrs. Holmstrom placed before him. There was nothing but pain for him in the past.

"Would you like milk to add to your coffee?"

"I'd appreciate that, ma'am."

Mrs. Holmstrom set a small delicate pitcher on the table near his cup.

The clink of china against lace-covered wood took another chink from the armor around his heart.

The back door swung open almost behind him. A strong wind breezed through the room. He could feel Linnea's presence even before he set down the spoon and turned.

Warm as spring, as welcome as the chinook. He moved without thinking, taking the bucket from her grip. His fingers brushed hers and lingered.

Her skin might be cool, from the temperature outside, but the feel of a woman never changed. She was like new silk. He felt her intake of breath, revealing her surprise at his bold action, and she tore her hand away.

Awareness fired through him, and he didn't move. Her face was gently shaped, and her pearl-pink lips made him wonder if they tasted as soft as they looked. His mouth tingled with a sudden wanting, but he was a wise man and he turned away.

Slowly, deliberately, he set the bucket on the floor next to the stove. Beside another bucket that was perfectly full. Baking and washing dishes could use a lot of water, he told himself. But Linnea blushed and he strongly suspected the real reason she'd fled his presence.

He was not a man who drew women to his side. He felt much older than his real age and looked it, too. A woman as plainly beautiful as Linnea Holmstrom would have no interest in a man like him. He didn't blame her.

Still that knowledge didn't make it easier to return to his chair. Mrs. Holmstrom's cheerful conversation and her exquisite pie couldn't begin to ease away the memories that came unbidden and unwanted. Memories of another kitchen with a woman of silk and beauty, who'd turned a simple shanty into a home with bits of fabric and lace.

It took all his willpower to answer Mrs. Holmstrom's genuine questions about his trip from Fort Benton, while her daughter sat wordlessly at her side. He ate quickly, hardly tasting the rich, sweet pie.

At last, he was able to turn down a third offer for seconds and rise from the table. But the memories lingered like night fog when morning came.

Feeling cold, Seth thanked the women, grabbed his jacket from the peg by the door and escaped to the restlessness of the high Montana prairie.

The sweet winds of the chinook had taken the sting from the cold air, and the icicles thick along the house's eaves dripped with happy music. The cheerful sounds only made him clench his jaw and wish for colder weather.

Sure, he was grouchy. He was overwarm from sitting in the Holmstroms' kitchen. His blood felt ready to boil in his veins as he marched across the yard. The past remained an echo and Linnea Holmstrom's quiet beauty was a clear image in his mind that refused to fade.

He couldn't tell if it was the past or the present that troubled him, as much as the knowledge that he could never travel that path again.

General nickered a welcome as he leaned over the stall door begging for a treat. Seth took a sugar lump from his jacket pocket and let the horse lap the treat from his palm.

Got a little attracted to her, did you, Gatlin? Yep.

It was attraction—and lust. Something he didn't figure a spinster like Linnea Holmstrom would appreciate.

The stallion nudged him, an old friend, and eased some of the emptiness away. Seth treated his horse to another sugar lump and then retrieved his hammer from the back of the sleigh.

It was best to get to work. And to forget the beat of attraction in his blood.

As Mrs. Holmstrom had promised, he found a wooden ladder at the back of the barn and he leaned it against the house. The old ladder didn't look trustworthy, but it took his weight when he tested it. A gambling man, Seth started to climb and ignored every groan it made.

He was grateful when his feet touched solid roof. The world looked different from up here, his troubles further away. The wind whipped across his face, whistling in his ears. The sheen of sunlight on melting snow glittered like strewn diamonds and it hurt to look at them.

Then, over the peak of the shimmering roof, a movement caught his gaze on the faraway hill. Shielding his eyes with one hand, he squinted into the glare of light.

Alone, on the distant crest of a low rise, stood a woman in a gray cloak and hood, her skirts lashed by the wind. She stared over the endless plains and looked as lost as he felt.

Linnea.

Why he kept looking, he couldn't say, but the sight of her held him spellbound. He could not tear his gaze away.

Her colorful skirt ruffles looked like spring flowers

cast against the winter white, like spring touching the land. It took all his willpower to turn his attention to the roof in front of him and not stare out at the horizon like a young man searching for a dream.

When he looked up, she was gone.

Just concentrate on the roof. That was why he'd come here. Judging by the looks of things, when this snow melted, he would be replacing the entire roof. Taking his hammer, he used the claw to rip away the crumbling shingles on the north side of the chimney. What a mess.

Ginny wasn't going to like it. She'd been hardly more than a shadow in her kitchen this morning, worrying over whether or not he was pleased with the meal of fried eggs and salt pork. His conscience stung.

Somehow he would find a way to take care of his sister. To erase the lines on her face made by time and fear.

He felt Linnea's presence before he heard her boots on the snow. Her gaze was a steady warmth on his back and he almost pretended he didn't know she was there. But he'd never been good at deception and, besides, he needed to fetch some shingles from his sleigh.

He made his way down the ladder slowly.

Stiffness tensed his back as he set foot on the slushy ground. "I need to grab my tools and some shingles from the back of my sleigh. Tell your mother I'll be hammering on her roof for a while."

"You intend to raise our rent, don't you? That's the real reason you're here."

Linnea was no timid mouse, nor was she a shrew.

Her eyes were too old for her face and it troubled him.

A woman so pretty shouldn't know heartache. She didn't have to say the words for him to know what a burden a higher rent would cause. He remembered her slim hands at the table while she picked at her uneaten pie and sipped her coffee. Hands callused from hard work, reddened from the cold winter. Hands that had sewn the dozen shirts he bought today, to support her aged mother.

"Please tell me the truth. There's no way for us to pay more."

"I said—"

"I know what you told my mother. But I can see what Ginny wants. What she's wanted all along. She wants us gone. I've paid every increase her family has asked."

"I have no intention of raising the rent."

"So you say now, but what about later? I can't do more and take care of my mother at the same time. She can't be left alone day after day if I take a job in town. And if we move, then she has to leave behind the home my father built for her with his own hands."

"I'm here to repair the roof, ma'am. Not to force you out of your rightful home."

"Ginny may have other plans."

"Not if I have something to say about it."

There was no mistaking the integrity in his words and the honor in his voice. Linnea's worries melted like the snow at her feet.

"If you're not going to be raising our rent, then I should help." She trailed him into the shadows of the barn.

"You? Hammer? I thought you were a seamstress."

"I've used a hammer a time or two when the event called for it. Besides, I have no intention of being indebted to you over fixing our roof. Since you're not going to raise the rent."

She'd made her point. "All right, then. You can hand my tools to me. Make things go faster."

"You've got a deal, Major."

"Call me Seth. Just plain Seth." The wind tangled dark locks across his brow and he didn't look at her as they crossed the yard together. Treated her like a woman who didn't make him look twice.

Seth. She longed to say his name, to feel the word take shape on her tongue and cross her lips. What was wrong with her? The foolish, daydreaming part of her just wouldn't stop. Even when she knew better.

"Be careful. This ladder's old and wobbly." Seth gazed down at her from the height of the roof. "Your mother would never bake pie for me again if I let you fall."

"I won't fall. I'm not the little girl she sees, and I'm not helpless like some women I know of." She couldn't help the small bit of pride that flared to life in her chest.

Heaven knows she had little to feel good about, and she wasn't going to be ashamed of it. She'd taken good care of Mama, more than a lot of girls her age could have done.

He held the top of the ladder steady against the side of the house. Why did she notice how strong his hands were? How attractively made? Stop looking at him, she told herself and started climbing.

"Why didn't you tell your mother about the quilt?"

"Why do you think that's any of your business?"

"Because I'm your landlord."

"Not technically. And that doesn't qualify you to be nosy."

"No, but I am curious." Seth's steady gaze felt friendly, like a man she could be safe with. "She doesn't know you took it to town."

"True, and I don't want her to know in case it doesn't sell."

"Why wouldn't it?"

Linnea hesitated, blinking hard against the bright sunlight that surrounded them. It wasn't as if she could tell Seth the truth. "The dressmaker thinks it will, and I sure hope she's right. The extra money would be nice, but to actually make my quilts to earn part of our living? What a wonder that would be."

"You don't like making shirts?"

"I love to sew, but it would be nice to do something different for a change."

"How long have you been selling shirts to support your mother?"

"Ever since I was sixteen."

He looked at her with wise eyes, as if he saw far too much. She lowered her chin, struggling against the old shame that weighed her down. "How about you? Are you going back to the army after you help Ginny?"

"No, ma'am. I'm retired. That part of my life is done for good. I plan to be a rancher. Raise cattle and horses and wheat."

Dreams, they erased the lines from Seth's face and made him look like a man standing at the edge of the world. Big. Bold. And more handsome than she had the right to notice.

"So you'll be moving on?"

"Yes, ma'am. After I help my sister get back on her feet. Shouldn't take too long. Figure I'll leave after the harvest." He hung the leather tool bag over the end of the ladder. "Let me push this snow out of the way, then hand me a few of the rags in there, will you?"

Linnea sorted through the scarred tools and found a few tattered squares of muslin. He took them from her without a word.

Busy at his work mopping up the snow from the edge of the chimney, he wasn't paying attention to her. But she couldn't see anything else. Not the fast-moving clouds playing peekaboo with the sun and blue sky behind him. Not the prairie dogs on the field frolicking in the slick snow. Not even the vastness of the horizon calling to her.

All she could see was Seth Gatlin, limned by the sun. He was big enough to take up the entire sky when he stood. He looked down at her and handed her the wet cloth.

"Ought to be dry enough for the pitch." He nodded toward the covered crock.

She uncapped it and handed it to him, the scent of pine resin sharp in the air. Watching him work was like a gift. She liked the way his broad hands spread pitch across the crack in the boards where the chimney stones and the wood met.

His brows furrowed with concentration, and his firm mouth flattened into a straight line. The wind tossed dark locks of his hair over his brow and caught the brim of his hat.

The Stetson went flying down the slope of the roof and tumbled over the edge.

"I'll get it!" Without thinking, Linnea tore down the ladder, her skirts flaring and billowing as the wind gusted hard enough to show her drawers.

Good thing Seth was on the roof and not on the ground.

Blushing, grabbing her skirts with one hand, she ran after his hat with the other. It wasn't easy. Layers of snow remained frozen beneath, as the top layers melted, making running a slick business. Her feet kept trying to slide out from beneath her as she half ran, half stumbled toward the barn.

Just out of her reach, the hat rolled end over end, pushed by the playful wind.

"Forget it, Linnea. It's not worth a twisted ankle," he called out as he climbed down the ladder.

"I can get it, if this wind will just—" She reached out and a powerful gust knocked the brim away from her fingertips. She smothered a chuckle and kept going.

Water splashed behind her. She looked surprised to see that Seth was gaining ground, running steady and powerfully, and more striking than anything she'd seen. Not even the wild mustangs could hold a candle to the way he covered the ground.

She leaped to catch the hat, but the wind spun it away from her, in a completely different direction. She tried to stop and skidded out of control.

"Let me fetch it," he told her. "I don't want you hurt."

"I'm not giving up now." She was laughing, and then he was chuckling, a rich melted-chocolate sound that drove the loneliness from the plains and from her heart.

Stumbling, Linnea dashed onto the road and let Seth overtake her. He was laughing, too, and it was slowing him down. The wind sputtered and sent his Stetson wheeling down the puddled road.

And into the path of an oncoming horse and rider.

The horse neighed in protest as the hat wobbled to a stop in front of its dainty hooves. The dark-cloaked rider, hood gathered low, managed a disgruntled frown.

It was Ginny McIntyre.

Linnea's laughter died. The warmth in her heart faded like the land before a sudden frost. Shame filled her, a shame there was no cure for.

"Seth," Ginny said stiffly. "There's a problem and you are needed at home. Right this minute."

Linnea could feel the other woman's disapproval, and like a cloud before the sun, she felt small and plain. This was just what she needed. To be seen running and laughing with a man—married or not. Think of what the gossips would make of this.

The happiness slipped away. A chill wrapped around her. She stared hard at the ground while Seth retrieved his fine Stetson. The hat was marked with wet patches and bent on one side of the brim.

"I'll be along shortly," Seth answered slowly as if he, too, could feel that something was wrong. "Go on back home, Ginny, and I'll be there. Got a couple of shingles I have to nail down now that I've got my hat back."

"I'll wait." Her chin lifted stubbornly, her gaze sharp as a blade on Linnea's face.

Heat flamed her cheeks, and she couldn't think of

a single thing to say in her defense. Nothing could make it right. She'd learned that from hard experience.

Right now, as Seth swept bits of ice from his hat, he wasn't looking at her with judging eyes, because he still must not know the truth about her. When he did, he'd never offer her a ride to town. Never show her his quiet, dazzling smile.

So she did the only thing she could do. She headed toward the house, hating the silence that followed her. Stumbling, wishing the earth would open up and swallow her, she finally made it to the front porch and flew through the door.

What would Ginny say about her? Linnea didn't have to guess. She had no doubt that if she pulled back the curtains she would see Ginny leaning over to whisper in her brother's ear.

"Linnea, is that you already? It is exciting the major is fixing our roof!"

"We are fortunate."

"Your feet are wet, *dotter*." Mama bustled from the kitchen, cradling a stoneware cup. "Here, I have tea ready. I knew you would go wading through the deepest puddles. Sit down and warm up before you catch a chill."

"Yes, Mama." Linnea took the steaming tea and eased onto the floor, close to the fire.

She took off her wet boots and set them on the hot hearthstones to dry. She jumped at the sound of Seth's footsteps on the ceiling directly overhead.

She knew what Ginny had told her brother. How could she face him? How could she return his shirts and ask for his money?

"Is everything all right?" Mama asked, always able to see what was important.

"Everything is fine. Just the way it should be." And it was true. The dreamy part of her might not accept it, but the sensible side of her did.

The fire popped in the grate. Mama's rocking chair squeaked as she settled into the cushions. With nimble fingers she gathered up her new wool and needles and began casting on stitches. "Major Gatlin must be a rather tall man, taller than my Olaf. Tell me, is he handsome?"

Oh, Mama. Linnea cringed, knowing exactly where her mother was going with this. "I'm afraid the major is quite unfortunate."

"Why's that?"

"He's terribly ugly, the poor man. He's pock-marked. He has a huge nose and long sallow face."

"I do not believe it. What a shame! And with that resonant voice."

"He's so homely. That must be why he isn't married at his age."

"Oh? How old do you suppose he is?" Mama's fingers hesitated as she listened to the pause in Seth's hammering. "He cannot be much older than you."

"His voice may sound young, but he's at least fifteen years my senior."

"Now I hear the lie in your voice, young lady." She resumed her work, talking over the comforting click-click of her needles. "It seems you have answered my question after all."

"There'll be no man for me, Mama, and you know it. Not even a man like the major."

It was only the truth. There was no denying it. No

sense in trying to daydream it away. Seth Gatlin would never want a woman like her.

Ginny's silent anger lay like a cold frost over the warm parlor. It had drained the taste from the chicken and dumplings she'd served for supper. And now, as darkness fell and the lonely night hours stretched ahead of him, Seth didn't think he could stomach more.

He closed his book and carried it to the kitchen table. The day had been long enough. Maybe he ought to spend what remained of the evening alone.

The door hinges squeaked softly in the corner of the parlor. One lamp's meager light, turned low to conserve kerosene, created shadows that hid Ginny as she closed her son's bedroom door.

"Jimmy's whiskey is still in the back of the pantry, if that's what you're looking for." Cold and empty, her words.

Seth winced and stilled his hand on the doorknob. "I need to check on my stallion. Make sure he's settled for the night."

"Oh." She eased into the orange glow made by the fire, the shadows licking at her skirt ruffles. "I can put on fresh coffee to warm you for when you return."

"That won't be necessary." He lifted his wool jacket from the hook and shrugged into it. "Thought we'd come to an understanding about this. I'm not here to be waited on. Take time to relax in front of the fire before turning in."

"Seth?"

His hand stilled on the knob. The dark night called to him, but he could feel Ginny's need trying to wrap around him like a child's desperate grip. "What is it?"

"I know you're here to help me. I've got no one else. The McIntyres have washed their hands of me. But I have to say this even if it drives you away."

He took a step closer, resigned. He'd wanted to avoid a discussion, but it looked like there would be no escape. Might as well face it now. "What do you need to say?"

"I want you to keep away from that Holmstrom woman."

"You mean Linnea."

"I saw how the two of you were laughing."

"We were chasing my hat."

"I know what I saw."

"You saw wrong." He felt the weight on his shoulders double, the burden in his heart become heavier than lead. "Don't make me talk about them. Don't make me go back there. My time for love is past."

"Not if you're looking for a woman's comfort without marriage." Ginny's chin shot up, and venom wrung all the prettiness from her face. "I know how it is with a man. Like a bull in a field of cows—"

"Put it aside, Ginny. Your husband deserted you and took another woman to his bed. Don't fire your anger with him at me or anyone else."

"But Linnea—"

"She's not your problem, Ginny. Providing for your son is." Seth headed out into the night, his anger hot as a well-stoked fire.

He could feel his sister's pain, and while he'd never been abandoned, he had lost the love of his life. He knew something about how much the heart could hurt. How it bled. How it would never be the same.

Had he made a fool of himself with Linnea Holmstrom today? Probably. Feeling the heat of Linnea's touch as she'd measured the new shirts and hearing the joy of a woman's laughter had lifted the winter from his soul for one brief moment.

The night felt suffocating and he was glad for the dark. How could he look himself in the eye? A man too old for such a young woman, whose time for loving had already been spent.

Silvery shafts of light pierced the land as he walked past the barn and listened to the ice crunch beneath his feet. The freezing air burned his lungs, and he drew it in deep. The cold settled into him, pumped through his veins and filled his heart.

He waited on the edge of a low rise, gazing at the vast prairie stretching black-blue toward the horizon. He stayed until every last memory faded. Until there was nothing but the sound of the wind in his ears and the rhythm of his own breath.

Linnea felt a welcome sense of freedom heading out into the crisp morning. The nearly thawed snow had refrozen overnight, and it was hard and slick beneath her shoes, but soon it would all be gone. The plains already gleamed with the first blush of spring.

The quick trills of lark song filled the air and gave her something to think about other than the newly altered shirts she carried and the man who owned them.

At the crest of the first rise in the roadway, she could see him through the glare of the cheerful sun. Seth was hard at work repairing the fence line, his hat tipped jauntily, head bent to his task.

Just walk up to him and give him the shirts, she reasoned. No lingering. No talking. No wishing.

It seemed so simple until she was in his shadow, gazing up at him against the brilliance of a new spring sky. She knew the instant he sensed her. His hammer's rhythm hurried and then slowed until he put the tool down with a clunk and swiveled on his boot heels toward her.

"Don't tell me that you've finished my shirts already."

"It's been a week, and there wasn't much to do. I'll just leave them here, on the wagon seat."

Remember, just give him the shirts and walk away. She ignored the desire to seek out his face in the shadows beneath his Stetson's brim. She laid the carefully wrapped package on the worn board seat.

His gaze felt like flame on her back. The black stallion tethered nearby lifted his head and allowed the wind to catch his gleaming mane, as if searching for admiration. She resisted the urge to reach out and stroke him, knowing the greatest reason for doing so was to keep her here, in Seth's presence.

She withdrew her hand and twisted away from the wagon.

"Are you planning on running away without letting me pay you?"

"You're busy. We can settle up later."

"At least tell me what I owe you." Already he was reaching for his billfold and thumbing through greenbacks.

"Twenty-five cents a shirt is what I used to charge."

"Used to?"

"Before Mrs. Jance moved to town and opened her shop. I'm not sure what the going rate is these days."

"Two bits sounds like a fine deal to me." He counted out three dollars. The greenbacks snapped in the wind.

Linnea stood tiptoe to take the bills from Seth's hand. His fingers were stained with dirt and his knuckles were nicked from small cuts.

Stop noticing him, she scolded herself and tucked the bills into her cloak pocket.

"Look at that." Seth stood, spellbound by something out of her sight. He straightened, gazing over the fence.

"The mustangs!" The faint off-rhythm of galloping horses grew louder. "I can't believe they're still here."

"Where do they go in the summer?"

"Up into the foothills of the mountains." She stood on tiptoe, straining to see the herd, but they remained hidden.

"Climb up so you can see." Seth climbed up on the fence and held out his hand to *her,* Linnea Holmstrom. "Come, watch them with me."

In the light of day, where he could see she wasn't pretty or young. And after all that his sister must have told him. His palm remained outstretched in an invitation that made her feel every inch a woman. Breathless and vibrant and sparkling.

How could she resist?

Chapter Five

She caught hold of the rails and climbed high enough to see over the rise of the land. There they were! The wild mustangs soared over the new shoots of tender grass, their manes and tails flying. The beat of their hooves drummed like music across the earth.

Without thinking, she laid her hand on Seth's arm. Heat flashed across her palm. An answering warmth fluttered low in her stomach. A desire so real she lost her balance. He reached out to steady her.

Good going, Linnea. He'd be able to figure out she had a crush on him if she kept that up. She'd vowed to keep her emotions under control, but she couldn't help wishing, just a little. Standing beside him and breathing in his man-and-wind scent made her weak.

Far too weak.

Just think about the mustangs, she told herself. They were nearly as grand as Seth was. They raced closer, so she could make out each individual horse. They wheeled like winged creatures, muscles rippling as they turned south, directly toward them.

"They're coming this way." She couldn't hold back her excitement.

Seth didn't seem to share it. He swept off his hat and frowned. "Gunfire. Listen."

A popping sound joined the music of the galloping horses, and their rhythm changed. The stallion trumpeted, stretching out to nip several mares, spurring them to greater speeds. The wind carried a frantic feeling of fear.

"Those are Mr. Neilson's fields."

"I wish I had my Winchester. Chances are he's only trying to scare them."

"They're pretty hungry this time of year." The mustangs disappeared down a rise and out of sight, trailed by a man on horseback. She could hear the report of a repeating rifle and the harsh cries of the stallion.

"Something's wrong." Seth leaped over the top rail and hit the ground running. "Stay here."

Not a chance. Linnea clutched the top board and slipped over it. Seth was already yards ahead of her, sprinting toward the distant fence line that separated the McIntyres' land from the Neilsons'.

A horse's neigh keened above the sounds of running horses and a man's angry curses. Had Neilson shot one of the mustangs? How could anyone harm such beautiful creatures? Anger fueled her as she raced behind Seth, but he was already leaping the section line fence and he, too, disappeared from her sight.

Suddenly a golden mare leaped over the wooden rails, platinum mane flying. A second and a third mare cleared the fence, eyes rimmed white with fear, their beautiful coats flecked with lather. Frantic, they balked at the sight of her and veered away.

Dozens of mares, heavy with foal, flew over the

fence. She could smell the heat of their coats and feel the breeze as they soared past. The earth beneath her boots vibrated and then they were gone, the ground still, the melody of their gait growing distant on the wind.

Angry men's voices remained, growing louder. Linnea pulled herself onto the middle rail of the fence and saw Seth in the small gully below, holding a mare to the ground with the force of his weight on her neck. Blood marked her golden coat in harsh red streaks.

"Linnea!" Seth called up at her, never taking his attention from the thrashing animal. "Run to my barn as fast as you can. I need wire cutters from the left shelf in the tack room and as much rope as you can carry. Hurry!"

"Worthless creature tore up my new barbed wire," Mr. Neilson complained as Linnea hopped to the ground and ran with all her might.

"Easy, girl," Seth murmured to the terrified mare. "We'll have you out soon. Just keep calm."

That was like asking a twister to become a gentle breeze. The mustang's powerful muscles bunched beneath Seth, and even though he held her head down and back so she couldn't rise, he had to sit on her and use his weight to keep her from breaking his hold. Sweat covered them both from stem to stern. Neilson wasn't helping.

"Know how much this newfangled fence cost me to put in? A fancy sum, dangnabbit. Thought it might be worth it to keep those worthless pieces of horse-flesh out of my fields. That's what the salesman told me. Horses won't touch it. Not even the wild ones. Oy."

"You got conned, Neilson. Horses can't avoid what they can't see or don't know to look for. You'll have the same problem when you move your cattle into these fields. Try tying red yarn on the wires a few feet apart."

"Yah. What a big help you are."

The mare tried to lunge beneath Seth, kicking hard, fighting with all her strength. Seth forced back a curse and spoke soft soothing words. The mustang stilled, stiff with panic, waiting for the opportunity to try again.

"Suppose she might be worth something at the stockyards," Neilson grumbled on, not caring how his rough, angry voice was affecting the mare. "They shoot her for the meat. Maybe I make more than it costs to haul her."

Seth strengthened his hold before she could begin to struggle again. With the wire wrapped around her back fetlock, she could lame herself permanently. This fine, beautiful animal didn't deserve that or a trip to the slaughterhouse.

"Neilson," he growled. "I'm only going to say this once. I'll fix your damn fence, but I'm taking the horse."

"This is my land."

"Too bad. Walk away before I get really mad."

The old man grumbled, and Seth felt the horse weakening. She was losing too much blood.

"Linnea!" he called when he saw her gray hood rise over the top of the small rise.

She climbed over the fence, her hood dangling from her shoulders and her blond curls tangling down her back. Her skirt hems were wet and muddy, but no woman had ever looked so good to him.

She slowed to a fast walk, gathering her skirts to keep from further panicking the mare. Concern bracketed her rosebud mouth as she knelt beside him.

"Here." She withdrew the cutters from her cloak pocket. "Do you want me to hold her?"

"No." The mare thrashed, and it took all his concentration to hold her down. "You'll have to cut the wires. Move slowly, but you've got to work fast. I can't hold her for long. She's tiring, and I am, too."

Linnea moved like morning sunlight, gentle but sure. She tore off her mittens with her teeth. Her slender hands seemed soothing to the mare as she tugged at the snarl of wire wrapped around the mustang's back leg.

The cutters snipped, the wire snapped with a twang as it broke free, and Neilson started up again, rattling on about the price of his fence.

The mare, sensing she was almost freed from the painful wire, thrashed, kicked and bucked, fighting hard to lift her head. Seth pressed her against the ground, hating the white rim of fear in her eyes. Lather slicked them both.

"Easy, girl. We aren't going to hurt you."

Linnea knelt at his side, holding a coil of rope. "I've cut away all the wire I can see."

"You'll have to tie a halter and hobbles for me. Do you know how?"

"No, but I'm good at embroidery, and that requires a lot of knots. Tell me what to do."

"Tie a slipknot," he began his instructions, his words raw and rough to his own ears.

Linnea didn't seem to notice as she knelt among the new shoots of grass and asked for Neilson's assistance in catching and holding the mare's rear legs.

She worked quickly and competently, her voice kind, her hair gleaming like new gold, her blue-violet eyes dark with sympathy.

Maybe it was the care she showed in tearing a strip of cotton from her petticoat to bind the mustang's bleeding fetlock. Or maybe it was just his sorrow for this majestic animal so badly injured.

Whatever the reason, his heart began hurting, keen-edged and fierce.

A hurt that came from feeling in ways he hadn't in a long while.

Linnea's stomach felt weak as she watched the frightened mustang limp through the plowed field. Freshly turned earth made the ground soft for the injured mare's foot, but she seemed too busy fighting against the makeshift halter to appreciate it.

The bandage was already bright crimson and dripping. "She's bleeding so badly."

"I can do something about that. *If* I can get her to the barn without dislocating both of my shoulders." Seth struggled to hold the mare's head low. The muscles in his arms and neck corded with the effort. "She's still got a lot of fight left in her."

"Can't blame her for being unhappy. Her family is running free on the horizon, and she's our captive."

"That she is."

"Will you have to put her down?"

"Not if I can help it. She injured herself pretty good, but she's strong as hades."

"That's a good sign." Lucky mare, for tangling herself up in a fence when Seth was at hand.

He was good with her. Strong and firm, but kind. More admiration burned in Linnea's chest, bright as a brand-new flame. "We aren't taking her to your barn?"

"Can we keep her at your place? She's going to need care, and I hate to take her home. Ginny's mad at me as it is."

"Over me?"

"Well, she did find out about the sewing. She wasn't happy about that, but she's really mad at her husband for leaving her. And for being forced to depend on me."

"I can see that would be a hardship."

He grinned at her teasing. "I'm an unworthy brother, but I do my best."

Lucky Ginny.

Seth paused to reach for the latch, but Linnea beat him to it and swung open the heavy gate. "Looks like you need both hands to hold her."

"She's tiring herself out. Look. She likes the sound of your voice. See how she's watching you."

"She's just getting too tired to struggle."

"No, she's figuring out which one of us is likely to help her out. I don't think she'll try to bolt if you come closer."

"You mean for me to touch her?"

"Sure. Let her feel it in your hands, how you only want to help her."

"How do I do that?" Linnea relatched the heavy gate.

"You've a gentle touch, Miss Holmstrom. This mare might be a wild thing, but she's got a heart. She's a herd animal and she's used to having someone around her she can trust."

"Other horses."

"True, but she'll settle for anyone kind in a pinch. Trust me. Come closer."

The mare seemed as large as the sun, and Linnea walked in her shadow, daring to edge closer. Such a beautiful animal. And a wild, powerful mare who stood much taller than Linnea was.

The mare turned her head a fraction and in those dark chocolate eyes she could read the mare's fear. And pain.

Seth was right. Trusting him, she pressed the palm of her hand against the mare's cheek.

The mustang's eyes widened. Her ears flattened against her skull. Her muscles tensed, but she didn't lash out.

Linnea stroked her again. How soft she was. Like sun-warmed velvet. It was like touching heaven, knowing this creature raced the sun and chased the horizon, and knew freedom like the wind.

"Linnea? Is that you? Goodness, *dotter,* you are nearly late for our noon meal." Mama clung to the porch rail. "I was beginning to worry. Is that the major with you? Is his horse limping?"

"It's not my stallion, ma'am. A mustang tangled herself up in Neilson's wire fence."

"Wire? Why, Lars Neilson never did have a lick of sense. We have room to spare in our barn."

"Mama, you shouldn't be out in this wind without a cloak and you know it. It's not warm enough." Linnea moved away from Seth and the wild mare, feeling Seth's gaze as heavy as a touch on her back as she hurried up the porch steps. "Come inside, and I'll get the soup warming."

"Warming? Why, I have everything ready. I only

need to set another place at the table and the major can join us.''

''He'll be with the horse for a while.'' Linnea could just see him through the corner of the window, leading the golden mare through the shadowed barn doors.

How strong he looked, and how gentle. Amazing that a man could be both. The sight of him made her pulse run fast and hot.

''Then we will pack a meal and you can take it to him.'' Mama breezed across the room, already making plans. ''It is good luck that we made two whole pans of cinnamon rolls yesterday.''

Linnea checked on the soup simmering on the stove. The fire was fed, the bread cut, the table set. She should have been here helping her mother. ''Mama, this is too much.''

''I am not helpless, *flicka*. The major likes coffee, does he not? Let me set a pot to boiling while you go see if he needs your help with that poor animal.''

Why did Mama look so happy? Unmistakable sparkles lit her eyes. Was she smiling? Awfully suspicious, Linnea decided, and she wasn't going to feed Mama's hopes for a son-in-law.

''Seth is only here for the summer. I think you should know that.''

''Seth, is it? Where is the knife?'' Mama rummaged around in the pantry. ''Here it is. I shall keep the meal warm, for tending an injured animal takes time. When you and the major finish, I will have extra bread cut and his coffee ready.''

Mama turned away, her hands busy as she began slicing fresh bread.

She's trying to fix me up with Seth. The realization

hit Linnea like a snowball right in the middle of the forehead. What was Mama thinking? How could she even believe that Seth would want her?

Poor Mama, always wanting the best for her daughter. She didn't understand. Linnea filled an empty pail with clean rags, grabbed a healing ointment from the pantry and the teakettle from the stove.

"Eat, if you get hungry, Mama. I won't be long."

"Don't hurry on my account. The major may need your help."

How cheerful Mama looked.

Linnea turned away, sadness filling her, brimming over so that she shivered from skin to bone. How did she break Mama's hopes? And how could her mother even imagine such a thing?

Seth swung two empty buckets over his shoulder as he met her at the barn door. "First thing I'm going to do when I'm done plowing the fields is build you a windmill."

"To pump our water? Are you serious?"

"Dead serious. How much water do you pack in a day?"

"Some days fifty gallons."

"We'll put an end to that." He said it the way a friend might, as if he cared about her welfare. "I've got the mare cross-tied and hobbled in one of the stalls. The barn's a scary place for her, since she's used to being able to scent the wind and look in all directions for danger. Move slow and talk to her, so she knows you mean no harm. Just go on in and wait for me."

"I've come prepared." She lifted the bucket she held.

"Good. I could use some help." His smile was

slow and lopsided, and friendly. Not a smile from a man looking to charm a woman. Or planning to come courting.

But a smile that made her feel less alone.

Mama was going to be sorely disappointed, Linnea realized as Seth disappeared down the path. *She* was going to be disappointed.

A curious moo from her milk cow greeted her the instant she stepped inside. The Jersey leaned over the rails and swiped her tongue at Linnea's sleeve. Dark eyes pleaded, and she couldn't resist giving the animal a quick pat.

Out of the corner of her eye, she could see the mustang watching, sides heaving, ears pressed flat against her skull.

"You're being quiet but you're angry, aren't you, girl?" Linnea moved on to the next stall, slowly, lowering her pail and teakettle to the ground so it wouldn't startle the mare. She stayed on the safe side of the gate. "You're bleeding, but Seth will take care of you."

The mare didn't move. Seth had her securely tied and hobbled so that she couldn't harm herself or them. Blood ran in rivulets down the mare's barrel and sides. Her left hoof was cocked off the ground, blood pooling beneath it.

Seth's shadow fell across the threshold, wide and masculine. His presence set Linnea's blood racing. She kept her eyes low and watched him secretly through her lashes.

He'd rolled his sleeves to his elbows. His skin was sun-browned and dusted with dark hair. Muscles corded as he carried the ten-gallon buckets easily. "How's our girl doing?"

"She's hurt worse than I thought."

"We'll have to see how deep that cut is to her fetlock." He upended one bucket into the small tub.

The mare startled, her fear wild. The ropes held, but her panic remained.

Seth eyed the mustang as he emptied the second bucket. "Think you can hold her for me?"

"I can try."

"Good." Approval flickered in his eyes. He moved toward her, so near her skin prickled as if they'd touched. He opened the gate.

One more step brought them so close she could hear him breathe. He towered over her, and she could feel his heat radiate through her. She couldn't move, which made no sense at all, because she was able to blink and breathe. A sensible woman ought to step away. He was far too close for respectability.

He brought his gloved hand to her face and she didn't care at all about what was proper. His gloved knuckles grazed against her left cheek, and she closed her eyes. The caress of the butter-soft leather was as gentle as the man's touch.

Her skin tingled and she felt the woman in her, dormant as if sleeping through a long winter, softly stir to life. Like new shoots to the sun, like the first buds of spring, she felt her heart opening.

"You should wear your hair down more often." His gaze traveled over her windblown locks, tangled around her shoulders. "I've never seen such beautiful hair."

Her heart stopped beating. Her lungs stopped drawing air. Everything within her silenced.

He didn't really mean it. He was being kind, that's all. She refused to take his words to heart. It was more likely that the stars would tumble from the sky than it was that Seth Gatlin would fall in love with her, a plain woman who was old enough to know better.

"I've got this as clean as I can." Seth didn't like the look of the cut, but he'd seen worse. "Linnea, do me a favor and loosen the knot holding her head. Not the ones to the cross-ties, but the hold keeping her nose to her knees."

"Is she going to be able to run again?" As she released the knot, Linnea's gaze met his.

In their blue depths he read her fear for the horse, fear that she might never be able to gallop the plains. He liked the sympathetic brush of her hand across the mare's neck. He liked it a lot.

The mustang snorted, her ears flat to her head, but she didn't try to bite. Linnea didn't look afraid, but awestruck. Her wonder touched him.

"She's such a beauty," she breathed, as if she were lucky enough to find a star shimmering on the ground in front of her. "I love her coat. She's as golden as morning sunshine when it first touches the plains. And her mane is as white as moonlight."

"It's called palomino." Seth straightened, deciding to leave the wounds uncovered for now. "I figure she's about ten years old. She's got another month before she foals."

"You didn't answer my question."

"No, I didn't." Seth regretted the truth, but what good was a lie? "The cut's shallow enough to give us hope."

"Good."

He watched lines smudge Linnea's brow beneath the windblown tangle of her bangs. The gossamer curls framed her oval face and his fingers itched to touch the golden strands. He knew they'd be as soft as they looked.

He shook his head at his foolishness, a man his age noticing a woman so young and beautiful. She could have her choice of men.

He shut the stall door and latched it tight. "Better to leave her alone for a while. Let her get some rest. That's the best way for her to heal."

"Should we leave her something to eat?"

"No. I'll be back later after she's calmed." He knelt in the aisle and placed the crock of Mrs. Holmstrom's healing salve into Linnea's pail. "I've got to get to town and pick up a coil of barbed wire before the day's end. Or I figure Lars Neilson will have my head."

"He put that wire up on purpose." Anger flushed her cheeks and drew up her slim shoulders. She was all fight and soft woman, and he *really* liked it.

"Course he did. He's not as bad as a man comes. He could start *shooting* the animals instead of shooting *at* them. Plenty of farmers do. He took the easy way and figured a few injured mustangs would teach the rest of them to stay out of his haystacks."

"You're siding with *him?*"

"That's not what I said. I'm only saying we're lucky she's not dead from a bullet, that's all. I don't like an animal being hurt. Never have. Never will."

"Okay. For a minute there, I thought I might have to knock some sense into you."

"A little thing like you?"

"I'm stronger than I look."

"Sure, if you're packing ten-gallon buckets full of

water to the barn every day.'' He grinned, he couldn't help it.

Linnea made him smile. It was that simple. And unexpected.

So he tipped his hat and headed straight to the door where sunshine and the safety of loneliness beckoned. ''Looks like you got a horse.''

''You saved her.'' Linnea breezed after him, her steps whisper soft on the earthen floor, her skirts rustling. ''When she's healed, you should keep her.''

''I'll be moving on soon. What would I do with her? You're the one who could use a horse.''

''I could never break her spirit.''

Linnea said the words wisely, as if she knew all that taking a saddle would cost the mare. His chest hurt as if the ice around his heart was breaking away.

''Here.'' He thrust the pail at her. The muddy hem of her blue dress edged into his line of vision and he turned away. It was the smart thing to do.

But he couldn't shut out her presence, the *feel* of her to his senses. Her soft lilac scent made his skin ripple. The sound of her breathing so light and gentle set his teeth on edge. Her shoes brushed the earth as she stepped back, and the hair on the back of his neck pricked, as if she'd pressed her hand to his nape.

What was wrong with him? Why was he reacting this way to Linnea Holmstrom? No other woman since his wife had affected him like this.

A gust of wind caught the edge of the barn door and tore it from his grip. The wood smacked into place with a bang, ringing like a gunshot.

He turned around and there she was, standing in the pathway, surrounded by new green grasses reaching up from the earth. The wind buffeted her skirts and had tangled her brilliant gold hair.

She looked as innocent as dawn and as tempting as sunlight and he couldn't help wanting to be warmed by her touch.

He'd been cold for so long.

"I'll be back to feed and water the mare. Don't worry." He resisted the urge to reach out and wind his fingers through her hair.

He was a man with needs and hungers. That didn't mean he had to give in to them. "Thank your mother for me. The salve may keep her injury from infecting."

"I'll tell her." Linnea merely gazed at him with her luminous violet-blue eyes, too large in her pale face.

Her cloak was stained and her dress rumpled. Her skirts dragged on the earth, hiding her patched and muddy shoes. With her hair fallen from its knot and dancing in the wind, she was far from the parlor-perfect image that ought to be the epitome of beauty.

At this moment, alone with the wind and prairie, she was the most beautiful woman he'd ever seen.

"I have been listening for you two." Mrs. Holm-strom eased into sight on the porch, a shawl wrapped around her frail shoulders. "Major, I hope you are hungry. The soup and sandwiches are ready. Come."

Anyone could see how joyful the older woman was at the prospect of being a hostess.

But his chest was tight and hurting with emotions he didn't want to examine, and he knew he'd never chase away the pain in his heart by sitting in her kitchen. He had enough loneliness in his life. Seeing all that he once had—a cozy home, a woman's touch, warmth and light—would only make the loneliness keen-edged and unbearable.

"Thank you, ma'am, but I have to be on my way. I appreciate the invitation. Hope you didn't go to too much trouble."

"Next time I will be quicker to coax you into my kitchen. I shall greet you with a plate of cinnamon rolls and we will see if you can walk away then."

"Greet me like that and you might never be rid of me," he teased, and was rewarded with her smile, more beautiful for all the years that had touched it.

"Thank you." Linnea touched his sleeve, and her beauty was the brightest of all. Honest and gentle, and everything missing from his life.

He headed down the road as fast as he could. Like a hot blade, he could feel Linnea's gaze on his back, or maybe it was simply his loneliness that hurt more with every step.

"The major said he would return?" Mama asked over the clack of her knitting needles. "I have not heard him."

Linnea looked up from her sewing. "He must have fed and watered the mare when we were out on our walk."

"A shame, it is. I wanted to thank him again. The repairs he made to the roof are good, yes? It rains and there is not a single drip. What a blessing it is he has come to manage things."

Mama cocked her head, listening as the wall clock bonged the hour. "Bedtime for an old lady. No, I need no help. Sit and enjoy your sewing."

"It's only a patchwork quilt, Mama." No matter what her mother said, she did need some help. Linnea set aside the block she was working on, a nine patch from scraps she'd been able to salvage. "Here, let me fetch your nightgown. I want you to change right here where it's warm."

"You spoil me, *dotter,* when you should be tending children of your own."

"Ah, but I am happy enough with you." Heading into the dark bedroom, Linnea found the warm flannel nightgown by feel. The room was damp from the evening's rain, so she headed to the kitchen to grab the iron warmer from the shelf.

"You spent much time with the major today." Mama set aside her knitting.

"He needed help with the horse is all." Linnea set the warmer on the hot hearthstones. She was careful to keep her feelings from her voice. "The mare was sleeping when I went to bed down the cow for the night."

"She is calm?"

"I wouldn't say that. She's afraid but too injured to do much. She took some of the grain I offered her. Who can turn down molasses-covered oats?"

"Ah, true wisdom. I wonder if the major likes molasses cookies."

"Mama." Linnea circled the chair and tugged at the older woman's dress buttons. "You have to promise to stop. You're making Seth uncomfortable."

"I merely invited him to eat with us."

"Yes, but it was the way you said it. Like you were ready to start planning a wedding."

"I did no such thing. You exaggerate, child."

"He ran off down the road, didn't he?" The buttons undone, Linnea took her mother's frail hand. "Stand and let's get this dress off you."

"Nonsense. I can do this myself and you know it. You cling to me when you should be making your own life. A man like the major can give you that."

"I know, Mama." Linnea could hear the wobble in her own voice, and she feared she hadn't fooled her mother one bit.

The woman was so stubborn! Choosing to believe in the impossible. Choosing to wipe the past clean like a slate and start anew. As if it were possible.

After her mother was tucked safely into her bed, Linnea welcomed the silence. No more Mama and her questions about the major. No secret hopes for a daughter's wedding.

Now all she had to do was to keep her own wishing under control. The parlor felt lonely tonight. A single light burned on the round table next to her rocking chair, casting a glow over the tiny parlor. Flickering over the rag rug where no children's toys had been left after a day of play. Over the furniture where no husband sat.

Orange firelight blazed a path across the room as she went about her nighttime duties. Banking the fire in the stove, filling the reservoir for the morning washing. She pulled on her father's old slicker and headed out into the dark to bring in wood for the morning's fire.

Rain tapped and blew on a low, moaning wind. The night felt cold and lonely, as if the entire world were weeping. Rain streaked like tears down her face as she splashed down the porch steps and into a mud puddle at the base of the stairs. The wind gusted and she tightened the coat's sash.

She hurried out into the darkness, the wind tearing at her clothes and the mud trying to trap her shoes.

There would be no mustangs pursuing the shadows, not on this stormy night. What about the mare? Was she listening to the night? Wondering if her herd would return?

The large dark lump that was the woodpile was hardly distinguishable from the dark. Linnea curled her fingers around a cold wet piece of pine and lifted it from the dwindling stack.

The hair prickled on the back of her neck and she froze. A shoe squished in the mud behind her. She wasn't alone. She spun around, but the high plains lay shrouded in black and hidden from her sight.

"Linnea?"

The wood slipped from her fingers and splashed into a puddle at her feet. Water sprayed up over her toes. "Seth. I didn't hear you."

"Or see me, I bet. Some storm. Guess it means spring is here for good. Did I scare you?"

"Just startled me."

"Sorry. Let me get that." He knelt before her, as substantial as the night, a man of shadow and worth that made her feel far too much. "While I'm at it, let me carry in all the wood for you. How much do you need?"

"I'm perfectly capable." Linnea grabbed the pitchy-smelling piece of wood from his arm and turned to the stack. "Did you come to check on the mare?"

"Yeah, thought I'd make sure she was bedded down all right." He snatched the wood from her and began filling his arms. "I missed you this afternoon. Figured you'd come out to the barn while I was there."

"I took Mama on an afternoon walk. She loves to

get outside when she can. She's pretty much trapped in the house all winter." Linnea shouldered past him and grabbed the piece of wood he was reaching for. "I can do my own chores, thank you."

"I never said you couldn't. I'm simply a gentleman who can't stand by while a pretty lady works."

"Save your sweet talk for the Widow Johanson. She might be impressed by it."

"And you're not?" Seth chuckled, so close to her that she could feel the heat of his breath. "Trust me, I'm not trying to sweet-talk anyone. I want to be neighborly. That's all."

"Fine. Then follow me to the house."

The night didn't feel as miserable with Seth by her side. She didn't mind the mud sucking at her shoes or the wind that drove rain into her face. The walk back to the house didn't seem as long. Before she knew it, she was crossing the threshold from darkness to light, from cold to warmth and Seth was emptying his load into the bin by the hearth.

"I'm dripping all over your clean floor." He straightened and lifted the wood from her arms. "I've learned from experience women don't always appreciate that. They spend a lot of time keeping their floors polished."

"True. I'll look past it this time, since you're being neighborly. And the mud on the floor, too."

"Sheesh. I can sweep it up."

"What? A man who sweeps? I've never heard of such a creature."

"Watch and learn." He stacked the last piece of wood into place and brushed the bark from his coat sleeves. "Where's the broom?"

"Don't worry about it. You'll track mud all the

way into the kitchen if you fetch it now. I'll take your word that you're a skilled sweeper.''

''Can't have my competence in doubt.'' Seth pulled off one boot, then the other. Sparkles lit his eyes and made him look younger.

She saw a man probably not much older than she was, the lines and burdens gone from his face. A glint of the devil flashed in his grin, slow and steady and only for her, before he disappeared into the dark kitchen. She could barely make out his shadow as he rummaged through the pantry. A loud clunk echoed through the house.

''Oops. I was lucky that didn't break.''

''I keep a row of crocks on the bottom shelf. If any field mice get into the house, I can hear them and chase them off with the broom.''

''You don't have a cat?'' The pantry door whispered shut, and Seth's footsteps padded through the dark.

''No, he died last summer. Cats are expensive in this part of the country. I couldn't find a kitten cheaper than a dollar fifty, so I figured we could do without for a little while.''

''That's what Ginny needs. A cat to do some hunting around the house and barn. She didn't need one in town.'' Seth emerged from the shadows, and the single light from the table lamp seemed to find his shoulders and worship him.

Her fingers itched to do the same. To know how a real man felt. To explore the tendons cording in his arms and feel the hard expanse of his chest. Just wishing, she told herself, because she couldn't very well reach out and touch him.

She might be a spinster, but she still had a woman's

desires. She wanted to be held safe in the shelter of a good man's arms. To know his kiss and his caresses. To feel the heat of his skin. The weight of his body. The pleasure of his loving.

"See what a good job I'm doing?" Seth's words came easy and unaffected over the rasp of the broom on the polished floor and he gestured to his handiwork. "True to my word."

Without a doubt, he was a man that a woman could believe in.

Chapter Six

Seth stepped into his boots on the rainy front porch, since he didn't want to muddy up the floor he'd just swept. The cool wind buffeted him, and water streaked down his face. As powerful as the storm was, it couldn't wash away the faintest scent of her lilacs.

Linnea hovered in the threshold behind him, her shadow cast long by the light inside. Her skirts snapping, her presence a warmth he dared not think too hard about. He pulled his coat tight and faced the storm where rain and darkness met.

"Want to come to the barn with me?"

Surprise, then delight shaped her soft face. "Let me grab my slicker."

Her footsteps faded away, and he made the mistake of glancing over his shoulder. She'd vanished from the doorway, but everything she represented remained—the snapping fire in the hearth, sewing left on the cushion of the rocking chair, a welcoming sanctuary made homey with ruffles and lace.

A woman. Home. Everything he'd never thought he'd have again.

Loneliness struck him like the miserable rain, driving through his coat to his skin, chilling him to the bone. Linnea's arms would be warm, her kiss like new silk. He'd never thought another woman could make him wish for a new start in life. Another chance to love.

A scary thought. He headed into the darkness and let the shadows engulf him.

Tonight the cold didn't soothe him, but left him hungry and restless, until Linnea appeared in the threshold, lamplight shimmering in her golden curls for a brief moment, and he felt whole. She pulled the slicker's hood up over her head and pulled the door closed behind her.

The light from the house faded, leaving only the overwhelming storm. He didn't know what made him do it as he reached out and took her hand. "The steps are slick."

"It's gentlemanly of you, but I go up and down these steps all the time, come rain, sleet or snow." She didn't tug her hand away, wet and warm in his, as he accompanied her down the stairs.

"I take it your mother's asleep?"

"Either that, or she was eavesdropping through the door when you carried in the wood. She's quite taken with you. Thinks you're a blessing because you fixed the leak in the roof. She praises you all the day long."

"After I finish planting, I'll be back to put on a new roof."

"Then she'll be indebted to you for the rest of her life. It hurts her to see the home Papa built for her needing repairs we can't do."

"Your parents must have shared a deep love."

"Very." She sighed, wistful, as if remembering better times. "It was beautiful to grow up basking in their loving marriage. To know that kind of affection does exist.''

''It's not easy to find.'' The wind gusted, and Seth moved to protect her from the brunt of it. The cold battered his back, but he hardly noticed it. ''I don't know any other woman who would give up marriage and a family to care for her aging mother.''

''You make me sound noble, but it's nothing like that. Nothing at all.'' The light drained from Linnea's voice, her words as dark as the night. ''But what about you? Not many men would come to help a stepsister in need, especially when there's nothing to be gained.''

''I had nothing better to do.''

''No wife or family, you mean.''

''That's right. I have no wife or family.'' The sadness struck like a sudden blow hard to his sternum.

He'd grieved, he'd found a way to survive, then to live each day. But that didn't mean he would never miss what he'd had. A wife to hold, who at the end of a long hard day would welcome him home with the gleam of love in her eyes. And the high shouts of his son and daughter as they raced through the house to greet him, shouting above each other to tell him the news of their day.

To be welcomed and loved and needed, to feel with a whole heart and have a real life.

This was what haunted him, what hurt beyond endurance.

The music of the rain hitting the earth and the low keen of the wind sounded lonely and relentless, and he swiped rain from his face.

He hefted open the heavy barn door and stepped aside, letting Linnea escape the storm first.

A sharp, warning neigh trumpeted through the darkness and echoed, almost like a woman's scream, in the hayloft overhead. The milk cow lowed softly, shifting in her stall, and the pad of Linnea's quiet steps to the gate made the cow calm, pleased with a little attention.

Listening to Linnea's soft voice as she talked to the cow, he found the lantern and lit it. The sharp smell of kerosene tickled his nose, but it cleared his head. "The mare doesn't seem glad to see us."

"Is she doing better?"

Seth shook the rain from his brim and headed toward the dark stall. Another frightened neigh tore through the darkness, and the loud smack of a hoof striking wood echoed in the rafters.

"Is she hurting herself?" Linnea asked anxiously.

"She must be doing better to have that much strength." Seth halted at the stall, taking care not to move too fast. "Easy, girl. I don't want you to hurt yourself."

The mare must have decided she no longer needed help and bared her teeth.

"Yep. She's better." The water in her trough was gone and some of the hay had been eaten. He took his time refilling both, knowing Linnea was watching him with her quiet gaze.

"If that hoof doesn't show signs of infection, I'll untie you in the morning, girl." He backed away, and the mare watched him with intelligent eyes, as if trying to measure the danger she was in.

Linnea said nothing, standing beside the friendly cow that was nibbling on the hem of the yellow slicker. The bovine appeared to be tame as a dog.

Linnea had a way with animals and he figured the mustang was a lucky horse to be trapped in her barn.

Maybe he'd be able to gentle the mare before he left at summer's end. Unless Linnea and her kindness tamed the mare first.

"I said something wrong, didn't I?" Woman soft, gentle as a hymn, Linnea watched him without moving, her bottom lip drawn between her teeth.

She looked vulnerable and so beautiful it took his breath away. The huge old yellow slicker with the worn cuffs and patched hood ought to make a woman look bulky, not gently feminine. She made the man he was ache with want.

"I'm sorry," she said. "I mentioned marriage and I shouldn't have done that. I didn't mean to make you feel uncomfortable. Or to think that I might be fishing for a husband, because I'm not."

She kept talking with embarrassment raw and trembling in her voice, and he couldn't find the words to stop her. "Linnea, I—"

"No, it's okay. I don't need to hear it. I know you're not looking to settle down with a woman with a mother to take care of. I'm not looking for marriage, so don't feel uneasy around me."

Her chin hitched up a notch, and with her spine straight and her small hands curled into fists, she looked ready to fight.

The glistening light in her eyes wasn't tears, but it was emotion. One thing he knew was the look of sadness. How it dimmed the light within a person. How it flickered like a candle at the end of its wick. And how hopes died like a sputtering flame until there was only cold and darkness.

She was lying to him. Plain and simple.

Linnea Holmstrom wanted a man to love her. He guessed that she didn't expect anyone would or could.

That was something he understood. All too well.

"It's not you, Linnea." He took a step closer toward her and the light, gathering up his courage because he didn't want her lie between them.

He didn't want her believing that she was undesirable. He could see that in her eyes, too. "You don't make me uncomfortable. Not like the Widow Johanson, for instance. She's been to the house three times to have tea with Ginny. And eyeing me the whole while."

"I'm not surprised. She's young and pretty and used to having a man provide for her."

"She scares me."

"Marriage-hungry women have been scaring men since the beginning of time." She almost smiled, a slight wobbling curve of her bow-shaped mouth. "Aren't men supposed to be commitment shy?"

"That's not what I am." He didn't know how to say it. He hadn't spoken of his loss since he'd walked away from the graveyard, leaving his heart behind. "I had a family once. A pretty wife who liked to sing while she did her housework. And a son and a daughter who had her smile."

"I didn't know." Linnea laid her hand on his sleeve. "What happened?"

"A fever. Hit out of nowhere. They were fine when I left in the morning and in bed when I returned at dusk. By midnight two days later, they were gone. Just like that."

His throat burned and he turned away from her. "When a man buries his family, it's like the sun going down on his life. A winter without the promise of spring. That's all. It isn't that I don't want a wife. It's that I had a wife. Everything changes, and that time for me is past. How could I be that fortunate again?''

He appreciated she didn't tell him how sorry she was for his loss. She simply let him have his silence. The burning in his throat wouldn't go away, and the night felt suffocating.

All that awaited him if he left was an empty bed in an unhappy house. Where a shadow of a child never made a sound, where his sister's silent anger lay hidden beneath her attempts to please him.

There would always be an empty bed and a lonely room, whether it was on Ginny's ranch or wherever it was he ended up. He'd faced that truth long ago when his grief hadn't killed him. He'd gone on living, but tonight the lonesomeness hurt too much.

Linnea's skirts rustled behind him. Her hand lighted on his shoulder and remained, comforting and steady. She didn't say a word, but he could feel her heart—her sorrow and her caring. Her touch was a softness he hadn't felt in what had to be forever.

A haven in a storm.

A light in the darkness.

Loneliness welled up, pushing out the memories and the pain until he couldn't breathe. His eyes burned and his throat ached. His chest felt tight and he couldn't stand it anymore. He reached out and pulled her into his arms.

Her golden hair felt like silk against the stubble on his chin, her soft woman body warm against his chest. She melted against him, her arms encircling his back. She was so small and yet he felt the strength of her, warm and caring. He buried his face in her hair.

Like night finding its morning, his loneliness began to fade. She filled his senses with her lilac scent and warmth, her arms tight around him, her soft hair on his skin, the warmth of her breath fluttering against his neck. He curled one hand around her nape. When she leaned into the crook of his shoulder, he could feel her tears hot on his skin.

Fierce, overwhelming tenderness filled him like a river breaking its icy dam. He turned to her blindly, finding the softness of her face and the silk texture of her skin. He pressed a kiss to her cheek greedily, like a starving man. Expecting her to break away.

As if a miracle, she turned to him. His lips found hers. She was satin soft and he kissed her hard and deep. He was breathing fast and his heart was pounding as if he'd run ten miles, but he couldn't move away. He cupped her chin, splayed his fingers around the back of her neck and drank of her like a man who'd been thirsty all his life.

She moaned, a small feminine sound that cut like cold water. He'd been too rough and it shamed him. He released her, letting go of her heat and her softness and hating it. Backing away a step, breathing hard, he tried to figure out what to say.

Her hair was tousled and her lips were shaped by his kiss. He could taste her still. He wanted to pull her back into his arms and never stop kissing her. To have the right to touch her.

What he wanted was simple. He needed her warmth and comfort.

She stared up at him with wide eyes. Afraid? Or maybe shocked. He couldn't tell.

"I had no right—" He felt like a fool, like a young

man without a drop of self-control. "I'm sorry. I just— I don't know what to say. There is no excuse."

"I understand." She dipped her chin, hiding her face.

He'd made a big mistake. How was he going to correct it now? He couldn't very well withdraw the kiss and erase the moment so it had never happened.

The sweetness of her pounded in his blood and he shook with a need he hadn't felt in years.

"You were overcome with your memories." She shrugged once, a vulnerable lift of her slim shoulder. A small gesture that wrenched his heart. "Don't worry. I know it wasn't me you wanted to kiss."

"I apologize. Just overwhelmed, I guess."

"It's all right. We can pretend it never happened."

"Sure." It would be hard to act as if he hadn't made an ass of himself tonight, reaching out for her. He was lucky she wasn't furious with him for taking liberties and taking advantage.

She looked sad. There was no other word for it. As he turned out the wick and lantern light faded into darkness, the image of her standing there in the middle of the aisle, looking forlorn and unwanted, remained.

He'd used her and hurt her. It was that simple. But as he opened the barn door and breathed in the scent of her as she passed, he had to wonder.

Maybe it was more than loneliness and memories that had driven him into her arms.

"You didn't ride over?" she asked at the top of the porch stairs, where the eaves partially protected her from the rain.

"I like to walk at night."

"The plains are beautiful in the dark. Even when it's rainy like this. It's like music."

"I suppose it is." He cocked his head, listening to the sound of heavy rains drumming across the prairie. There was a melody and rhythm to it, like a thousand hymns whispered all at once.

"You won't be uncomfortable around me, will you? Because of the kiss?" she asked. "I would hate that."

"I would, too." He tipped his hat, already taking a step back. "We're friends. No uneasiness allowed."

"Good." She smiled and even in the shadows she was a beautiful sight.

He felt brittle, as fragile as blown glass. He didn't trust his voice, so he kept walking, letting the night engulf him and the rain wash away the ache in his heart.

But another deeper ache remained. One that was fiery hot and strident. The feel of Linnea's kiss haunted his lips on the mile-long walk through the night.

She'd kissed him back. Gentle and ardent and uncertain, but she'd definitely kissed him in return.

Realizing that, the rain didn't feel as cold. Or the storm as dark.

She couldn't see him anymore. Linnea let the curtain fall into place across the cool glass. Shivering from her damp clothes, she crossed the room and knelt before the crackling fire.

The flames had burned low while she'd been outside, but the coals glowed hot. Hot like Seth's kiss.

Don't even think about it. She had no right wanting to kiss him. Her mouth was still tingling from his lips.

How was she going to forget that? Or how he'd held her to him with a need so fierce her heart was still racing from the power of it?

She would be sensible. She'd take him at his word. He'd been overwhelmed by his painful loss and needed comfort. That was all. His kiss didn't mean a thing—not to him.

Seth had been hurting and needed comfort. That was all. She would do well by not losing her head and reading anything more into it than that.

But the parlor felt emptier than it ever had. The shadows fell across the rug where no man's boots were set to warm, in a room where no man would hold her in his arms.

Seth's scent lingered on her clothes—a rugged, masculine scent, clean like the night, charged like thunder, and she breathed it in. What was she doing? Hadn't she just vowed to be sensible?

You have more common sense than that, Linnea Holmstrom.

She banked the coals and turned out the lamp. Her steps echoed in the house. After checking to make sure the door was locked, she made her way through the dark. To the single bedroom where Mama slept, hardly a shape beneath a thick pile of quilts.

She changed quickly, then knelt to pull out the trundle bed. When her fingers brushed the quilt she'd made long ago, she dropped to her knees on the cool floor.

Although it was dark, she didn't need light to trace the perfect appliquéd circles of pastel calico she'd purchased at McIntyre's store. The wedding ring quilt she'd made for her marriage bed. For the wedding she dreamed of like any sixteen-year-old girl.

Lessons learned. Lessons she would do best not to forget now that a man's kiss once again burned on her lips like a brand.

Dawn came with a wisp of bright color in the east, where low blue-tinged hills touched the horizon. Streaks of crimson, orange and purple twisted along the underbellies of dark clouds.

The storm was long gone. Warblers and finches trilled in the new grasses, greeting the sun with their song. The new day came with quiet reverence that made Linnea feel renewed. And strengthened.

Today she would not think about Seth Gatlin. Not once.

She ambled across the soft earth made fresh and green by last night's rain, swinging the buckets in both hands.

This is a good life. She may not have a husband of her own. She may never know the precious weight of her newborn child in her arms.

But she did have this, the hush of a new day. And the quiet companionship of a white-tailed deer, who raised her dainty head from her grazing, sides rounded with the weight of her unborn fawn.

Chickadees lifted from the fields, and the deer fled. Linnea heard the muted clomp of metal against stone and spun around, the bucket banging against her shin.

A man, with his Stetson's brim shading his face, rode toward her on the golden spears of the newly rising sun. Astride his big black stallion, Seth Gatlin looked as powerful as the landscape and as impressive as the sky.

"Morning, Linnea." He tipped his hat. "Thought I'd get an early start on checking the mare."

"I haven't made it to the barn yet. I was going to start packing water."

"Good thing I happened along when I did. I'll make you a trade." He dismounted with a creak of leather and held the reins to her. "You take General to the barn for me, and I'll fill those buckets for you."

"I'm capable of carrying my own water." The buckets clanged against her shins as she turned, her pride getting the better of her.

If she planned on sticking to her resolve, then she'd do better to act more like a self-reliant woman than a spinster searching for romance.

"Yeah, I'm going to stand by and let you do the work." He sidled up to her and stole the bucket right out of her hand.

"Hey. That's mine."

"I mean it, Linnea. I'm an army major and I'm used to having my own way." Teasing lights flashed in his eyes. "I'm not giving in."

"Neither am I." She held her remaining bucket with both hands. "I've been packing water since the day my father took ill and I don't mind it one bit."

He fell in stride beside her. "You've been taking care of your mother for a long time. And doing the field work, by the look of things. You don't sublease these fields, do you?"

"No." She knelt down, but Seth was beside her, his firm shoulder brushing hers as he drew aside the well cover.

Since he was so darn determined, she let him take the second bucket and tie it to the fraying rope. "We rent these twenty acres back from Ginny, but the neighbor to the east rents the rest of the quarter section."

"What do you do with the twenty acres? Hay it?"

"Yes. I keep a small herd of cattle to sell every spring. You probably didn't notice the cows in the field across the road."

"All twenty of them? I noticed."

"I sell the gentlest milk cows in the county. It brings in enough money with my sewing to make ends meet."

He hauled up the heavy bucket hand over hand. "Do you have any coming fresh soon?"

"Anytime now. Are you interested?"

"My nephew Jamie is about the sickliest lad I've ever set eyes on, and she doesn't have a cow. I figure a few glasses of milk a day might do him some good."

"Ginny's lucky she has you for her brother." Pain filled her, heavy as stone, and she twisted away. She did feel sorry for Ginny, but it was hard to forget all the hurt over the years.

"I'm glad to be here." Seth was at her side, carrying the brimming ten-gallon buckets handily. "Deciding to retire from the army wasn't easy. With my family gone, I felt kind of aimless. But Ginny wrote she needed help, and I volunteered. Thought it might give me a chance to dust off my ranching skills before I buy a place of my own."

"Do you know where you'd like to go?"

"Hadn't much thought about it. Figured I'd know the place when the time was right."

"Major?" Mama's sweet voice trilled on the morning breeze. "Is that you again? How lucky we are. I was just whipping up my specialty batch of pancakes. Can I tempt you to join us for breakfast?"

"I'm busy, ma'am." Seth's hard-set face softened

when he looked at her mother. ''Maybe another time.''

''I've got fresh sausages to fry up. Does that tempt you enough?''

''You're going to be disappointed if I turn you down, aren't you?'' Seth squared his shoulders, even more a man for his kindness. ''I'd be pleased to join you.''

''Wonderful.'' Mama clasped her hands together. ''How do you like your eggs?''

''Mama, you've embarrassed the poor man enough,'' Linnea protested, for she suspected that Seth could see her mother's true motivation.

''I haven't eaten yet. Mrs. Holmstrom, fried eggs are fine.''

''My specialty.'' Mama waltzed into the house, her happiness as bright as the sparkling morning.

''Forgive her. She's a misguided mother.''

''There are a lot of those around.'' A slow grin curved along his mouth, the mouth that had kissed her with need.

Tingling, Linnea took a deep breath. *Remember, you vowed to forget about that kiss.*

If only it were that easy.

The barn loomed ahead of them, and General lifted his head high. His neigh shattered the morning's peace. The stallion that had been trailing Seth now took off at a tail-high gallop heading straight for the barn.

Seth couldn't grab the dangling reins, and he shook his head. ''It's no use calling him back. He wants to show off for the pretty mare in your barn.''

''She's loud this morning. That must mean she's stronger.''

"Angrier," Seth corrected. "She's going to be a handful now that she's rested. I'm glad you're here. We've got to get her used to you being around, since she's yours now. Believe me when I say, in six months she's going to think of you as her family and not the herd."

"I don't believe you. How can a wild creature be tamed? The first chance she gets, she's going to fly over the fence and take off with the mustangs."

"It depends on how she's treated." Seth shouldered General away from the barn doors and set down the buckets. "She's likely to be mighty angry over being cross-tied all night, but that's all right. We'll untie her and she'll be grateful we came along."

"That's your horse-training philosophy, is it? Make an animal grateful and she'll stay?" Linnea grabbed the door and pulled before Seth could stop her. "You might have gotten lucky with General, but you don't sound like any horseman I've heard."

"Then you've been listening to the wrong sort." His mouth crooked in a jaunty grin.

When he was smiling like that, it was hard not to look at his lips. Harder still to forget the heated caress of his kiss. The brush of hot mouth and hotter tongue. Impossible to forget his steel-hard arms that clutched her to his equally solid chest.

She tugged open the door, grateful for the wind that cooled her overflushed face. Seth's stallion raced past her in a black blur of mane and tail.

"General, for heaven's sake, be a gentleman." Seth left the buckets just inside the doorway and loped down the aisle to retrieve his horse. "Linnea, leave the buckets. I don't mind filling the troughs."

"Are you going to do all my chores?"

"Sure. Why not?"

She shook her head. He was too much of a gentleman. If he was any nicer to her, it was going to be impossible to forget the kiss that still buzzed on her lips and reminded her of her loneliness.

"Just check on the mare. I can handle the milking." She emptied the water bucket into the cow's trough, chasing out the last drops before lowering it to the ground. She grabbed the second bucket. "Did she drink and eat last night?"

"Her water's down, but she didn't touch her food." Seth looked up from tethering General to the center pole. "Don't look so worried. She's probably protesting her treatment here. Some wild horses have been known to starve to death in captivity."

"That makes me feel much better about keeping her tied up in here."

Linnea approached the second stall. The mustang was huddled in the corner, just out of sight. She lifted the bucket and water tumbled into the empty trough. The shadowed mare neighed a sharp, high warning.

Seth's hand closed over the metal handle, his arm hard and warm against her shoulder. "Let me finish up. You need to talk to her. Reassure her. Yesterday a barbed wire fence, today a stall and rope. It's tough being a horse."

It was tough being a woman around Seth Gatlin. Although Linnea's pulse was thudding in her ears and her blood zinged through her veins, she reminded herself of her goal. She wasn't going to give in to the temptation to dwell on their kiss.

He'd been lonely. She'd been lonely. That was all there was to it.

But the part of her that was always dreaming called her a liar.

"It's healing up, girl. You won't be hurting much longer." Although he loosened the mare's hoof, his grip on the hobbles remained firm. She fought, but she couldn't kick him.

"She's not affected by your charm," Linnea pointed out from the other side of the stall.

"Give her time. I'll win her over." Seth released the rope and moved fast enough to avoid a powerful hoof to his knee. "I'm going to be sorry I didn't leave those hobbles on her."

"At least she can lie down."

The mare lunged, teeth snapping.

So close, Seth could feel her breath on his forearm. "Take it easy, girl. I know you're afraid, but just be glad you're here instead of in Neilson's barn. He'd be ready to haul you in for slaughter about now."

"Don't even joke about that." Linnea's chin shot up, and she was pure anger. Fire danced in her eyes, and it was a beautiful sight. "I don't know what's got into Lars Neilson, but I won't come down on my price when he buys his next milk cow."

"I'm glad I'm on your good side, since we haven't negotiated the price of my cow." He swung the gate shut behind him. "I want you to come into the barn every few hours. Leave her any treat you can think of."

"Sugar cubes?"

"Or a piece of peppermint candy. A part of an apple. Maybe you've still got carrots in the cellar. Talk to her, leave them for her. See if she starts associating you with something good to eat."

"Just what I want. She sees me and bares her teeth." Linnea chuckled, a soft, low sound that slid across his skin. "Her leg is going to be okay?"

"It'll be like new. The cut wasn't deep, so she's lucky. I don't feel any heat, so she may have skirted an infection."

He latched the door and grabbed the milk pail from Linnea's slender hands. Too bad she moved so fast that he'd missed touching her. He liked the way her hands looked—slim, graceful, long fingered.

The morning sun was drying the dewy grass as they headed for the house, and Seth couldn't remember a finer morning. Spring was transforming the land, and last night's storm had brought a change to the prairies.

And maybe to his heart.

He could feel it like the breeze on his face and the ground at his feet.

Across the road, cows leaned on the split rail fence and their plaintive moos rose to earsplitting levels.

"Those are my girls, who are spoiled something terrible. I've started to feed them grain in the mornings and they aren't going to let me forget."

"See? If it works with the cows, it will work with the mustang."

She shot him a warning look, that behave-or-else look he was starting to like. The cows mooed so loudly, it hurt his ears.

"Quiet down over there." Linnea's voice warmed as if she were talking to old friends. "I'll feed the bunch of you in a little bit."

"Doesn't look like they're going to accept that. Can I take a look at them?"

It was nice simply walking across the road with her. Listening to the wind in her skirts and the light step of her dainty boots on the earth. Breathing her scent. Being next to her made him feel more like the man he used to be.

The cows crowded close, straining over the top rail to be the one to receive a brush from Linnea's hand. Seth didn't blame them one bit.

She drew him like sunlight and he couldn't look away as she greeted each Jersey by name and ran her fingertips over their light-brown noses.

She had six cows ready to come fresh, their pregnant sides inflating heavily as they breathed. Six heifers ready to be bred this year. Yearlings clung to their mother's sides, eagerly crowding close to nip at Linnea's skirt through the fence rails.

He could see why her animals were in demand. "How about I take this one?"

Linnea followed his hand. "That's Patches. She's a friendly cow, and she doesn't kick. She'll be good around Ginny's son."

"That's what I figured."

"I'll let you know when she's ready." Linnea moved close, her arm brushing his, to rub Patches's ears. "It shouldn't be much longer."

"Do I pay you then? Or now?"

"Why don't we wait until you take her home." Linnea turned and ignored the cow's deafening protests.

He fell in stride beside her, feeling the sun on his face and something stirring in his heart.

Maybe it was nothing. Maybe it was because he'd kissed her last night. Or maybe this feeling sharp and new was something else entirely.

He'd have to wait and see.

Linnea hopped up the steps, calling out to her

mother, and kicked off her boots at the door. Then she took the milk pail from him with a smile, one that made him remember the beauty of her kiss, the taste of it, the texture.

He didn't question why his heart was pounding as he stepped into the house. Or the memories that did not come with pain as he sat down to the table with the scent of pancakes and sausage sizzling in the air.

He'd learned in his thirty-three years of living that it was best not to question when something extraordinary happened.

So he accepted it. Just like that.

Across the table, Linnea smiled as she handed him the platter of eggs fried just the way he liked it.

For the first time since he'd arrived in this small corner of Montana, he was damn glad to be here.

Chapter Seven

"There's no need to hurry." Linnea gently guided her mother away from a pothole in the road. "I don't want you turning an ankle."

"How exciting it is to be heading to town. I have waited for this all winter."

"And you'll be waiting longer if you're not careful." Linnea tightened her hold on her mother's arm. "Over here, where the road's not so rough."

"How sweet it is to have a daughter to fuss over me."

"How nice it is to have you with me today. A new fabric shipment came into McIntyre's the last time I was there. I think with the extra money I've made sewing, we can choose enough for a new dress for you."

"For me? What good will a new dress do me? I have my sprigged lawn that serves me fine for trips to town, and I need for nothing more. What about a new dress for you, *flicka?* A pretty blue calico that brings out the beauty of your eyes?"

"I need for nothing and you know it. With you, I have all I need."

"Ah, a daughter's love. How fortunate I am."
Mama squeezed Linnea's hand, and a lifetime of love
could not be mistaken.

Sadness wedged like a blade in Linnea's chest and
she was glad her mother could not see it. How dear
Mama was, and yet endlessly misguided. "A new
dress will not make the major court me."

"Ah, but it could not hurt."

"He's a widower. He buried a wife and children
and he doesn't yearn for another family."

"I would not be too sure." Mama's chin bowed,
as if she'd lost some of her grand hopes. "What loneliness there is in his voice."

"He'll be leaving after the harvest."

"He need not leave alone."

"Oh, you are stubborn when you want to be!" Linnea nearly dropped the starched and pressed shirts she
carried. "This is a good life we have, and I know
how lucky I am every morning when I awaken and
every night when I go to sleep. End of discussion."

"We will buy *you* cloth for a new dress. A single
mistake should not a lifetime make, Linnea."

But it did. She bit her bottom lip, holding back the
words that would cause her mother only pain.

The sun, warm on her back, was like a soothing
touch. Linnea listened to the song of the prairie—the
melody of the wind through the new grasses, the trill
of larks and the harmony of chickadees. She felt the
tension ease from her clenched jaw.

Yes, this life was good. She did not want for more.
And if it was a lie, she would not give it voice as she
watched the prairie grasses ripple like a brilliant green
ocean at the wind's touch. The drooping blossoms of

yellow bells nodded patiently, turning the meadows a bright yellow with their solemn peaceful presence.

A peace that comforted her like nothing could.

The rattle of a wagon wheel in the road behind them drew her attention. She spun around, gently tugging her mother to the far edge of the road.

"Goodness, it sounds like Ginny's wagon, but could it be the Neilsons' oxen?" Mama wondered, turning her blind eyes to the spot in the road where the team of black oxen drew a sturdy wagon.

Seth sat on the bench seat above them, holding thick reins in his capable hands. His hat was tilted at a jaunty angle to shade his eyes from the sun. "Look what a lucky fellow I am coming across two beautiful women on my way to town."

"Major!" Mama clasped her hands together in delight. "You must be breaking sod. Where is your fine stallion?"

"Grazing in the shade back home, no doubt." He drew the rattling wagon to a stop beside them. "I got a good price on these oxen, so I up and bought them. Would you ladies like a ride to town?"

Seth's eyes sparkled, because he knew darn well Linnea wasn't about to say no, not with her mother along. "Thank you. It's a long walk for Mama."

"Glad to be of service." Seth hopped down.

Clods of dirt crumbled off his work boots as he touched the ground. Dressed for hard work, he wore trousers with a patch at the knee and one of her muslin shirts.

"I see they fit just fine." She commented when he held out his hand to help her up into the tall wagon.

"Now, see here one minute," Mama interjected.

"I do not wish to be in the middle. Always have hated the middle. You help me up first, young man."

"Are you sure? I might hit a bump in the road and the wagon might buck you right off the seat." Holding back his grin and failing, Seth caught hold of Mama's elbow.

"Did anyone teach you not to question your elders?"

"Yes, ma'am, but I couldn't help playing the devil."

He stepped up on the frame, holding the frail woman steady as she climbed onto the seat. His grip on her bone-thin arm was gentle but steady. There was no mistaking the care he took with her.

Something sharp passed through Linnea's chest, leaving her strangely vulnerable. What a wonderful man he was. Good to the core. As he settled her mother on the seat and made sure she was comfortable, she felt the pain again. Harder this time. Sharper.

With the sunlight blazing around him, he came for her. His hand lighted on her shoulder, and desire for him burned all the way to her soul.

She wanted him. More than she'd wanted anything in her life. She wanted *this* man to hold her close when the night was cold. To know the depths of his kiss and the strength of his heart. To share with him her body and to hold him deep inside.

She could smell the tart scent of the earth on his clothes and the hint of salt on his skin. Dark stubble clung to his jaw, as if he hadn't taken the time to shave before starting his work in the fields.

"Let me take your package." He slipped the bundled shirts from her arm.

She was hardly aware of anything but the pressure

of his hand on her elbow as he helped her up. Of the worn-smooth seat back and the rhythm of his breathing. Breathless, she climbed onto the bench seat and accepted the package he held for her.

While her heart raced with emotions too frightening to name, Seth looked at her with gentle regard. The way one neighbor looked upon another.

You've fallen in love with him, just like you swore not to do. She had no one to blame but herself. Certainly not the wonderful man settling onto the seat beside her.

She was too much a dreamer.

One thing was certain. She'd keep this secret in her heart. No one—*ever*—would know how foolish she was, loving a man she could never be worthy of.

She was like touching spring. The fire of it. The beauty. Seth gritted his teeth and refused to so much as look at Linnea out of the corner of his eye. Her thigh pressed against his and as the miles passed, the constant soft, firm pressure had built into a tingling heat that flowed like molten lava through his veins.

The town neared and the roads became busy and the oxen were young and needed his attention, but the truth at the back of his mind remained.

He couldn't believe it. He'd never thought he'd feel this way again.

"My, but the mercantile sounds busy." Mrs. Holmstrom turned toward the store as if she saw it. "Shoppers are everywhere. I can hear their shoes on the boardwalk."

"It's a popular day to come to town." He pulled the oxen to a halt in the street. "That's the closest I can get."

Linnea's hand curled around his wrist. "This is fine. You don't have to help us down with the traffic so busy."

"I'd be disappointed if I couldn't. Helping beautiful ladies is my calling in life."

She blushed, an innocent bloom of gentle pink across her porcelain cheeks. "I know a sweet-talking con artist when I hear one. Mama, don't pay this silver-tongued devil any mind. Give me your hand."

How she could make him laugh! He felt alive in a thousand different ways and it was as precious as a dream. He circled the wagon and held out his hand to her mother.

It had been a long time since he'd been courting and for the life of him he couldn't remember the first thing about it. But he had no doubts about what he was going to do. Seth guided the older woman to the boardwalk, and then returned to find Linnea climbing from the seat.

He caught her before she landed, his hands banding her arms and holding her in midair for one brief moment. The jangle of the harness and the drone of voices faded into silence. He met her gaze, wildflower-blue, and his heart tumbled in his chest.

Yessir, he had no doubt. Not a single one.

"Wait for me and I'll drive you back," he offered. "Your mother doesn't need to walk all the way home."

"You're a thoughtful man." Linnea looked at him as if he'd hung the moon, with her eyes wide and lit from within. Then the light faded and she withdrew to a proper distance, reaching to tug at her bonnet ribbons. "We won't be long at the mercantile."

"I've got a few errands, and I'll be back." He tipped his hat.

He hopped into the wagon and released the brake. The oxen were edgy from the noise around them, but they seemed to settle a bit when he took the reins. Talking low to them, he glanced over his shoulder just in time to see Linnea slip through the glass-fronted door and out of his sight.

But not out of his mind. He pulled the team up in front of the seamstress shop where sun reflected in the window around a dazzling red-and-white quilt, the one Linnea had sewn with her two hands.

He wasn't sure what made him tether the team and hesitate outside the door. With his dirt-streaked clothes, he wasn't dressed to step inside the elegant shop, but he turned the brass knob anyway.

A dainty bell tinkled over his head as he pushed inside. He took one look at the half a dozen women, their backs to him, looking through thick books at the counter, and almost turned around. He swept off his hat, feeling more awkward than he'd felt in his entire life.

"May I help you?" a handsome woman asked quietly, approaching from the side.

"I'm not sure," he answered truthfully. He couldn't say why he'd even stepped through the door. "I'd like to look around."

"I have plenty of gifts for a courting man," the woman said wisely, keeping her voice low so that it wouldn't carry. She gestured toward the racks of satin and silk dresses and the display of fancy bonnets. "Or, a smaller token. Take your time and please ask if you'd like help in choosing."

"Thank you kindly, ma'am."

He couldn't imagine Linnea would have much use for a huge hat with feathers or imitation fruit on it. And as pretty as the dresses were, he figured it'd be forward to buy clothing for a woman he wasn't married to. So he stepped up to the display counter where silver and gold gleamed.

"When are you going to take that quilt out of the window, Ellie?" one of the women from the group asked.

"When I sell it," the proprietor answered from the far end of the shop. "You may well consider it for your daughter's wedding bed. What a beautiful remembrance it will make."

"I'll not buy something made from Linnea Holmstrom's needle, thank you very much."

"Be charitable. The poor girl paid well enough for a single mistake," another answered.

Seth glanced at the door and back at the gaggle of women in their tailored dresses. Small towns, small minds. It happened in the best of places, and here was no exception.

"Do you see anything you'd like?" The shop owner turned away from the women and approached him, back straight and chin up.

"I'll take those things. Right there." He had no idea what they were called, but they were pretty enough. A gift a country woman like Linnea Holmstrom with her love for sewing and beauty could use.

"What a fine choice. Let me wrap these up for you. It will only take a moment."

"Thank you, ma'am." He ambled over to the window display.

That was Linnea's quilt. He couldn't imagine having the patience and skill to make those tiny stitches.

No doubt about it, that was the most beautiful quilt he'd ever seen.

"—stole the woman's husband. *Twice*—" a whispered voice rasped just loud enough to carry the length of the room.

Seth glanced over his shoulder and saw one of the women looking at him. He turned his back, troubled by the harsh words.

"Poor Ginny, stuck out in the country right next to *that* woman—"

They were talking about Linnea. Seth clenched his jaw and tamped down his anger. He had no doubt the women were speaking just loud enough so he would hear. So that he couldn't help wondering about her past. Part of him wanted to know the truth, but it wouldn't be right or respectful to Linnea. He willed himself not to listen even when the woman grew louder.

Maybe he'd wait out on the boardwalk until his gifts were ready—

"Major." The shop owner approached, her face tight. Although he didn't know her by name, she knew who he was. "Here you are. That will be nine dollars and fifty cents."

He reached for his billfold, feeling the curious women's stares and the rapid thud of his pulse. "I'll take that quilt, too. You're right. It would look mighty fine on a wedding bed."

"What a good man you are." The seamstress beamed at him and he had the strange idea she knew exactly why he was buying the quilt. "I'll wrap it well in paper. Just two more minutes."

She stepped away, hugging the quilt to her.

The well-dressed women remained silent, staring at

him as he counted greenbacks from his billfold and laid them on the counter. He recognized a familiar face. "Good day, Mrs. Johanson."

The widow turned beet red. "Hello, Major."

"I found someone to sew for me." He said it quietly, so there would be no misunderstanding. To any of these women with more time on their hands than they had principles.

He had no doubt of the gossip that would result from this, and he didn't care. He had nothing to hide. A man who'd just realized he still had a heart, that it wasn't dead and buried, didn't care much what busybodies thought.

When he left the shop, the quilt slung heavily over his forearm, happiness hit him full force.

"These are the last shirts I can accept, I'm afraid." Mrs. McIntyre looked as unrelenting as a northern blizzard as she laid the shirts on the counter. "Shannon will pay you up front."

"But I've already come down on the price." Linnea kept her voice low so her mother, shopping an aisle away, couldn't overhear. "I need this work, Mrs. McIntyre."

"It can't be helped. Mrs. Johanson made a more reasonable offer and I've chosen to go with her from now on. Do not bring your work here again because my decision is final."

"But I don't understand. You've never made one complaint about the shirts."

"The shirts aren't in question." Mrs. McIntyre's cold gaze turned sharp.

"The sewing I do for you is most of my income." She felt her face flush, because the store was quieting.

She could practically feel the dozens of shoppers listening. And her mother was one of them. "I've done nothing wrong."

Shame filled her. Somehow her wobbly legs took her one step forward. Then another. She made it across the silent store. Anger lashed through her and she fought to keep her temper.

At the counter, Shannon filled an envelope with dollar bills. "The customers are always pleased with your shirts. I thought maybe you'd like to know there's never been one complaint."

Linnea pushed the envelope in her pocket, wishing she could thank the woman who'd once been her best friend. Humiliation balled hard and hot in her throat, and she didn't dare try to speak as she turned away, the heat of so many glares making her feel small and ashamed.

"—strapped with that old mother of hers, the woman can't have an easy life. You can't blame her for looking for a little affection—" whispered a voice on the other side of the canned goods aisle.

"A decent sort of woman doesn't go looking for a man's affection. You'd think one nine-month's shame would be enough."

Linnea fisted her hands and kept walking. Her vision dimmed around the edges and her shoes rang unnaturally loud. She caught sight of her mother at the yard goods counter. "Mama, it's time to go."

"But I must wait for Donna to cut the cloth." Her mother appeared as cheerful as ever, but Linnea could see the lines of strain around her mouth and how her eyes lacked their usual sparkle.

Pain tore through her like a summer twister. How

dare Mrs. McIntyre say words that would hurt Mama! "We will buy fabric somewhere else."

"But here it is cheaper and I have chosen what I think you will like."

"We cannot afford a new dress now. Let's head outside for some fresh air."

"This is to make you happy. To show my *dotter's* beauty." Chin high, she clung to the counter's edge and refused to move. "Donna helped me choose the right color of blue to match your eyes, and enough to make a bonnet."

Across the store, boys stood openly in the aisle and snickered. Boys old enough to have manners.

"Mama, come."

"Ah, here is Donna. How much do we owe you?"

Linnea read the pity in the clerk's quiet gaze. She hated the way her hands shook as she counted out the few dollars from the envelope in her pocket.

No shirts to sew. She'd hated sewing them, it was true, the endless basting and piecing and interfacing. The careful repetitive detailed work that gave her a knot in her neck and a pain in her wrist. But it provided for Mama.

Now what would she do?

Taking her mother's arm, she led the way down the aisle. Shoppers had returned to their browsing, but the boys were still pointing. She could read on their lips the nasty words they were saying. Words that made filthy the foolish love she'd felt—once so pure and innocent—for Jimmy McIntyre.

"Is the major waiting for us?" Mama asked, stubbornly cheerful, as if that had been the real reason Linnea had pulled her out of the store.

"Not yet."

She felt her heart was exploding. Long ago she'd been a stupid girl believing a handsome man would choose her to love. And she was being just as ridiculous now, a grown woman who knew better.

"Now do you see why you must stop with this hoping?" Linnea hated her harsh words. "I'm too old to marry. And a woman who's made my mistakes doesn't get a second chance."

"You were young and in love."

"You are too forgiving and I can't stand it." She didn't want to hurt her mother, but she stared down the street and saw everything she couldn't have.

Women climbing out of their buggies, holding babies in their arms. Healthy, beautiful babies that wiggled their tiny fingers and waved their chubby arms and cooed adoringly.

The hole in her heart opened a little wider.

Mama touched her brow. "I did not mean harm, my *flicka*. I did not think. Of course you are right, but then I love you, my own precious daughter. I know the beauty in you that no one else can see because they are blind."

Linnea guided her mother out of the way of passersby, tears blurring her vision when she'd vowed not to let them. Love for her mother so bright that it hurt filled her. What would she do without Mama, whose love never dimmed or doubted?

A man's rumbling "whoa" drew her attention and she saw Seth perched high on the wagon, drawing his oxen to a stop. How wonderful he looked, even streaked with dirt from the fields. So noble her soul sang from simply looking at him.

"Are you two lovely ladies ready to head home?" He set the brake and jumped down.

He looked at her with respect, treated her as if there were no taint to her reputation. As if people weren't whispering about the time Seth had been spending at her place.

"Why don't you take Mama home?" she choked out, managing to hold back the hot, aching tears. "I need the walk."

"But Linnea—" Mama reached out.

Linnea caught her frail hand. "I need to be alone. Besides, you'll have the major all to yourself."

"You will walk safely?"

"Linnea, I'm not leaving you behind." Seth's dusty boots strode into her line of sight, and she couldn't look at him. Had he heard the rumors, too? "I'm a gentleman, remember? I can't ride knowing you're walking in the hot sun."

"I love to walk," she lied the best she could, and hurried off, nearly tripping down the boardwalk.

She would not make matters worse by reading anything into his kindness. He was a good man, through and through.

And she was done with wishing and dreaming for what could never be.

From this moment on, she would pack away her hopes into a box and close the lid. No matter how lonely she was, how empty the house after Mama went to bed and the night lent itself to dreaming, she would never hope, never imagine. Never believe.

Her arms would remain empty.

Nothing—and no one—could change it.

Seth's wagon stood in front of the barn, and his oxen were picketed in the shade, grazing. Dread filled her as she took off across the fields. Seth was probably in the house, held captive at her mother's table by yesterday's batch of cinnamon rolls. Knowing Mama, she probably wouldn't quit hoping for a son-in-law, even after today.

"Linnea!" Seth's call resounded across the plains. There he was in the corral behind the barn, holding the wild mustang with rope and the strength in his arms.

She wasn't going to go near him. Not with the tongues wagging in town. So she turned away, letting the restless hush of the prairie soothe her.

A white-tailed jackrabbit stood up on his hind legs to study her with his long floppy ears laid back and his nose twitching. Then he leaped in long strides, disappearing in the thick prairie grasses.

She climbed a rise and stared out at the horizon where land and sky made forever. How she wanted to let the wind blow her there, where there were no troubles or pain. A red-tailed hawk cried out in the blue skies overhead, sailing on wide reddish-brown wings. He circled lazily as if no worries could tether him.

What was she thinking? She couldn't go anywhere. She had Mama to care for. The dear, sweet, stubborn woman who refused to stop loving her no matter the mistakes she'd made.

The crosses stood barely seen amid the calf-high grasses and the nodding yellow bells. Linnea knelt in front of them, tracing the words she'd carved there herself. Olaf Holmstrom, her cherished father. All the guilt in the world couldn't bring him back or change the existence of the second grave.

She could barely look at the marker she'd made years ago. She'd been shaking with weakness from a prolonged labor and it showed in the unsteady writing. Christopher Olaf Holmstrom, it read, Beloved Baby Son.

She let the tears come, hot and steady, ripping through her like claws. Tears she had refused to shed in the mercantile where Mrs. McIntyre, her baby's grandmother, scorned her. Where others pitied or disdained her for this child resting in the earth, this child who'd never taken a first breath or wiggled his tiny perfect fingers or gazed with wonder at the world.

Shame, they called him. But he was her son and her whole heart.

Nothing hurt like broken dreams, buried and without life.

She cried until there were no more tears. Until there was only emptiness and the wind racing across the prairie, leaving her behind.

Coyote song haunted the night, making the prairie eerie. Linnea hesitated on the bottom step the instant she spotted light through the cracks in the closed barn doors. *Seth was here.*

She almost turned around and went back in the house. It was well after midnight and she couldn't put off going to bed any longer. As she filled her arms with wood for the morning fires, she kept her back firmly to the barn. With any luck, he'd stay inside until she was safely locked in the house.

"Who-who?" asked a barn owl as he glided on soundless wings to the ground. He captured a field mouse with his hooked talons. Like a phantom, he lifted into the air and disappeared from sight.

"Are you all right?" Seth asked from behind her.

She dropped the wood with a ringing clatter. "That's twice now you've done that to me."

"Sorry. The coyotes are loud tonight. Full moon." He knuckled back his hat but his face remained in shadow. "You didn't come to the corral today. I called out to you."

"I had some things on my mind."

"I noticed. Did you want to come with me now?"

"I need to go in. Chores are waiting." She knelt to gather the wood, but he was already there, so close their arms brushed.

His eyes darkened. His gaze slipped to her lips. Her lips buzzed as if he'd closed the distance between them. She jerked away, leaving him to gather the wood.

As she headed back to the house, she could feel his question in the air. And like the haunting cries of the coyote packs, it made the hair stand up on the back of her neck. She marched into the front room and grabbed the empty wood tin. Without a word, she dropped it onto the porch outside the door.

"How are you and the mare getting along?" He ambled up the stairs and into the light.

"Well enough."

"She's nearly healed. I let her run around the corral today. Kept her hobbled so she couldn't jump the fence and take off. Are you two becoming friends?"

"She won't eat from my hand. But after I'm gone, she'll eat the apples I leave for her."

"Give her time." He dumped the wood into the bin, his movements relaxed and easy. "I've nearly got the fields plowed and sowed. Bought the rest of the seed today."

"I'm sure Ginny appreciates it." Her stomach

twisted and she retreated toward the safety of the house.

"Linnea? I'm sorry about what Ginny did." His apology stopped her just as she was about to shut the door. He stood like a warrior on her porch, strong and as unconquerable as the night. But it was his tenderness that touched her.

He moved close. Too close. "Ginny speculated to a few of her friends on what you and I have been doing together. She had no right to hurt you."

"She didn't hurt me." Words came easily, because she wasn't going to malign Seth's family. Whatever manner the woman, Ginny McIntyre was his rightful sister. "I don't think you and I should be spending time alone together from now on. I'm certain it would only give the neighbors more fat to chew."

"I don't care about the neighbors." He caught her hand and pulled her away from the safe haven of her parlor and into the shadows. His grip was strong, but his touch tender. "I've learned the hard way what matters in life."

"I have, too."

"Good." He leaned closer, his gaze arrowing to her mouth. The air buzzed between them, and Linnea watched in horror as he dipped his head and tilted just enough so he could fit their lips together.

"I've got Mama to tend to." It was the only excuse that came to mind as she splayed her hands on his forearms and shoved him hard enough to dodge his kiss. "She's asleep, but I need to keep an eye on her."

"Listen." Seth caught her wrist so she couldn't escape into the house. "The horses."

Across the prairie beat the drum of a hundred

hooves. Faint and growing louder across the face of the night, pounding with life and power. Closer they came, soaring like magic, manes and tails shimmering in the moonlight, barely earthbound. The stallion lifted his head and neighed. The forlorn sound echoed across the plains.

The mare inside the barn answered, the sound strangely melancholy.

"She sounds lonely."

"She surely does."

Linnea listened again to the stallion's call and the mare's answer. The remaining herd sailed over her fence and into her pasture.

"I've never been so close to a wild herd. Look at them." Seth swept off his hat, gazing with awe and desire at the beautiful horses gleaming in the silvery light.

The mare's cries filled Linnea's ears until she couldn't stand it anymore. She tore away from Seth and ran. Her skirts caught the wind and nearly tripped her, but she kept going. Ten feet away on the other side of the road, the dangerous stallion's neighs rang shrill with warning and he pawed the air with his hooves.

"Linnea!"

Seth was behind her. He was going to stop her, and she couldn't bear it. She'd had enough loneliness. Enough sorrow. With all her strength, she pulled open the door and raced into the darkness.

"She could hurt you. Linnea. Wait!" As if he knew what she planned to do, he was already trying to stop her.

His hand caught her shoulder, and she twisted

away. Dodging the center post, she dove toward the stall and pulled the latch.

"I'm not keeping her captive." She wasn't crying, but her cheeks were wet as she tugged open the gate.

"Linnea." He wrapped his arms around her.

But she squirmed away. She found the rope holding the mare and jerked the slipknot free.

The mare reared. Seth hauled Linnea against the back wall and the mustang galloped away with a clatter of hooves and high triumphant neighs—calls to her herd that she was free.

Linnea felt better, stronger. Crushed against Seth's chest, she could hear his rapid heartbeat. Had he been afraid for her?

Their gazes met in the darkest shadows. In the scant glow of moonlight through the weathered boards, she could see his fear.

"You could have been trampled." He tightened his arms, trapping her against him. "I'm glad you're safe."

"I'm fine." She could feel him breathe, feel the flex of his muscles as he moved.

His hand smoothed across her brow. She wanted to give in to the warm caress. To close her eyes and let him take away the loneliness. She needed his kiss, she craved his touch.

It took all her strength to tear away from the shelter of his arms. Away from the comfort he promised.

She headed toward the large swatch of light made by the open barn door. Anything to get away from him.

"Linnea?" His step pounded after her. "I'm getting tired of chasing you. Maybe you can tell me why you let the mare go. I made some progress with her today.''

''She deserved to be free.''

''Freedom is a dangerous place. That's how she wound up in your care.''

''Life is a dangerous place. It can't be helped.''

''Damn it, that's not what I meant. You had something to offer her. A safe place to live. Hay and grain and a comfortable bed at night.''

''She wanted her freedom.''

''In time, she would have made a good saddle horse. She would have been happy.''

''Do you see her staying around? Look.'' She swept her hand toward the prairie, where the galloping mustangs were distant silhouettes against the horizon. ''She made her choice, and I'm glad.''

''You are the darnedest woman, Linnea Holmstrom.'' He shook his head. He sounded angry; he sounded amused. ''Is there a chance now that you'll invite me in for a cup of tea or something?''

''Not a chance on this earth.'' She left him standing in the yard, bathed in moonlight, looking as confused as she felt.

She'd been mean to him. It weighed on her conscience as she bolted the front door and turned down the light. Darkness filled the parlor. *There.* Maybe that would stop him from coming back to the door and knocking. Trying to get the kiss she'd denied him tonight.

But she sat at the window and peered through the night shadows. She spotted him against the dark night. He walked home, his head bowed, his hat in his hands.

She'd hurt him. When she'd only meant to keep a proper distance between them. Troubled, she leaned her forehead against the cool glass. She'd done the right thing, but it didn't feel that way. Not one bit.

Chapter Eight

"Wait to wash the cloth, *dotter*. Until you've made your trip to town."

"I'm not going to town." Linnea scooped the dipper into fresh well water and drank it gratefully. She felt sticky and dusty from packing water for the garden, and her arms and back were aching. She returned the dipper to the bucket. "I'm late on starting the washing."

"Linnea. Tell me why the wood is on the porch."

"I didn't want Seth in the house last night."

"He was here?" Mama marveled, as if the greatest miracle had occurred. "To think I slept through it. Did you offer him my cinnamon rolls? How highly he praised them yesterday."

"When he brought you home?"

"Why, yes. He left this for you. To continue sewing for him." She reached into her pocket and withdrew a greenback. "I told him to run home and fetch his favorite trousers and you would make a pattern from them. He wants four pair, Linnea. Three for work and one for good."

"I'm not sewing for him." Her step faltered when

she noticed the twenty-dollar bill her mother was waving.

"Whatever for? If this is about yesterday—"

"This is not about yesterday," she bit out, hating the harsh strain in her voice. She yanked open the front door and loaded her arms with wood. "This is about what's right. He has a sister to sew for him and half the unmarried women in town."

"But he prefers you."

Linnea stomped across the room and dumped the wood on the floor in front of the stove. Raw and hurting, she tried to stop thinking about yesterday. How could she?

Ever since she'd let Jimmy McIntyre get her pregnant when she was sixteen, the gossips had been relentless. And inventive. If what they said were true, she'd have slept with half the men in the county.

But they weren't going to gossip about her and Seth. She stabbed sticks of wood into the meager fire and watched the flames flare.

"You have lost work in town. What can it hurt to make a few garments for a bachelor? He cannot sew for himself, and there is trouble with his sister, I think. He cannot rely on her."

"That's none of my concern." Remembering last night and how Seth had walked away in the darkness, his head bowed, raked like hot coals across her conscience.

"Please reconsider—" Mama paused in midsentence. "I hear a rig in the yard. A little buggy drawn by a single horse. We don't know anyone with a small buggy."

"I'll see who it is."

Sure enough, there was a polished lady's buggy

parked in the shade of the barn, a single mare already grazing in the grass. A handsome woman dressed in a slate-blue shirtwaist and black skirt swept down the dusty path toward the house. Her matching bonnet framed her face.

Linnea's heart sank. She knew exactly why the woman had come. She was returning the quilt. "Mrs. Jance, welcome."

"It's good to see you again, Linnea. Please, call me Ellie. Is this your mother? Pleased to meet you, Mrs. Holmstrom."

"Oh, how wonderful you have come to pay us a call." Mama clasped her hands together, beaming with happiness and beauty. "I cannot tell you all the good things I have heard about your shop. What a talented seamstress you must be."

"I don't know about being talented, but I try to run a good business, which is why I've come. I've sold your appliquéd rose quilt, Linnea." She snapped open her pocketbook and counted out several large bills. "This is your share at sixty percent."

It couldn't be true. Linnea's knees wobbled and she caught the carved back of the sofa. "You sold it?"

"And now I'd like to know if you have another I can display in my window."

"You *really* sold it?" She couldn't believe this was happening. Someone from town had bought her quilt? And paid so much money for it?

"A young man bought it for his bride-to-be."

"*Dotter,* what is this? You have kept this from me." How happy Mama sounded. How proud she looked as one hand flew to her heart. "My daughter's work was displayed in your fine shop, Mrs. Jance?

Oh, to think my horrible, bad daughter did not tell me so that I could boast!''

''Mama! Guess why I didn't tell you.'' Linnea still couldn't believe it and that Mrs. Jance had come with more than money. ''You want more quilts?''

''Does my *dotter* have more quilts!''

Mrs. Jance's eyes sparkled and she held back her chuckle. ''That must mean she does.''

''I'll bring out what I have.'' Linnea took the crisp bills and folded them into her pocket. ''You already sold my best one.''

''That's all right. I'm sure whatever you have is lovely.''

Her hands were trembling as she knelt in front of the cedar chest in the bedroom. What if Mrs. Jance didn't like them? She had only a few that had never been used. They were all traditional patterns she'd learned from the book Papa had given her for her fourteenth birthday.

Suddenly the simple blocks didn't look fancy enough. If only she'd had the chance to start something new.

''This is stunning.'' Mrs. Jance knelt beside her and shook her head at the calico pattern of pink buds and green leaves, pieced with pink calico and plain white.

''It's a Double Irish Chain. There's no appliqué.''

''It's feminine and beautiful.'' Mrs. Jance lifted the quilt from the chest and draped it on the bed. ''Look at that. May I take this one?''

Linnea nodded. ''I have a flower basket pattern here. I made it from memory of a drawing I saw in a book.''

Mrs. Jance ran her thumb over the feathered circle

stitch that set the theme for the quilt. "I'll take this one, as well. Now, how would you feel about sewing a quilt for me? You select the pattern and I'll give you the pick of fabric in my store. We split the proceeds fifty-fifty."

"Yes." How could she refuse? There would be no more collars to set, no more pesky sleeves to baste and rebaste into place.

"Good, then I'll take these and expect you to show up in my store soon. I know I'll enjoy doing business with you, Linnea."

Ellie Jance left, hugging the quilts against her.

"Shame on you for keeping this secret from me," Mama scolded. "To think what good fortune this is. What do I always say? When a door closes, a window opens."

"Yes, Mama." Linnea laughed. She couldn't help it. She was so happy. She had more blessings than she could count. She would not ask for more.

"Are you leaving?" Ginny asked quietly in the night shadows.

The muscles in Seth's neck clamped into a tense knot. Instead of turning around and looking at his sister, he kept folding his shirts and placing them on a pile on the bed. "I'm moving into the claim shanty."

"But it's been abandoned for years. It's falling down."

"I'll fix it." He kept his voice neutral. Getting angry at Ginny wouldn't solve either of their problems.

"But I promised to cook for you and keep house. In exchange for you helping me." Sorrow filled her words.

And, he hoped, regret. "I can cook my own meals. Or you can invite me over, if you've a mind to."

"I shouldn't have said those things about Linnea."

"Damn right you shouldn't have." It grated him that she hadn't thought. Ginny had learned from her father how to strike and then hide, always sorry. "I've got more work than I've got daylight to do it in. But you seem to have enough time to make a mess of everything you touch."

"I didn't mean to."

"Yes, you did." He refused to be fooled. They'd grown up in the same house for a time. Her father had been a cruel man, always attacking and retreating, jovial until he found a person's weakness. Seth didn't have to live like that now, in the form of Ginny's apologetic silences and attempts to please him. And her hatred for it.

"I gave my word, and that's the only thing keeping me here." He grabbed socks from the top drawer. "The only thing."

"If you left, we'd go hungry. I married into one of the richest families in town so I'd always be cared for. So my son would never know the life we had growing up."

"Rich or poor, town or county, that doesn't make the difference." He jammed his socks into the leather pack. "You ought to know that by now. Your fancy house didn't protect you from life, did it?"

She hung her head, staring at the floor, and her refusal to own up to what she'd done, to be responsible, angered him more.

He buckled his packs and swung them over his shoulder. "You've got a son who's alive. I'd be grateful if I were you. I'd spend my time making his life better instead of cutting down a defenseless woman who's done nothing wrong.''

''You think I'm wrong.''

''I know you are.''

''I see.'' She bit her lip, waiting. ''You're angry because my son is alive and yours isn't.''

''Fine. Turn it into that if you want.'' He'd had enough of her house, dark and bleak. Of the jabs that came passively so she could deny them.

He pushed past her and climbed down the ladder from the attic, taking the rungs two at a time. Like a thousand pounds pressing on his chest, he felt claustrophobic. He couldn't breathe. He'd stayed in this bleak place long enough.

''Inga Neilson saw Jimmy in the fields one night when she was coming home late from a church meeting. Riding back to town as happy as you please, whistling. He had to have been at the Holmstrom farm. He'd been with Linnea, I know he was.''

Seth pushed open the door and stepped out into the shadowed porch. Lamplight from the kitchen spilled over the weathered boards and lit his way as he kept going.

''Your friend Linnea had been with him before, when Jimmy and I were promised. Did you know that? She—''

''That's enough,'' he growled, and meant it.

He watched the realization dawn on her face, pinched hard with bitterness and anger, and she bowed her head.

''I just thought you should know,'' she bit out. ''I won't let her hurt you.''

''You have no say in how I live my life. I don't want to hear another word against Linnea.''

"But she's—"

"Not another word."

The night deepened, and Ginny became only shadow as the moonlight faded behind clouds.

"All right. I'm sorry." She whispered the words, laced them with defeat.

He wasn't sure if she was telling the truth. Time would tell. "Just so you know, I won't bend on this. No more gossiping. No more cruel remarks."

"She's not the woman you think she is."

"Neither are you." He left, choosing the darkness instead of Ginny's passive rage. He could hear her tears, but he didn't turn back. He felt sorry for his sister, but she had some growing up to do.

The shanty was little more than a shack perched on a small rise behind the orchard. The front door listed on its rusty hinges and great patches were missing from the roof, but he could fix that.

He set his packs on the floor. The night wasn't cool, so he didn't build a fire in the chimney he'd repaired a few hours before. He spread out his bedroll and took off his boots.

There were changes to be made in his life. He wasn't certain he knew what to do about them. How should he go about making Linnea his wife? He reached into his pack and took out the gift Mrs. Jance had boxed. With a tug, the strings came loose and he pushed the paper aside. Surely she'd like a pretty bauble like this. He traced the pattern on one of the thimbles.

Linnea had certainly been angry with him. Maybe she had a right to her anger. He *had* been trying to kiss her. All he had to do was think of her and joy filled him. He could picture the way her golden curls shone like treasure at the sun's touch.

He loved her face and her smile, the way she laughed and who she was. Desire for her pounded in his veins and he grew hard wishing he had the right to do more than kiss her.

Did she love him? His entire future hinged on that question. Judging by the way she'd behaved last night, he had no idea.

One thing was for certain—he wasn't going to sit here wondering. His life had been empty for too long.

"I haven't seen you in a while." That's how Linnea greeted him when he rode into her yard.

He tipped his hat back, taking his time to figure out exactly what to say. He sensed the wrong thing would put her on edge and that was the last thing he wanted. "I've been fairly busy in the fields."

"Are your crops surviving the drought?"

"All seventy acres, so far."

"Good for you." She nodded politely, then plunged her arms deep into the washtub and fished around in the sudsy water. "I told you I'm not going to sew for you. Let me return your money."

"Keep it and apply it to what I owe you for the cow."

"She's ready. Had her calf a few days ago. When you're ready to leave, go ahead and take her with you."

She scrubbed a garment against the washboard with great fury and said nothing more.

Looked like she was still mad about the kiss.

"Major! How wonderful to see you again." Mrs. Holmstrom's greeting was as gracious as heaven.

"Give me a few moments and I will have *tosca* cake right out of the oven."

"A man can't say no to your baking. I brought something for you." He reached into the back of the wagon and cradled the soft furry animal in his palm. "I bought one for Ginny this morning from Mrs. Neilson and thought I'd pick one up for my favorite ladies."

"No, not one of her kittens!" As if she could see, Mrs. Holmstrom turned toward the nearly silent mew from the tiny creature. "Major, this is too much. We cannot pay you for this."

"No payment necessary, ma'am. This is for all the kindness you've shown me. It's a little female calico. She's mostly orange and black with a little white thrown in." He set the kitten in the palm of her hand.

"Oh, she's darling. I've always had a cat, and the last one we had was a cuddly tom who fell ill last year. How I've missed him keeping me company. Linnea, come see what the major brought."

"Isn't he generous?" Linnea's step padded on the earth behind him and her presence brushed like a caress across his skin.

It was tough to keep from thinking about kissing her. "I've come to put in the windmill I promised."

"A pump for the water?" Mrs. Holmstrom gasped, as if the words were too good to be true.

"That's right, ma'am. Linnea won't have to carry another heavy bucket to the house or the barn."

"Praise be, what a blessing you are. I'd best get back inside and check on my *tosca* cake." Cuddling the kitten, she counted the steps back to the porch.

"You've made my mother happy."

"Good. Because I was hoping that would make it harder for you to be mad at me."

"I'm not mad at you."

"Sure. That's why you winced when you saw me driving up." That had a corner of her mouth fighting a grin, so it was progress. "I owe you an apology."

"No, I owe you, because I released your horse back into the wild. I was rash and I didn't think. She would have been worth a hundred dollars, maybe two. You caught her and treated her wounds. She rightfully belonged to you."

"I'm not troubled by that. I shouldn't have tried to kiss you."

"That's right. You shouldn't have." She spun away, her step jerky as she headed back to her washing.

He'd hurt her more than he realized. A beautiful woman like her having to face rumors like that. She was innocence itself, unassuming and gentle like the flowers blooming in the fields.

"I'm sorry for wanting to kiss you."

Kneeling at her work, she gazed up at him, her face soft and undefended, her anger gone. "You're forgiven, it's forgotten."

"Not forgotten." He brushed her cheek with his fingers, and the velvet warmth of her skin fired his blood. "I can't figure why you aren't married, a beautiful woman like you."

"You've been to town. You ought to know why. There will be no wedding bells for me."

"Someday a man's going to come courting. You wait and see."

She withdrew from his touch, the light in her fading like day into night. Water splashed as she scrubbed a bedsheet against the washboard. "A man courting me? That's never going to happen. I'll forever have men, even men like you, trying to steal kisses in the dark."

She kept scrubbing and he had the odd feeling she was crying, but he saw no tears on her cheeks. She kept scrubbing as if she hadn't understood what he'd been trying to say.

The sun blazed on his back and his muscles burned from cutting the heavy lumber, but that didn't stop him from thinking of her all morning. He dug his gloved fist into the nail bucket and loaded his shirt pocket. His gaze drifted eastward toward the rise in the road that hid the Holmstrom farm from his sight.

He could see Linnea in his mind's eye—slim and graceful, the wind in her skirts, the sun in her hair. The quiet smile that softened her face and made her heart show in her eyes. Had she cried when he'd driven away? Or did she save her sadness for nighttime when no one was looking?

A movement against the prairie made him blink. But her image remained, her skirts snapping in the wind and hugging her soft woman's curves.

A sunbonnet shaded her face and capped her golden curls. He wanted to rip the hat from her head so he could see the wind tangling her hair. So he could wind his fingers into her soft curls and hold her in another kiss.

"Working hard, I see." She shaded her eyes with one hand.

"Trying to. Hope to get this done in a few days."

The wind plastered her dress to her like a second

skin. Not even her petticoats or her corset could hide the curve of her hips and breasts.

Such nice breasts, too, he realized. It wasn't gentlemanly of him but he noticed.

"My mother sent you this." She held out a covered plate, one he noticed now through the glare of the sun. "She didn't want you to have to head home for lunch. This time I think the motives are pure. She's finally accepted you won't be a permanent fixture around here, so you're safe."

"As long as she shares her baked goods with me, I'll forgive her for anything."

"Why? I'm not about to." Linnea's smile said otherwise.

He stepped close so that only the wind separated them. Close enough to see the violet sparkles in her deep-blue eyes and her bottom lip quiver. Their fingers brushed as he took the plate. Through leather gloves, his skin tingled.

She was beautiful when her cheeks turned as delicately pink as prairie roses.

"Mama added a second helping of her *tosca* cake. She's playing favor to your sweet tooth. But don't worry. I've already told her you're not looking for a wife, a man who looks the way you do."

"What way is that?"

"Oh, there's your complete hair loss and the unfortunate size of your nose."

"She believed that, did she?"

"Sure. She's still charmed by you, so I'll have to enlighten her to your other nasty qualities."

"I have nasty qualities?"

"Bad enough to discourage her." Her grin dazzled.

''I have yet to tell her about your gambling habit. Mama will be appalled.''

''Break it to her gently, Linnea. I don't want her to stop feeding me completely.''

She laughed and he felt renewed. Her mouth was lush and relaxed, her lips a dusty-rose shade that made him salivate like a bee circling a flower. He was hungry and wanting and buzzing.

She spun around as if she couldn't wait to get away from him.

''Hey, Linnea. Are you just going to leave me like this?''

''Sure, why not? You're a grown man. You can eat by yourself.'' She tugged at the blue brim of her sunbonnet. ''Mama wanted to invite you into the house, but I talked her out of it. Said you probably didn't want to interrupt your work.''

''Sure. Why would I want the chance to get out of the sun for a while?''

''That's what I thought. You're a tough army major. You're used to eating outside with flies for company.''

''Flies? I'm not attracting flies.''

''That's what you think.''

She left him laughing, and he watched her amble through the meadows bright with brown-eyed Susans and cheerful bluebonnets. With the wind buffeting her calico dress against her like a second skin, Seth couldn't look away.

She stopped to pick a few flowers, probably for her mother, before heading to the house. That was Linnea, always doing for her mother.

Had anyone ever picked flowers for her?

Tenderness welled within him so sweet and bright

it hurt like a wound, but he wasn't afraid of it. Love had come to him a second time in his life like the miracle of summer to the plains.

He wasn't going to let it pass him by.

Morning came to the prairie not with a whisper but a celebration. Birdsong announced the dawn before the first ray of light breached the colorless horizon.

Seth breathed in the fresh scent of the morning. The fragrance of wildflowers and wild grasses lifted like the sweetest perfume he'd ever known. The scent reminded him of Linnea as he picked a fistful of the purple-blue flowers.

The first peep of gold over the eastern hills made the world glow with a strange half-darkness. Then the rays of golden lengthened and deepened. Rose and lavender lashed together at the horizon and streaked out to touch the clouds. The sky turned peach at the farthest edge of the plains.

The land waited with a sudden hush. Seth laid the flowers and a thimble on Linnea's front step. Emotion slammed into his chest like a runaway train. And as the sun rose and brought light to this corner of the world, he swore it did the same to his heart.

"Mama, I've got the cows to milk," Linnea's voice came muffled through the wall. "We're going to need to churn butter this morning."

The doorknob creaked as it turned, and Seth hurried into the field. He heard the hinges squeak open as he knelt in the tall grass. If he took off his hat, he didn't think she could see him.

She carried two empty milk pails, one in each hand, and closed the door with her foot. Her skirts swirled around her shoes as she skidded to a stop on the porch. Her jaw fell open as she stared at his offering.

He rubbed his clammy palms on his trousers. He'd never been so nervous. Didn't she like the flowers? Had he done the wrong thing?

She set the milk pails to the ground with a clink and knelt to gather the bluebonnets. She cradled them in her lap and ran her fingertip over the delicate blossoms.

Was that a smile on her face? He couldn't tell, but if his heart kept beating this fast, it was going to kill him. He was too old for this.

She lifted the flowers to her face and breathed deeply. Her eyes drifted shut as if she were savoring the fragrance and the beauty.

His knees weakened and he sat fully on the ground. Spellbound, he watched her, joy dawning in him so bright and unexpected it left him reeling.

She snatched up the thimble and studied it. Ran her thumb over the delicate flowers on the enamel surface. She looked down the road in either direction. Then the corners of her mouth curved.

He saw his future in her smile.

Chapter Nine

Linnea simply stared at the thimble in her hand. The baked enamel surface gleamed pale as new butter. She traced her finger across its surface made bumpy by a spray of painted-on flowers.

So delicate. And expensive. Finer than anything she owned.

Who could have given such a thing? Surely it was not meant for her mother.

All through her morning chores, it bothered her. She'd left the bluebonnets in a cup on the table. The thimble remained a weight in her pocket, real and undeniable.

She milked the few cows that remained in the pasture, met the dairy wagon come to buy the milk and fed the new calves. Mama had toasted bread, eggs and ham ready by the time she returned to the house.

Don't even think someone's courting you, Linnea. Romance was not likely to come looking for her.

Midway through the meal, Mama set down her glass of fresh milk and cocked her head. "Goodness, is that the major already? Should I fry more eggs?"

Seth? Linnea bolted out of her chair and pushed aside the curtains snapping in the open window.

He sat on the high wagon seat looking like a man from her dreams. Self-assured, trustworthy, kind. He drew his oxen to a stop in the yard.

"How are you this fine morning?" He tipped his hat and his blue gaze snapped as if he thought himself so charming.

Oh, the man was far too saucy. "Better, but then you drove up. Still attracting flies, I see."

"Well, ma'am, I'm a male of the species, so I guess that can't be helped. But if you want running water piped into your kitchen, you might consider holding back your remarks until I've finished."

"Major, can it be?" Mama crossed the room in a flash and bounded out onto the porch.

She turned her sightless gaze toward him. "I thought you only meant to put a pump in the field. But to think we will have the luxury of water in our house! I cannot thank you enough."

"He'll probably raise the rent, Mama."

"Or I *could* be sweet-talked into making a trade. Say a batch of cinnamon rolls and we call it square."

She wanted to stay mad at him, she really did. But he winked at her, that impudent man who thought he could kiss her anytime he wanted, and heaven help her! Every bit of her anger blew away like leaves on the wind. She was helpless to stop it.

What had he told her? *Someday a man's going to come courting. You wait and see.*

He didn't bring the flowers, Linnea. But she wanted him to be the one. Because that would mean he saw *her,* the woman she was and not the reputation gossip and judgment had made.

A fluttery, excited feeling gathered deep within her. What if he'd left the flowers?

"Major, come join us for our meal. I shall fry more eggs for you."

"I'd love to accept, but I've already had my breakfast. Tomorrow?"

"Wonderful." Mama clasped her hands.

"I don't know, Mama. We're already feeding him lunch. Maybe we should start charging him. Let's say a dollar a meal."

"Any chance I can bargain you lovely women down to fifty cents?"

"She only teases, Major! *Dotter,* behave yourself."

Laughing, Seth snapped the reins, his dazzling gaze meeting Linnea's, bold and confident.

What on earth was she going to do about that man?

The next morning there were bluebonnets on her doorstep. They were only wildflowers, she told herself, but they were her favorite.

Who had left them?

She wandered down to the road, where no recent tracks disturbed the dust from town. But Seth had already arrived, judging by the two-toed hoofprints of oxen and the deep impressions from a loaded wagon.

She ran to the back of the house and spotted him in the field. Shovel in hand, he waved to her and went back to work.

He hadn't left the flowers, she reasoned with herself. Why would he?

Maybe he'd seen who had.

Forgetting about her waiting chores and every reason why she'd vowed not to be alone with Seth Gatlin, she marched through the tall grasses and dancing wildflowers.

He glanced up, adjusted his hat as the breeze dallied across the prairie between them, then went right back to work. He didn't look back up, either. He kept shoveling and emptying the shovel in a smooth rhythm as if he were hoping she'd walk right on past him.

Sure, now that she wasn't handing out free kisses in the night and maybe more, he refused to speak with her. How could he make her angry when she'd just forgiven him?

"Isn't it a little early in the morning to be picking wildflowers?" Seth commented when she drew near. "Or did you decide to come over and pick on me next?"

She felt ashamed. She'd been the one who had started this, angry with him, determined to keep him at arm's length. Then she saw the small crook in the corner of his mouth. So, he was teasing her.

"A man who's about to be served breakfast might think about being nicer. My next chore this morning is gathering the eggs, and all it would take is one little misstep and all the fresh eggs might wind up falling. Mama won't know the difference if she's scrambling eggs already broken in the basket or ones I've scooped off the chicken coop floor."

"You win. I'm bein' nice from now on." He leaned on his shovel and grinned at her. A captivating, saucy, far-too-tempting grin that ought to be illegal. "I saw those flowers on the doorstep when I drove over. Got an admirer you're not telling anyone about?"

The devil danced in his eyes, but his words rang

with such sincerity she didn't know whether to believe him or not. "You didn't see anyone?"

"Nope. Not a soul." He didn't blink once. Not once.

"This is the second morning in a row. You wouldn't happen to know who picked these for me, would you?"

"No idea." He shook his head, but his gaze felt soft as a touch to her face. "See? Didn't I tell you someday a man could come courting?"

"Yes, you did." She took a step back, studying him thoroughly. "If you ever see anyone leaving flowers on the step, would you tell me who he is?"

"You have my solemn word on it." He grabbed his shovel, his gloved hands so strong, yet she knew how tender they could be.

Remembering the feel of his fingers against her face and the heat of his kiss, she hugged the flowers carefully in her arms and headed back to the house.

Linnea rubbed the sweat from her brow with the edge of her apron. Although she'd banked the fire, the iron stove radiated heat.

Exhausted from her morning's work and from preparing the meal in sweltering temperatures, she covered the fried chicken with a cloth.

A tiny meow came from Mama's chair cushion. Linnea pushed aside the hem of the lace tablecloth to find the new kitten making her way toward the chicken.

"No cats allowed on the table, sorry." She curled her hand around the kitten's tummy and lifted her gently. The calico meowed in protest because the chicken did smell good.

Linnea grabbed her sewing basket on the way to the door and welcomed the merely warm breeze and fresh air. Summer was on its way. She could smell it in the ripe, sharp scent of the grass and the tartness of the earth.

The leaves on the fruit trees behind the house rustled merrily, dappling sunshine. The sweet scent of the tiny growing apples, peaches, pears and plums blended together and made her stomach growl.

Mama's needle paused. She sat on a bench in the dappled shade. "Are you done cooking so soon? I was of the mind to get off my backside and help you."

"You'll stay out of the heat. End of argument." Linnea set the kitten in Mama's lap, and the calico leaped right off. "Maybe it will be cooler tomorrow."

"Ha! I think our summer has come early. It is hot in the shade."

"Want me to fetch you some water?"

"You are too good to me, *dotter.* Sit down and keep me company. I have been listening to the major's progress with the digging. Already he is halfway to the house."

Linnea eased down onto the bench, which happened to give her a perfect view of Seth Gatlin. His shovel drove into the ground over and over again. His masculine form was pleasingly proportioned, she noted, with wide shoulders, narrow hips, powerful legs.

She shouldn't be noticing.

"I am going in to fetch more thread." Mama set down her crocheting. "No, I need no help, and the house will be cooler now that you are no longer cooking. Sit and rest, Linnea. You work too hard."

"There is much to do." She didn't mind, and as soon as her mother was safely inside the house, Linnea closed her eyes. The breeze played with her damp bangs and cooled her heated skin.

"Dreaming of your admirer?"

She opened her eyes to the sight of Seth Gatlin striding past her vegetable garden. "You think that's funny, don't you? An old maid like me getting flowers from somebody."

"Not at all. You're a beautiful woman, Linnea."

"Not with a ruined reputation."

"A wise man might not care."

"Like who?"

Seth leaned one shoulder against the tree trunk. His eyes were as dark as midnight while he considered his answer. "Take the man who bought your quilt from Mrs. Jance, for example. *He* might have left the flowers."

"How would you know a man bought my quilt?" She couldn't bear to think he was teasing her, not about her feelings and not like this.

"I was in Mrs. Jance's shop that day running an errand, and saw the whole thing. The Widow Johanson was there, too, and she was speechless, I'll tell you."

He swept off his hat and the wind tousled his dark locks. He looked rakish and impudent and so desirable she didn't dare hope.

"You think the same man who bought my quilt left me these flowers?"

"One and the same, I'll bet."

"Well, you saw the man who bought my quilt. Who was he?"

"I'm not telling you. That would ruin the romance." He knelt until he was eye-to-eye with her and only the breeze separated them. "I wouldn't want to do that."

"I didn't know you were a romantic man."

"No, but life is dull over at my place, so I figured watching you and your secret admirer might be fun."

"Fun, is that what you call it? Torture would be more accurate."

"Now, see, that's a matter of perspective." His gaze fastened on her mouth. His eyes went completely black.

The air between them crackled.

"Major, are you still here? I heard you two talking, and so I made a plate for you. I bet you are as hungry as a wolf!" Mama hesitated on the threshold, holding one of the serving platters in both hands. "I do not dare take another step for fear of spilling. Come rescue me."

"Gladly."

Linnea stopped breathing. Seth's mouth softened as if he intended to lean forward and claim her lips with his. Then he pulled away and stood, jogging across the yard to the back steps.

"I have forgotten how hungry a man working gets," Mama trilled on, unaware of what she'd interrupted. "I fear we did not make a large enough breakfast for you, Major. You came in search of food, did you not?"

"This ought to tide me over until supper time. Thank you." Seth took the platter into his capable hands.

"We did not have a large enough platter, so perhaps this will do as well. I hope you like the potato salad. Linnea made it from my mother's recipe."

"Potato salad is one of my favorite things in the world." Seth's charm left Mama grinning ear to ear.

He touched her sleeve and offered her his hand to help her down the stairs and across the lawn.

"Here." He tossed something into Linnea's lap and flashed her that saucy grin of his, the one that left her unable to breathe. Then he strode back to the fields.

"What did he give you?" Mama asked as she settled onto the bench.

"A silver dollar." Linnea didn't know if she should take off after him and give the money back or smack him upside the head. "Payment for the day's meals."

"Oh, that man!"

Linnea couldn't help it. She burst into laughter.

Seth snapped the reins, guiding the oxen down the shadowed road. He yawned. It was early, but he had the feeling he'd sparked Linnea's curiosity. If he wanted to leave the flowers he'd picked, he figured he had to do it before she was awake.

If only the rattling wagon didn't make so much noise. Antelope leaped away in the fields. Some secret admirer he was, announcing his presence to the entire county.

The Holmstrom farm lay quiet in the gray twilight just before dawn. He guided the oxen into the grass, where there were no ruts to rattle the wagon, and studied the house. The windows were closed and the curtains still drawn. Didn't look like anyone was up yet.

Victory.

Then a movement caught his attention. A curtain

was moving, as if someone in the parlor had released it suddenly. So she was up early and keeping watch for her admirer.

Determined to outsmart her, he drove the oxen into the field, unhitched them and tethered them as usual. Then he gathered the fresh flowers from the wagon seat and hurried to the house, keeping out of sight of the windows the best he could.

Yep, she was watching the front steps like a hawk. He laid the bouquet on the back porch in plain sight of the door and sneaked back the way he came. He poured himself a cup of coffee from the jug he'd brought and hunkered down to wait and watch.

The sun gave birth to another day, bringing golden light to an awakening world. Deer grazed peacefully in the thigh-high grasses, and a prairie falcon circled high overhead, hunting for breakfast.

He poured a second cup and savored the rich, biting flavor. Too bad he hadn't brought any sugar.

At last the back door swung open and Linnea froze in the middle of the tiny porch. Her long silken hair cascaded down her back, thick and unbound.

When she knelt to collect the flowers, locks of gold tumbled across her face. His fingers itched to brush back her hair, lift her into his arms and kiss her until neither of them could think.

She stood and her gaze shot straight to him. He was going to have to talk with a forked tongue to make her think he wasn't her secret admirer. To his surprise, she ducked inside the house. He slurped his cooling coffee and, sure enough, she reappeared with a water bucket swinging from her hand.

She was sure walking fast. She wasn't smiling.

He'd seen an angry woman before. But for all his

experience, he'd never figured out the knack for dealing with an angry woman. He didn't know what to do as Linnea marched straight toward him with her skirts snapping and golden hair fluttering in the wind.

"Morning," he greeted her.

Wrong thing to say. Her pretty mouth compressed into a puckered line. "How long have you been sitting here on your behind?"

"You ought to know. You saw me drive up."

A muscle jumped in her jaw. "You saw me looking out the window?"

"Hell, he probably did, too, whoever that admirer of yours is. Must be why he came around back to leave the flowers."

"You saw him?"

"Not exactly. I was pouring my coffee. When I looked up, I could see the flowers on the back porch, but nobody was around. Then you came out and saw the bluebonnets."

"From here. You could tell there were flowers on the step from here?"

"Sure. Look." He gestured with his cup toward the house.

She sidled up beside him and squinted into the sun.

"Can you believe he came and went and we never saw him?" He did his best to sound innocent.

"Probably because he's a sneak. A man of the worst sort."

"That's likely to be true. He probably wouldn't appreciate hearing the object of his affections talking about him like that."

"Oh? Is he nearby? Can he hear me right now?"

"I suppose if he's hiding on the low side of that knoll over there. Or in the field. This grass is so high all a man would have to do is kneel down. You wouldn't see him.''

"Just proves my theory. A man of the worst sort. He's probably a liar, too.''

"Probably.'' He swallowed the rest of his coffee. "Want some? I brought another cup.''

"Nice of you, but I have a secret admirer hiding like a snake in the grass. I wouldn't want him to see me with you. He might get the wrong idea and stop leaving me flowers.''

"He wouldn't do that. A man with any sense would fight for a woman like you, Linnea.'' He couldn't hide his grin any longer so he dug around in the wagon bed for the other cup. "Since I know the identity of your beau, I know he's an upstanding man.''

"Upstanding? A sneak and a liar?'' She quirked one brow.

"Well, any man has his flaws.'' He handed her the cup. "He's a hard worker. Handsome fellow, too. Probably the best-looking bachelor in the county.''

"Beauty *is* in the eye of the beholder.'' She held the cup while he poured. "Maybe when I finally meet him, I won't like the way he looks. Maybe he has dark hair and I like blond.''

"It's a possibility. But keep an open mind. He's obviously in love with you.''

"Obviously?''

"Sure.'' He capped the jug. "A man doesn't go courting for the fun of it. Marriage is too much torture for that.''

She choked on the coffee. Her laughter chased away all his loneliness and her bluebonnet-blue eyes sparkled with quiet affection. "You are a bad man, Seth Gatlin.''

"I try." He wanted to wrap her in his arms and feel her against him. He wanted to spend the rest of his life making her laugh.

She thrust the bucket at him. "Fill this for me, and I won't charge you for breakfast."

"Sure. Do you like my coffee?"

"You call this coffee?"

"That's what the outside of the bag said."

"I'll show you coffee. Come with me."

The next morning she was waiting for him even before the birds were awake. This time, she *would* catch him. She planned to sit on the knoll in the field where she could see both the front and the back step at once.

Let Seth Gatlin try to fool her this time!

The warm morning breeze whispered through the grasses as she chose a spot in the grass. Birdsong came with the gentle dawn. Sure enough, before the golden glow at the horizon became bright, two gray oxen pulled a wagon toward her house.

Seth didn't stop in the yard. He didn't even glance at the windows to search for her as he guided his team into the fields. He stopped the animals at the end of the deep trench he'd dug from the well, a third of the way from the back door.

There were no flowers in his gloved hands. He made no furtive glances toward the house. And it didn't look like he'd noticed her sitting there on the incline where the grass didn't hide her.

He unhitched the oxen and picketed them. She liked the easy way he moved while he worked, and the muscles shaping the shirt he wore—the one she'd made for him. She'd never seen a shirt look so good on a man before, hugging the curving breadth of his shoulders and the corded strength of his arms. She sighed just a little.

He grabbed a small jug and two battered tin cups and strode straight toward her. Had he known where she'd been sitting all along?

"Morning, Linnea. Up early watching for your admirer, I see."

"I'm simply enjoying the dawn, Major."

"Major, is it?" He quirked one brow, towering above her, casting her in his shadow. "I figured I'd come over here early and watch for him with you."

"How kind of you, but I can't see the house when you're standing in the way."

"Sorry about that." The corner of his mouth lifted and he didn't appear contrite as he settled on the ground beside her. "He could have been standing right in front of you and you would have missed him again."

"It doesn't look like he's going to leave me any flowers this morning."

"Maybe he figured you'd be watching for him and so he outsmarted you. Since he's the most handsome bachelor in the county, he's probably the smartest, too."

"He sounds conceited."

"Nothing like that. He's the nicest man you'll ever come across. Want some coffee?"

"No. I suffered through one cup and that's enough torture for anyone. I can only hope my secret admirer makes better coffee than you." She fought laughter. "I've got to draw some water for breakfast. I've got a morning full of chores ahead of me."

Seth poured steaming coffee into his battered tin

cup. He'd teased her enough for one morning. "Anders Neilson ought to be coming along in a few minutes. He's going to help me sink the pump and raise the windmill."

Linnea stood, her skirts rustling. "I can't thank you enough for being so kind to Mama."

"I like your mother, but I'm not doing all this for her."

"Oh?" Her blue eyes widened and filled with hope.

Before he could say another word, she snatched her bucket and stalked off toward the well.

He had to admire the sway of her hips as she walked and the swish of her skirt against her nicely firm backside. The wind helped matters by blowing just right, making her dress cling against her long, lean thighs. She wasn't wearing a petticoat, probably because of the heat, and he took his time enjoying the sight of her.

When she was ready to let him, he was going to caress every inch of her. By the time he was done, he'd know her every curve and texture—the smooth weight of her breasts, the silken dip of her stomach and the heat of her thighs.

Her unbound locks danced in the breeze and hid her face as she knelt beside the well. He waited for her reaction.

She stared at him across the waving grasses and scooped up the bouquet of bluebonnets. He'd crept through the fields in the dark before dawn and left them on the well lid.

"Tomorrow, I'll catch him," Linnea vowed when she swept past, flowers in one hand, the water bucket in the other. "You just wait and see."

He watched her go, already making plans.

* * *

The next morning there were bluebonnets in front of the barn doors, a thimble of gold tied to their stems. But she hadn't been able to catch Seth leaving his gift. He arrived later with his wagon full of rattling pipe and Anders Neilson riding a bay gelding alongside him.

Mama hurried out onto the porch to offer them breakfast, but they'd already eaten in town. With a quick wave, Seth led the way to the fields where they worked all morning.

They didn't stop at noon, even when she and Mama brought them heaping plates of food. The men took turns working while the other ate.

It was baking day, to make matters worse. Linnea was stuck in the sweltering kitchen and she couldn't sneak glances at him. It was hard to keep her mind from wandering as she formed the loaves into neat doughy logs and placed them in the greased bread pans. It was hard to keep a drop of hope from burrowing into her heart.

He was leaving at summer's end. He'd told her he didn't want a wife.

So, what did it mean? That he'd changed his mind? Or was he paying her a kindness and that was all?

By the end of another week, Seth and Anders had raised the windmill, sunk the well pump, laid the pipe and brought water into the kitchen.

As Seth drove away that evening, lifting his hat to her, she knew he'd be back early tomorrow with his bouquet of wildflowers.

And she'd be waiting.

*   *   *

Seth slipped the note between the string and the gift box and realized his hands were shaking. No surprise, considering his stomach was tied up in a knot. He'd written and rewritten the note seven times. When she read it, what would her answer be?

"Seth?" Ginny called from outside the shanty. "Are you in there?"

"I'm here." He grabbed his hat and plopped it over the gift. What he felt for Linnea was private, and he knew Ginny had her own reasons for not approving. "I bedded the cow down for the night. I'm glad you finally took to milking her."

"She seemed uncomfortable." Ginny hesitated in the shadows just outside the cabin. "I felt sorry for her, and I knew you were busy. The crops are looking good."

"I'm no farmer, and I'll be the first to admit it, but the wheat seems to be growing."

"Did you finish up your work at the rental property?"

"Yes, the Holmstroms'." He knew she was trying. He knew she was scared, but there was so little of the young girl he remembered in the woman who stood before him, clinging to the shadows. "Is the boy in bed?"

"Yes. He wanted to know if you're going to stay with us after the crops are in and sold." Ginny leaned against the threshold, her need as tangible as the deepening shadows. "You are all that's standing between us and going hungry. I know I was wrong before. About Linnea. You are a fine man, Seth, and I doubted your morals. I just couldn't bear to think that woman could tug you away when Jamie and I needed you so much."

"I'm not going to move back into the house. You can be as polite and helpful around the farm as you want. You can keep quiet about Linnea, but it won't change my mind. I can't live with your sadness. It reminds me too much of my mother."

"Oh." Ginny's head bowed. "You're a man. You wouldn't understand, but marriage is hard for a woman. Hard in more ways than it's possible to count."

"I had a happy home and a happy marriage. Don't take the easy road, Ginny. I never struck my wife. I didn't fill my home with anger and hurt. A woman isn't a punching bag for everything that goes wrong."

"Well, I disagree," she said quietly, her voice full of pain, her once-pretty face twisting with bitterness. "You're a man. You have all the rights and the freedom. While a woman has to turn herself inside out trying to be what her husband wants until she has no pride left, just trying to make him love her."

"Love isn't earned. It doesn't judge and it doesn't put down conditions."

"A man's love does."

"Not all men's."

Silence stretched between them like a barbed wire strung too tight. He pitied his sister her marriage, thinking Jimmy McIntyre's leaving could be the best thing that ever happened to her. Then Ginny shifted and the boards beneath her shoes moaned.

"You fixed up the place well enough. At least you have a roof that won't leak." She rubbed her sleeve cuff across her brow as if her head ached. "I invited Sidney Johanson to Sunday dinner tomorrow after church. She's a good woman, Seth."

"Ginny—"

"I know you don't want to hear this, but I'll say it anyway. If you wind up marrying the right kind of lady and staying here permanently, I wouldn't mind at all, since I'm not sure I can run this ranch by myself come next spring."

"I'm not listening, you know." He said it tenderly, because he knew the shadows that haunted his sister's heart. And a childhood that knew too much of poverty and the end of a willow switch.

"Well, it was worth a try. Good night, Seth. I know I haven't said it enough, but thank you."

"Good night, Ginny." He waited until she was gone before he ambled out into the night.

It was a lover's moon, big and round and shining like a dream. Fistfuls of stars twinkled across the heavens, flickering night after night without end, always battling the dark.

Like a man's heart, he supposed.

Or a man's fortune.

Tomorrow he would find out one way or the other how his luck would fall. If there would be a light that forever burned. Or if there would be darkness.

Chapter Ten

Where was he? Linnea had been watching the yard since before sunup, and still there was no sign that he'd been here. No flowers and no flash of his impudent grin as he tried to outsmart her.

The sun blazed above the horizon, bright on a world of rustling grasses and fragrant prairie. Wildflowers streaked color through the fields as she tried to keep an eye out for him while she worked.

Plunk. The tin bucket flew out of her hand. Milk splashed across the front of her skirts and onto the dusty ground. The spray-legged, knobby-kneed calf hopped back a few steps in alarm and bawled at the top of its powerful lungs.

"Easy, little one." Linnea held out her hand, and the doe-eyed calf raced back to the safety of her skirts. She rubbed velvety ears until the animal was comforted and then retrieved the pail. "Next time, don't butt the bucket."

The calf bleated and rammed his head against the pail.

Laughing, Linnea turned just in time to see a splash of purple-blue on the porch step.

That man! What had he been doing? Waiting for the one minute her back was turned?

She scanned the tall grasses, seed heavy and nodding drowsily in the warm morning breeze, but she couldn't see him. He could be halfway home by now, hidden by the gentle roll and draw of the prairie. The day ahead of her suddenly seemed bleak because she hadn't seen him.

There were the happy yellow faces of brown-eyed Susans in the bouquet today, mixed with the delicate bluebonnets. Beside the bouquet of flowers sat a small box tied with a pretty blue thread.

What was Seth up to? Heart pounding, Linnea eased down on the steps and cradled the box in her hand. She tugged at the bow, and the string fell away from the package. A folded note fluttered to her lap.

"Are you done with your chores, *dotter?*" Mama called cheerfully from inside the house. "We need to get an early start cleaning. What a hot day it promises to be."

"I'm nearly finished."

Linnea stared at the note in her hand, too afraid to open it.

It was only a piece of paper, she scolded, and unfolded the square of paper.

"Linnea," she read in a man's bold, disciplined handwriting. "I would like to come courting this afternoon. I'll be by with my buggy at two o'clock and hope that you say yes."

There was no signature, just, "Respectfully, your secret admirer."

She folded the note into careful quarters and hid it in her skirt pocket. Her hands shook so hard she didn't try to open his gift.

I would like to come courting. His written words echoed in her heart. He was a handsome, successful army major with a kind manner and a sense of humor she loved, and he was courting her. *Her.* Linnea Holmstrom.

She set the box she held on her lap and found the courage to lift the lid. Inside was a seamstress set, glistening with gold accents and hand-painted enamel.

Seth took one look at Linnea walking down the road in his direction and knew what she was doing. Meeting him without her mother noticing.

She looked beautiful—there was no other word for it. She wore a blue dress that showed off her trim curves perfectly. She flicked her gaze nervously up at him.

"Looking for your secret admirer, are you?" he asked.

"Sure, but then you came along. You've probably scared him off."

"Probably. But since it's hot and you're without a ride, want to come up here with me?"

"I might as well."

She smiled, demure and lovely, and placed her hand in his. He helped her onto the seat just like he planned to do for the rest of his life. Tenderness filled him, sweet and powerful.

"So did you ever catch sight of the fellow leaving you flowers?"

"I did." She settled her skirts on the seat. "I'm not sure I like him. He's homely."

He released the break, trying not to laugh. "That can't be. You don't think he's handsome?"

"Not in the slightest." Humor glinted in her eyes.

"But a single woman my age can't be too choosy. Considering the shortage of eligible men in this county, I'll have to look past his rather bad looks and make the best of it."

"Maybe next week he'll invite Sidney Johanson to go driving with him instead."

Linnea couldn't help the laughter that bubbled through her like joy. Was she really here with Seth and not imagining it? The wind on her face was real. She was out on a Sunday drive, like most courting couples.

He took her hand in his and held on. Warm, sure, possessive.

He didn't let go.

The silence lengthened and he turned off the main road and drove along a meandering route that followed the river. She couldn't think of a thing to say to this man she'd had no trouble talking to for so long. To this man whose hand remained on hers. Warm, sure, possessive.

The silence became unbearable. *Think of something to say, Linnea.*

"I haven't been courting in a long time, and I've forgotten how miserable it is." He swept off his hat and dropped it onto the floor well. "This jacket is as hot as hades. Want to go take a dip in the river?"

"Sounds like heaven. I wore petticoats and I'm dying."

He guided General off the road where old cottonwoods cast welcome shade. The buggy rolled to a stop, and she couldn't help admiring what a fine vehicle it was. Polished oak accents and fine upholstery. Real springs that had made the ride feel as if they were floating.

He climbed down and helped her to the ground, holding her a moment longer than necessary. He reached behind the seat for a folded blanket. Her pulse roared in her ears as he splayed his hand at the small of her back and walked beside her.

He treated her like a real lady, laying out the blanket in the shade. Giving her his hand to help her to the ground. Taking her foot to loosen and remove both of her shoes and stockings. She felt like a princess.

Shocks of dark hair tumbled over his forehead as he unlaced his shoes. Tenderness unlike any she'd known filled her, made her heart hurt and her throat ache.

When he'd rolled up the hems of his trousers, he stood and helped her to her feet.

Like a gentleman, he settled beside her on the bank's edge and plunged his feet into the rushing water. "Now that's a welcome feeling."

She held her skirts so the lace Mama tatted for the hem wouldn't be ruined and slipped her toes into the water. The cold current tugged at the soles of her feet and it tickled.

"Why did you buy a new buggy?"

"Figured I might need it. A dashing man worth his salt can't be seen showing up with a beat-up work wagon to court the loveliest lady in three western territories."

"You didn't buy a buggy to take me for a ride."

"No." He cupped her face with his hand. "I bought the buggy because I'm not planning on leaving."

"You're staying?"

"I want to see how the romance between you and your secret admirer turns out."

His thumb caressed the underside of her jaw in slow circles and sent ripples of tingling pleasure shooting down her spine. The rough, warm texture of his skin and the solid sense of him made her ache for more. Much more.

She leaned into the heat of his touch and closed her eyes. Drank in the sensation of being with him. The excitement of his touch. The pleasing way he smelled like soap, leather and man.

His lips claimed hers, tender the way a summer breeze caressed the land. The icy water, the squawk of waterbirds, the whispering chorus of the cottonwood leaves faded away until there was only his kiss. His gentle, all-consuming kiss.

His hand curled around her throat, holding her as he deepened the kiss. The sweep of his tongue and the brush of his lips made her breathless, weak. She curled her hands in his shirt and held on tight.

This felt more right than anything she'd ever known.

When he broke away, he held her against his chest. Simply held her. The rapid beat of his heart against her cheek matched hers, and she dreamed—just a little.

What if she could spend the rest of her life in the arms of this man?

Ginny hefted the bucket from the trough and hated how water and dust made mud at her feet. She'd tucked the hem of her skirts in her apron band to keep them from becoming soiled, but the bulkiness was hampering her as she took a step.

Mud squished between her toes. Water in the bucket sloshed and the metal rim slammed hard into her shinbone. Pain ricocheted up her leg and she silently cursed Jimmy McIntyre for running off on her. Cursed him again as her shoulder socket burned from the weight of the ten-gallon bucket. And again when her entire spine ached as if she'd been kicked.

That man who had looked more handsome than ever while time had only seared lines on her face and robbed her figure. That man who hadn't had to pay for a thing in his life and left her to this. Working like a common country girl.

Memories from her childhood rushed through her, leaving her weak and nauseous. The smell of Pa's whiskey, her stepmother's broken crying. The endless work and gnawing hunger that haunted her even while she slept.

When she reached the garden, she dropped the bucket on the ground. Pain twisted in the small of her back, and her neck and arm ached. When she looked down, she saw the bucket was half-empty. She'd spilled that much water carrying it from the trough.

Tears burned in her eyes. She'd had enough of this, living poor and helpless. If only Jimmy were here, she'd make him pay! But he wasn't and that only made the anger worse.

She missed her house in town and the pretty little porch with the wide benched swing. She missed her friends in town and being able to buy whatever she wanted. Frilly things, useless things, a new hat even when she didn't need one. She missed her housekeeper and her weekly book club meetings.

"Are you sad, Mama?"

Jamie's little-boy concern tore apart her thoughts.

He sat in the dirt with two toy horses she'd spotted in a fine catalogue and had the McIntyres order for his last Christmas. Seeing the expensive toys at odds with his dirt-smeared face, his trousers handed down from his cousin because he'd outgrown his store-bought clothes raked her pride across hot coals.

She hated to think her son would grow up as she did, laboring in the fields all summer, wearing handed-down clothes to school in winter. Fury blinded her, but she managed to keep her voice calm as she answered him. "No, sweetie. I'm just a little tired is all."

He seemed to accept her explanation and returned to his play. She poured the water remaining in her bucket into one of the garden rows. Water trickled halfway down the trench, so she turned around and went for more.

The jingle of a buggy harness echoed in the yard. Seth? She'd seen him drive his new vehicle down the old shanty road on the other side of the orchard, but he hadn't said a word about where he was going. To town, dressed the way he was. Maybe to see her father-in-law.

She left the bucket in the trough. The milk cow watched it bob up and down in the water with concern, but she hardly cared. Maybe the McIntyres had changed their minds. Maybe they would put the land in her name and then she could sell it. Take the money and buy a house in town.

It wasn't Seth's stallion hauling the big comfortable buggy up the driveway. It was Sidney's prized gray Arabian. Sidney waved from the shaded seat, and Ginny waved back. Of all her friends in town, Sidney had stood by her when Jimmy abandoned her just after the new year. Quickly she untied her apron and let her skirts fall to cover her bare feet.

"You've caught me watering the garden," she explained, smoothing her skirt.

"I didn't mean to drop by unannounced, but I have some news." Sidney drew her horse to a stop and climbed down from the buggy, her fashionable skirts sweeping gracefully with her movements.

Envy stabbed through Ginny. She wore a plain gingham dress, and she felt like the country girl she'd lived her entire adult life trying to cover up. "Let me dash inside and change. I couldn't wear my good clothes to work in the garden."

"You look fine, Ginny, don't worry yourself about that. I can't stay anyway, I'm expected back at my in-laws for supper. Just came to tell you that my brother was over to see Mr. Hansson about the upcoming haying and saw your brother's new buggy."

"Yes, I know about that. He bought it in town just yesterday. Out of the blue. Spending money when he could have borrowed mine."

"That isn't why I came." Sidney glanced over her shoulder. "I thought you should know. I don't mean to spread gossip, but you've been a good friend to me since my husband's death and I don't want to see you hurt."

"What do you mean?" Panic fluttered behind her breastbone. "What is Seth doing?"

"He was seen driving down along Rose Creek with Linnea Holmstrom."

The sick feeling returned to Ginny's stomach. "Maybe he'd come across her on the road and was giving her a ride. He's done it before."

"Dressed in his Sunday best? I don't think so."

Sidney wagged her head. "Mark said it looked like Seth had come courting. You know what that means."

Ginny swayed, and she grabbed the top rung of the split rail fence. "He *couldn't* be courting her. A decent man like my stepbrother wouldn't marry a woman like Linnea."

"Whatever his intentions are, it looked as if he was serious about her. Out on a Sunday drive. You know that's what courting couples do around here."

He'd marry Linnea and Linnea would turn him against her. And she needed him. Ginny knew it with absolute certainty. Linnea was going to find herself a husband after all, and Seth was vulnerable. He'd been too long without a wife in his bed. Linnea was giving out what Seth needed. It was that simple.

"He doesn't know the kind of woman she is, that's all." Sidney offered what comfort she could. "When he finds out, he'll no longer want to court her, let alone marry her."

"He swore to leave me if I said one word against her."

"Then this is worse than it looks. He's serious about her."

Ginny stumbled into the shade. "I can't risk angering him further. He's moved into the old claim shanty as it is. What can I do?"

"I don't know, my friend, but I wanted to warn you. I know how precarious things are with your husband gone. If you need to, there is room with me. The cottage out back is yours for the asking."

Ginny flushed with embarrassment and anger. What kind of friend was Sidney? Offering her the servants' quarters? "I'll be fine. Linnea might have destroyed my marriage—"

"It's not as if he ran off with her, as Ellie Jance pointed out. We don't know they were even together and we should not assume—"

"He got her pregnant long ago, remember? Right before he proposed to me. For all I know she was trying to steal him away from me." That was proof enough to blame Linnea forever.

"I must be going." Sidney climbed back into her fancy buggy, lifted the reins and drove off, waving goodbye.

Ginny couldn't help noticing Sidney's expensive French-made gloves. She looked down at her fingernails stained with dirt and her skin browned by the sun.

Linnea Holmstrom would not sink her claws into Seth. She'd make damn sure of that.

The sun was low in the sky. Looked like the first Sunday drive she'd ever taken with a man had come to an end. Seth headed General down the road toward her house.

"Let me off at the bend in the road. That way Mama won't suspect I was with you."

"We can't let her think you'd be alone with an ugly bald-headed man." He winked.

"I teased you something awful. I'm sorry."

"I teased you back so we're even." He climbed down and offered her his hand.

He swept her to the ground, and she wished there was a way to push the sun back up into the sky and steal more time with him.

"Thank you for today."

"I want to ask you to drive with me next week, but I'll be busy haying. The neighbors have invited me to join them. Hansson has a cutting machine, and if we go from ranch to ranch, the work is done faster than if I hand-cut the hay alone."

"I'm glad they've included you. Papa used to do that and, oh, I remember having to cook for the hayers. Mama and I worked from dawn until midnight for two days in the sweltering kitchen. Is Ginny going to be able to cook for the men?"

"Ginny and I haven't discussed that yet."

"I wouldn't mind helping, although Ginny and I are far from friends."

"I noticed something like that."

She smiled, relaxing a little at his touch, and he ran his hand down the outside of her arm. She felt like paradise, all fine bone and a woman's softness, even through the fabric of her sleeve.

"Figured you probably hand-cut the hay on your farm, so I included that acreage in with mine. If that's all right with you."

"What? And not spend the next two weeks swinging a sickle in the hot sun? I'd gladly feed the men in exchange."

"It's a deal then." This felt right, starting to take care of her. Acting on the tenderness he felt for her. "There's one more thing before I let you go."

Her mouth softened. So she wanted his kiss, did she?

"A bouquet of flowers." He snapped off a handful of bluebonnets swaying in the grasses alongside the road. "Got to keep that secret admirer of yours jealous."

"I figured out who he is."

"Is that so?" Trouble glimmered in her eyes and he couldn't resist playing along. "Do you think he's the most charming bachelor in the county?"

"Anders Neilson? Well, he *is* blond and he is fairly good-looking. But you have a new buggy, so that decided it for me."

"That makes me a damn lucky man." He handed her the flowers. She was sunlight and summer and everything good in the world and he wanted to take her into his arms and kiss her again. To taste her sweetness and her passion.

In time, he told himself, he'd be able to make her his. And to discover the soft curves she kept hidden beneath that pretty blue dress.

"I hope you like bluebonnets."

"I do." She traced a fingertip over the delicate blossoms. "I love the way they grow so thick the prairie turns purple-blue with them."

"They match the color of your eyes. That makes them my favorite flower." He pressed a kiss to her cheek, pure gentleman, instead of tugging at those buttons on her bodice as he wanted to. "I'm glad I came along before Anders did. It's going to be a long two weeks until I can do it again."

He pressed a kiss to her cheek and breathed in her soft scent.

The afternoon sun was low in the sky, the grasses rippling and whispering with the lazy wind, and contentment filled him. He didn't want this to end, but he was a practical man, and so he let her go.

When she set out across the field, he sat in the buggy while she waded through the tall grass and vibrant bluebonnets.

He watched until she was a tiny spot of gold and blue on the distant rise, and then she was gone. The brightness leached from the sun, the beauty drained from the day, and he was alone.

He snapped the reins and headed home.

"Seth, is Jamie out here with you?"

"He sure is." Seth asked his nephew to hand him the small mallet.

"I'm helpin', Mama!"

"I see that." Ginny's face softened when she looked upon her son. "I bet you're a wonderful helper."

"The best I've ever seen," Seth agreed.

Jamie beamed, pleased as he fished the mallet from the toolbox. Dark locks fell across his brow and reminded Seth of another little boy, one who hadn't lived to reach his fifth birthday.

It was a sorrow and always would be. Seth swallowed hard as he accepted the mallet from the boy. "Thanks, Jamie."

"Sure thing."

He showed his nephew how to hit the spoke just right—not too hard and yet firm enough to drive it into place in the rim. "There. That's one wagon wheel repaired."

"Jamie, it's time to take your bath. I've got your wash water ready."

"Aw, Ma, I'm bein' a help."

"Yes, you are, but your uncle Seth is done."

"Go take your bath, Jamie. I'm done and heading in myself." He snapped the box closed. "Thanks for your help."

"You're welcome."

The boy stood, small for his age. He had to be the littlest boy in his class in town, Seth figured. A sick child Jimmy McIntyre hadn't wanted to be responsible for.

Some men were fools.

He grabbed his tools and carried them to the back of the barn, head pounding.

"Seth?"

He hoisted the box into place on the back shelf and kept his back to her. He didn't want her to see how upset he was.

"Do you think we'll get a good price if I want to sell the hay?"

"I don't know, Ginny. I figured I'd worry about that when I knew how much extra hay I had to sell."

"You didn't see my father-in-law like I hoped you would, did you?"

He heard the faintly accusing tone and closed his eyes. Tension knotted his muscles. "No, I took Linnea for a buggy ride. But you knew that, didn't you? I didn't know gossip traveled so fast."

"You drove around with her in your buggy. People noticed."

"They should mind their own business. Just like you should."

"You are my business."

"Then you should be damn glad that I've found someone who makes me feel again." He pushed past her, anger growing with each step. "Not a word against her, Ginny."

"Fine." Her reply came tight-lipped and rang of censure. "Then at least let me ask you about the land. Do you think you can convince my father-in-law to deed it over to me?"

"I won't have time to find out until after the haying. You'll have to wait."

"A few weeks? Fine." She breathed her disapproval. "Whatever you think is right."

"Linnea offered to help you with the cooking come Friday."

"I don't need her help."

"That's what I figured you'd say. Remember, twenty men will be at your kitchen door as hungry as oxen."

Ginny paled, but her chin went up a notch. "I can handle the cooking. I helped your ma when I was little and the threshers came."

"Good. I can count on you?"

She nodded but refused to meet his gaze. "I'd better go check on Jamie's bath."

He nodded, watching her go, wondering if she had any idea what she was doing with her anger. Wasting precious time with her child. He wanted to shake her, but he doubted it would do a lick of good.

Some lessons in life had to be learned the hard way.

The ache in his heart seemed cavernous. He sat in the glow of a flickering lamp deep into the night, staring at the small tintype of his family. Studying with sweet painful memory each detail of his wife's face, of his son's and tiny daughter's. How proud he looked seated with them, Angelina on his lap, his arm around his gentle wife.

He would always miss them. But one day soon, the loneliness would end. He would have the chance to have a family again. And he would cherish every moment, every day.

"Mama, are you sleeping?" Linnea whispered. Lamplight tossed a dark glow across the page of her book and the corner of the bed.

No answer. Linnea closed the Dickens novel and set it on the night table. Her mother didn't move, her gray locks fanning the embroidered pillow slip, her pretty face relaxed. She was so frail she hardly appeared to breathe.

Linnea smoothed the sheet and stood. The bed ropes squeaked and the feather tick shifted. Warm air puffed in through the open window, fluttering the ruffled curtains.

Love warmed her heart and she bent to brush Mama's papery cheek. The older woman didn't stir, lost in dreams, and so she turned out the light and left the room.

The house was silent, the perfect time for dreaming. She lifted the kitten from the cushion of her rocking chair. The calico purred, and the only other sound in the room was the wall clock ticking the seconds by, measuring time.

She didn't feel much like working. Her sewing lay in a stack on the bookcase, pieced squares for the new quilt Mrs. Jance had commissioned. She didn't feel like reading, either. Too many thoughts raced through her mind—and too many worries.

Seth was courting her. In spite of her past. In spite of what others said about her.

It felt too good to be true. But the sewing gifts he'd given her were right there in her sewing box. The golden crown of a thimble reflected the lamplight.

She remembered Seth's kiss. A deep happiness filled her, a feeling that softened the shadows in the room and drove the loneliness from the night.

Chapter Eleven

Linnea skidded to a halt in front of Mrs. Jance's sewing shop. *That was her quilt.* Sunlight glinted on the glass panes caressing her Double Irish Chain made of pinks and greens. A simple pattern, but it looked almost elegant next to the veiled straw hat and a pearl-beaded summer dress.

She couldn't believe her good fortune. Her neck ached from sewing into the late hours of the night, but it was worth it. Her luck had changed.

Feeling a little more confident, she turned the brass door handle and stepped inside. The bell above her chimed and the women sipping tea at the pattern book table turned to stare at her.

Let them think what they wished. She wasn't going to let them affect her. Not on such a beautiful summer's day when her past no longer branded her. Seth was courting her and that knowledge gave her strength. She smiled at the women, recognizing Ginny McIntyre among them, and headed to the back counter.

"Linnea." Mrs. Jance's greeting rang warm and sincere as she stepped out of the back room, a silvered

tray filled with china cups and plates of sliced cake.
"Let me serve my customers and I'll be right with
you. Oh good, you finished the quilt!"

Linnea laid the heavy wrapped bundle on the sparkling glass countertop and couldn't resist inspecting
the new shipment of threads. She rubbed her thumb
across silk-woven strands. What fine quality.

"I'll give you a discount on anything you decide
to purchase for yourself. Or your wonderful mother."
Ellie returned and reached for the paper-wrapped bundle. "I can't wait to see what you've done. The doctor's wife bought your quilt in the window, but she's
letting me leave it on display."

"The doctor's wife bought my quilt?"

"She said it reminded her of the very quilt her
grandmother patched for her, but it was lost on the
trip from the East." Ellie pushed away the paper and
gasped when she saw the alternating blocks of appliquéd summer flowers and white squares of stitched
hearts. "Perfect. I know just the lady who will buy
this. How did you complete it so quickly?"

"I stitched on it every chance I got."

"I haven't seen better. You didn't trace this, did
you? This is a true art, Linnea. Have your pick of the
place, anything you want. I have to admit I'm greedy
for another. Take your time and browse. I'll get your
money and bring you a slice of cake. Be right back."

It was better than Christmas. Hundreds of colors of
embroidery floss vied for her attention on the display
rack. How was she going to choose? First she would
pick gifts for Mama. Then she would decide on the
colors she needed for her next project.

In the middle of choosing a pretty fine thread for

Mother, Linnea heard footsteps across the polished wood floor, drawing closer. Ginny McIntyre.

"It's a shame when a woman has to work." Ginny eased next to the rack and ran her gloved fingertips over the fanciful threads. "I may have fallen upon hard times, but I haven't become a common laborer."

"Good for you, Ginny." Linnea's hand shook as she tugged tiny skeins of gold floss from the stand.

"A woman in your circumstances with an old mother to feed tends to make eligible men shy away. What man wants to support a mother-in-law? Add that to the child you bore out of wedlock and no decent man is going to come within ten miles of you."

"This is about Seth. I'm not going to talk about him with you." Linnea began piling spooled white thread into her basket.

Ginny moved closer. "I know you're desperate to get yourself a man to support you. But not my brother. He's lonely and, as men tend to do, he'll reach for the comfort of any woman willing to satisfy him."

"You must not think very highly of your brother if you think him capable of that."

"It's you I don't think highly of. I know my mother-in-law is no longer buying shirts from you, and a woman with no morals has to earn her rent money some way—"

"I'm not doing anything wrong and you know it." Linnea said it loudly enough that the women at the counter, straining to hear, could get it straight when they began gossiping. "The only reason you care is that you need him to support you."

"Damn right I do. I want you to stay away from him."

Linnea's jaw dropped at Ginny's curse and her venom. "I never wanted to come between you and your brother. Courting me is his decision."

"If that's what you call it." She looked docile and frail, but she was nothing of the sort. "Be careful, Linnea, or I'll raise the rent on your pathetic little house so high you'll have to move out. And good riddance it would be."

"Seth wouldn't let that happen."

"Seth doesn't know the truth about you, Linnea." Ginny's gaze narrowed, not caring that her voice traveled the length of the shop, where her friends listened on the edges of their seats. "He doesn't know about the baby you bore without a ring on your finger. To a man who was planning to marry me."

"Jimmy had broken things off with you, Ginny, and you know it. And of course Seth knows. I can't imagine you haven't told him—"

"He won't hear a word against you, but that will change. My brother knows what decency is. Mark my words, he'll not come courting you again."

Visibly shaking, Ginny marched away, hands fisted, greeted with assenting voices from her friends.

"Ginny, I'm shocked at you. In a place of business!" Ellie Jance marched into the room, a package under one arm. Her face was flushed and her usually well-styled bangs mussed. She'd clearly come in from outside. "I cannot hear another unkind word in my shop. Please leave if you can't respect my wishes."

"Fine." Ginny grabbed her reticule from the small table. "I'm not planning on shopping here again."

Ellie set a small tray on the counter near Linnea. "Are you all right? I can't help but think the woman is desperate."

"I'm sure you're right." Linnea couldn't stop trembling. She felt as if the floor at her feet was bucking and spinning. Her vision blurred and she fought to sound calm, as if Ginny's words hadn't obliterated her. "I'll take ten yards of the cream calico."

"This right here? It's lovely." Ellie hurried to comply. She tugged the bulky bolt from the shelf and unrolled it with heavy thumps on her measuring counter. "What else? Did you want to give me your order and take the cake and tea into my office? It will be a quiet place to sit and recover, if you'd like."

"Yes, thank you." Linnea blushed, not knowing why Ellie's kindness hurt the way it did. She rattled off her fabric order, enough for her next quilt even though she feared the seamstress would cancel their arrangement. Without thinking, she requested a few extra lengths of fabric and new silken thread for her mother.

She grabbed the small tray and fled to the back room, where the cozy office sat in the corner, windows and curtains drawn against the relentless summer sun. It was hot, but it was private, and she collapsed into the chair. Her mind reeled with Ginny's words. *Seth doesn't know the truth about you.*

How could it be? He'd said he didn't care about rumors or gossip. Maybe that was true. Maybe he'd had too much integrity to listen to what everyone was saying. She still couldn't believe it. It can't be true. How can he not know? *Everyone* knew, or thought they knew, what happened. Just as they'd gossiped anytime she was seen within six yards of a man.

Her head pounded and the tea didn't soothe it. Her hands wouldn't stop shaking. She still had the mail to check and grocery shopping to do for the meal she'd promised Seth and the hayers.

Ginny was lying, that was all. Trying to scare her away. She was a desperate, hurting woman and she was afraid of Seth abandoning her, too.

Ellie rapped her fingers on the door. "Linnea, I have your order ready. I'll leave it behind the counter. Help yourself to it when you're ready to leave. You sit there as long as you need."

There was no point in putting off what had to be done. The doubt Ginny placed in her mind made the trip to McIntyre's more formidable.

She went to gather her purchases and left the shop.

"I'll put your order in for delivery right away," Shannon promised at McIntyre's front counter. "I imagine with an order this size you're cooking for hayers."

"Yes, thank you." Linnea was grateful for the thoughtful treatment as she gathered her change from the counter. She was even more thankful for the bell jangling overhead signaling she was finally on her way home.

With the sun blazing down on her and her packages already heavy, she headed down the busy boardwalk to the edge of town. Few people were walking in the heat, and it was another thing to appreciate.

Never had she been so glad to leave civilization behind as she followed the road heading out through the ripening fields, where dust swirled at her feet.

The sound of a horse and wagon rattled above the lark song and the plaintive winds. Linnea cringed, her stomach twisting tight. It had to be Ginny. That was the kind of luck she was having today.

Hugging her packages tightly, she stepped off the dusty road and onto the uneven shoulder where grass caught at her skirts. She walked faster and stared hard at the ground in front of her.

If Ginny says anything, I'm going to ignore it. She refused to let a bitter woman ruin another minute of this beautiful day.

A team of bays drew even with her—not Ginny's pretty mare. It was Hansson's team, but she knew the men were in the fields working today. Like sharp blades to her back, she could feel the scorn from whomever it was sitting on the wagon seat.

She didn't turn her head. She kept walking, clutching her packages tightly, keeping her gaze on the road in front of her. Go on by, she silently pleaded.

The horses pulled ahead of her, then slowed. The big wagon wheels kicked up dust at her shoulder. She could make out a dirt-caked pair of boots and denims. The Hansson boys.

She walked faster.

The wagon remained at her side.

"Hear you like to go drivin'." One of the teenaged boys taunted her, dipping his voice in a suggestive way. "I like to go drivin', too."

"Oscar," his brother scolded. "Leave the lady alone."

"She's no lady." Oscar nosed the horses in front of her, trapping her between the fence and the front wagon wheels. "How much is the major payin' you? Hear she sews for him. *Sews.* If that's what you want to call it, then I got me a rip in my denims I'll let you—"

"*No.*" She felt trapped. The horses were sidestepping in their traces so she couldn't risk squeezing past them and the fence posts. She spun around and tried to run.

Oscar Hansson swung from the wagon seat and blocked her path. He was tall and wide. There was no mistaking the strength in his arms as he faced her with his beefy hands fisted on his hips.

She was trapped. The barbed wire fencing was impossible to climb over quickly. "Please, stand aside and let me go."

"How much do you charge? I hear you come cheap, which is damn lucky because I don't got much. Six bits? How about a whole dollar." He reached into his pocket and withdrew a shining silver coin.

"Let me go." Panic made her chest tight and she fought for air. "My mother is expecting me soon—"

"That old hag? She can wait a few minutes while her daughter earns a little rent money." He flicked the coin through the air and it thunked against her chin.

Pain scored across her bone and she jumped back. The coin fell into the dust, and her spine slammed against the wooden wagon box.

"Hey, Oscar, you're scarin' her. Get back in the wagon. Pa sent us to town for a new mower bit. He told us to hurry."

"Stay out of this, Bo. Unless you want to come down here and help me. She ain't as cooperative as the whores in town, but then she's a whole hell of a lot prettier."

She could taste fear in her mouth, hear it in her shallow breath, feel her body grow numb and wooden. He came at her, malice glittering in his narrow eyes. He tore the package out of her arms. The beautiful fabrics, flosses and threads tumbled to the dust. He marched over them, grinding the finery deeper into the dirt.

She stared in shock at the beautiful things at her feet and at the mocking amusement in the grin he flashed her. He was playing with her, that was all, and humiliation swept over her.

His hands seized her shoulders. Shaking, she kicked him hard in the shin and pushed away from him. It was like hitting the side of a barn, but she startled him. Panic drove her forward and fear made her leap toward the fence. Metal dug into her palms as she grabbed the top wire.

He grabbed her by the hem of the skirt and hauled her back to the ground. Her hands tore, her skirts ripped and she tumbled to the ground.

"You boys! What in the hell do you think you're doing?" Like thunder, the newcomer's words snapped Oscar to attention.

He snatched his dollar from the dust. "Nuthin'."

"Looks like something to me." Elderly Mr. White, the delivery driver for McIntyre's, set his brake as if he were intending to stay. "You apologize to Miss Holmstrom and be on your way."

"Sorry, ma'am." Oscar didn't look sorry as he walked over her yard goods on the way to his wagon. He swung up. "Let's get a move on, Bo."

The brothers drove off, and Linnea breathed a sigh of relief. "Thank you, sir."

"Young men can cause trouble easy enough." He strolled close. "Looks like they hurt ya."

"It's nothing." She ignored the blood dripping onto the dust. "I appreciate what you did, scaring them off like that, but I'm fine, so you shouldn't make yourself late. I know how the McIntyres are."

"Seems only right to offer you a ride." He knelt in the dust and shook his head. "Looks like you dropped your things. Let me pick them up for you, and I'll take you on home."

"No. I'll be fine. Please, just leave."

"It don't seem right—"

"Please." She couldn't look at him. "When you deliver our groceries, please don't say anything to my mother. I don't want her upset."

Seconds ticked past and finally he stood and ambled over to his wagon. He walked slowly enough so she could change her mind, but she didn't.

He drove off, kicking up dust as he passed.

Tremors rocked through her, making it hard as she tore strips from her petticoat, her best one, to make a bandage for her hands.

Careful not to smear blood on the fabrics, she lifted them carefully from the dirt. Her heart sank at the ground-in dust that stained the pretty crochet thread she'd chosen for her mother.

Ginny's buggy rolled past without stopping. Although the woman didn't say a word, her amusement felt as damning as the sun that blazed from the sky.

With her purchases clutched in her arms, Linnea trudged home. The beauty of the day was lost, the treasured respect Seth had given her as soiled as the cloth she held.

"Dotter, I was so worried when Mr. White came here and you were not yet home. Then I thought you must have been having fun at the sewing shop." Lines eased from Mama's face as she stepped down from the porch. "Did you have fun? You work so hard. Goodness knows you deserve it."

"I chose fabric for my next quilt."

"That means Mrs. Jance was pleased with your work. I am not surprised. I am the one who taught you to sew."

Pride sparkled rare as diamonds in Mama's eyes. Misplaced and stubborn and so incredibly priceless, Linnea's eyes burned. She could never let Mama know what happened. "After the hayers have come and gone, you and I will head to town and treat ourselves."

"We cannot afford such luxuries for an old woman like me."

"You are as young as can be and my whole heart, Mama. I want you to have something special. And Mrs. Jance is giving me a discount."

"That woman is an angel from above." Mama stooped to pet the calico lazing in the shadow of the porch. "Come inside and tell me of the fabric you chose. Tell me what you are planning. I wish to picture it in my mind."

"I chose a cream calico for the backing and the alternating squares," Linnea began, following her mother into the house. Her hands smarted and she was still shaking, but she was safe. "I plan to wash the fabrics this afternoon."

"Child, it is too hot to boil the water! You must already be warm from your walk. Wait until morning."

"But I must start the baking for the hayers." The thought left her feeling weak. All those men would be staring at her, and probably the Hansson boy who'd accosted her today.

Spools of thread tumbled from her wooden fingers. They clattered to the floor and rolled on the polished wood. Chiding herself for her clumsiness, Linnea emptied the load in her arms onto the sofa cushion and knelt to rescue the errant spools.

"Goodness, you bought more than you claim." Mama sounded delighted as she reached out and ran her sensitive fingers over the small skeins of embroidery floss. "What a treat."

"Mama." Linnea pulled the soiled fabric and crochet threads away from her mother's very sensitive fingertips. "I almost forgot. I have a letter from Aunt Eva."

"My dear sister! Come into the shade out back and read it to me. I cannot wait to hear how she is doing."

"All right, but first I want to get those fabrics soaking while I have the chance," she insisted, struggling to keep her voice cheerful. "Go sit and I'll be right out."

Mama ambled outside where her crocheting and a comfortable seat in the shade awaited her.

With her hands pounding with pain, Linnea gritted her teeth and built a fire in the stove. Her dress was torn, but she would mend it tonight after Mama went to bed. At least the bleeding had stopped. She cut off the bandages so her mother wouldn't notice.

Humiliation settled over her like the dust in the air. She wouldn't cry about it. She *wouldn't*.

Hadn't she known it all along? A woman like her had no right to dream.

She set the stained fabrics to soaking and joined her mother in the shade. Mama fidgeted with anticipation as Linnea slipped a pin from her hair and tore open the envelope. The letter inside was folded carefully and writing covered every spot on the page.

Linnea smoothed open the letter, scanning the page

quickly. The word *wedding* jumped out at her. "It looks like your sister has remarried."

"*Married?* Truly? After all these years?" Mama beamed with joy. "Quick. Read on. I must hear!"

As Linnea read the aunt's letter, telling every detail of her wedding, her mind kept wandering to Seth. Always to Seth. And to the ugliness that had happened to her on the road.

"Can you picture the reception? All those flowers. And an arbor. Think of how beautiful it must have been."

"Yes, Mama. I'm happy for Aunt Eva."

"What joy for my dear sister. To think she found her true love. Just as I had with my Olaf. Eva was so unhappy in her first marriage, it broke my heart. We were so far apart and could never afford to visit. But now all is well. See? There is always good news to be thankful for."

"Yes, there is." She was grateful for what she had.

Happy endings were for some people, but not for her.

Seth arrived at the Holmstrom shanty before dawn, the flowers in his hand. His body ached from the hard days working the fields, but it was satisfying to work alongside his neighbors. They were accomplishing something grand. After tomorrow, he would have enough feed to keep the horses he thought about purchasing. Or enough to sell so Ginny could buy coal to last the winter.

Satisfaction outweighed the exhaustion, and at least now he knew for a fact he would stay here on this land and spend the rest of his life as a rancher. With Linnea at his side.

He stopped in the fields as he had every morning, choosing a bouquet of blue, yellow and red flowers to make a summery bouquet. A man didn't get a lot of second chances in a lifetime. He wanted to do this right. To show Linnea all she meant to him.

Curtains fluttered at the windows. The calico slinked around the corner of the house to greet him. He gave her a few scratches between her soft ears and was rewarded with a raspy purr. That's when he saw them, the flowers wilted and faded on the edge of the porch.

The bouquet he'd left yesterday.

It wasn't like her to forget his meager gift of wildflowers.

Was she all right? Had something happened? He glanced around the yard and saw the calves had fresh hay in their mangers. A washtub was upended against the side of the house that hadn't been there yesterday.

Maybe she was busy. She had the hayers coming. Yes, that was it. She'd been overwhelmed by the task of cooking for so many men and had forgotten his flowers. It was nothing personal.

Then why had the faded bouquet been moved to one side, off the top step, out of the way?

A rooster crowed in the henhouse, reminding him he had places to go, obligations to meet.

He left more flowers. Linnea stood in the parlor and watched Seth leave. She could just see him through the fluttering curtains in glimpses that rose and fell in cadence to the breeze.

Leaving yesterday's bouquet haven't discouraged him today. But maybe if she moved this morning's blossoms aside and left them unattended, he'd figure things out.

It was going to take a little time, but he would stop coming.

And her heart would be forever broken.

"Linnea, come and see if the beans are ready. They smell warmed through to me." Mama called through the open kitchen window. "I cannot find the bread knife."

"I'll be right there." The sun was almost directly at the zenith. The men would be here any minute, and she wasn't ready.

She set out the last of the plates and dashed to the house. The warm scents of baking beans and steaming ham welcomed her as she hurried into the kitchen.

She found the bread knife and rescued the warming pots of beans from the oven. She checked each crock and gave them a stir. They looked presentable, so she carried them out by the handles to the waiting trestle tables.

"Are they making good progress in the fields?" Mama asked as she cut slices of thick bread.

"They are across the road right now, so I can't see them." Linnea grabbed the butcher knife and began cutting meat. The fragrant ham fell in juicy slices onto the platter.

Mama tilted her head, turning toward the front windows. "Here they come, *dotter*. I am finished."

"Right on time, too." She couldn't slice fast enough. "At least the potatoes and beans are on the table. And the pitchers of water."

"I will take out the platter of bread and then a

pitcher of milk. Some have brought their sons and
they are still growing boys.''

''Mama, I don't want you serving food. Wait—''

''Do not fuss. I can find my way.'' She lifted the
thick and fluffy slices of bread and searched for the
cool pitcher left on the counter.

''I'm nearly done, Mama.''

''Here comes the major.''

Sure enough, his step rang with authority as he
climbed the back steps. His shirt and denims were
covered with bits of mowed grass and his hair looked
as rakish as a pirate's. But his smile shone warm and
welcome as he took the platter and pitcher away from
Mama.

''Let me help you two beautiful ladies. We've got
hungry men out there.''

''We have only the ham to slice,'' Mama answered.

Linnea turned her back, refusing to look at him.
She kept slicing, barely able to see the meat in front
of her. Seth's steps tapped away without saying another word.

She sighed in relief. At least she'd avoided speaking to him. So far.

Finished, she set aside the knife and wiped her
hands on a towel. As a last thought, she grabbed her
sunbonnet and tied it on. She was ready to face the
hayers out there, she told herself. But the platter felt
heavy as lead in her hands when she stepped onto the
porch.

There were twenty men gathered around the table,
spooning heaping piles of beans and potatoes onto
their plates, passing around the bread, talking loud
and gruff. She recognized neighbors she'd hardly seen

over the years, but two faces caught and held her attention.

The young men who'd accosted her on the road.

Just take the stairs one at a time, Linnea. Keep one foot in front of the other. Give Seth the meat platter and head back to the house. It was that simple. Nothing was going to happen.

Her feet moved forward, carrying her down the steps and toward the table.

"Linnea." Seth stood—wonderful Seth—and lifted the platter from her hands. "This is a mighty fine meal you made us."

"Thank you kindly, ma'am," Anders Neilson grumbled politely, and others joined in, murmuring their thanks.

"Thank you for coming to hay for us this year." Linnea's tongue stumbled over the words, and she stared at the edge of the tablecloth where Anders was digging his knife deep into the butter crock.

A movement caught her eye. Oscar Hansson gave her a broad wink.

"Respect the lady, boy," Seth reprimanded him, authority booming in his voice. "Jon, your son could use a lesson in manners."

"I'll see to it," the father agreed, glaring at his son.

"Your fingers are like ice," Seth whispered, and only then did she realize he was holding her hand. "You have nothing to fear."

Only losing you. He was nobility through and through, a good-hearted man who had no idea what others thought of her.

"I'll be in the kitchen if you need anything. I'll be cutting strawberry pie for dessert."

''I bet that's delicious.'' His smile deepened, became more tender, and his fingers tightened around hers. ''I'm proud of you. This is a fine meal.''

Her throat closed, and she fled to the house. To the safety of the four walls that had sheltered her all her life.

Something was wrong. Seth noticed it as Linnea returned with fresh pitchers of cool well water. Returned again with platters full of bread, ham and another bowl of creamy mashed potatoes. She refused to meet his gaze, and he saw the same sadness in her he'd noticed when they'd first met.

She's tired, he told himself. She had to be. She'd clearly been baking and cooking for more than a day, and dark circles bruised the delicate skin beneath her eyes.

But even so, she looked like heaven to him breezing out of the house in her blue calico dress and matching sunbonnet. Her golden curls were tucked up out of sight except for the spill of gold over her brow, but he knew what was hidden beneath the soft fabric of her bonnet.

She cleared the table, quiet and pale. Without a word to him, she returned with generous slices of pie dolloped with whipped cream. Probably without a doubt the best pie he'd ever eaten, but he didn't get the chance to tell her that. She kept her back to him.

She stayed in the house until the men departed for the field, but he headed straight for the house.

''Major, is that you?'' Mrs. Holmstrom asked from the counter where she was busy covering extra loaves of bread. ''Did the men get enough to eat?''

''More than enough. It was a mighty fine feast.''

"Linnea worked so hard. I am pleased, because she does not have to cut the hay herself this year, working like a man in the fields. I owe you a fine supper when this is all over."

"I'll be happy to take you up on that. You know I love your cooking." Since Linnea was nowhere in sight, he headed back outside.

There she was, like an angel from heaven, with her skirts swirling around her like poetry and her golden curls escaping from her bonnet. The plates clattered as she stacked them.

Her back was to him and he couldn't help admiring the fine cut of her neck or how delicate she looked there, where her collar hugged her soft white skin. She would be like that all over, porcelain fine and creamy soft.

His blood heated and he reminded himself that she was a lady. She demanded his respect.

For the rest of his life.

"Hi, beauty." He stepped closer.

She gasped and dropped the plates. They clanged together, the chime of enamel against enamel. She spun around to face him, her eyes wide, her face so pale.

"You made me proud," he told her, reaching out to her. They were alone. The men were on the other side of the house and heading toward the field. They couldn't see as he pulled her close to him.

"Seth." She wrestled her wrist from his grip and backed away. "You should be in the fields."

"I wanted to see how you were. To thank you—"

"It's not necessary." She took a step back and turned to gather the fallen plates. "You'd better go."

The hair on the back on his neck prickled. "You're

mad at me. That's why you left the flowers. You didn't forget them.''

"I'm not angry with you.'' She took the stack of plates and swung away from him. "I'm busy.''

"I don't have much time now, but I want to straighten this out later. When I'm done with the haying.''

"There's nothing to straighten out.'' Her chin lifted and she took off for the house. "Don't bother leaving me flowers. That's not necessary.''

"But I—''

"Goodbye, Seth.'' She retreated into the house, his angel and his heart, and slammed the door.

Ginny. It had to be Ginny. Angrier than he could ever remember being, he stormed past the house and into the field. He worked hard well into the afternoon before the sting of his fury faded.

Chapter Twelve

Here it comes, Ginny thought the minute she caught sight of Seth through the open kitchen window, striding toward the house.

She felt sick inside at what she'd done. For days the anxiety had been eating her up until she could hardly concentrate on her work. She'd ruined an entire batch of corn bread telling herself how foolish she'd been, letting her pride get the best of her in Ellie Jance's shop.

The pleasure of putting Linnea in her place was long gone. Now she was afraid of what Linnea had told Seth. And what he would do to her. Ginny rescued the corn bread from the oven before she let this batch scorch, and set the thick fragrant loaves on racks to cool.

"Ginny." His knock rattled the ill-fitting screen door in its frame.

He was furious all right. "I'll be ready for the men tomorrow. Got everything done that I can tonight."

"You have more bread than this, right?" Seth frowned at her table and the steaming loaves.

"That's enough," she insisted, but seeing the disapproval in his eyes, she wanted to dig in her heels and fight. She couldn't risk angering him further, so she kept her voice down, her mind searching for the right way to phrase things. "The only income I have is the rent money, and my son has to come first—"

"We had an agreement," he said quietly, his words vibrating with leashed anger. "You feed these men and feed them well. Every other neighbor woman has done the same."

She hung her head, sensing she couldn't win, hating that she was considered one of the neighbor women, a country woman with homemade clothes and a cellar full of preserves. "I'll do my best."

"I want the men well fed tomorrow. At noon sharp. This is important."

"I know." She tried not to think about the money the food would take out of her budget. She looked past the hard day of work awaiting her to the end result. That hay would bring her money. She'd sell it and add it to her funds when she sold the land.

Feeling better, she turned toward the stove where a pot of bacon and beans cooled.

"There's something else. What did you say to Linnea?" His accusation came cold as a winter's night and drew the warmth from the room.

A spoon tumbled from her fingers. Feeling stupid, she knelt to retrieve it only to drop it again. "I'm so clumsy."

"You didn't answer me."

He was still glaring at her with sharp-edged accusation that made her shake all the way down to her toes. How could she explain? She'd lost her temper, her pride had flared and she'd said words she now regretted?

"I said nothing out of the ordinary."

"I hope you're not lying to me." Instead of flaring with anger and lashing out with a closed fist as Jimmy would do, Seth remained in the shadowed doorway, just out of reach of the light, looking lost and hurt.

Hurt? How could that be? His power as a man remained as tangible as the night. But so did his sadness.

"I've heard the rumors that she supposedly made your husband cheat on you. I know you don't believe that."

"She would have if he'd wanted her."

"Ginny." Seth sighed, a weary sound that cut through her defensiveness. "You have no idea what I've lost, buried and thought I would never have again. I've lived alone feeling as if I'd died right along with my family for so long. Now I have the chance to be happy."

The screen door creaked as he gave it a shove. "Don't take that away from me. If I find out you've lied, I can't in good conscience stay."

"I said nothing out of the ordinary to her. I promise you."

Seth didn't want to call his stepsister a liar, but he didn't believe her either. Whatever she'd done, he would repair it. He would make Linnea understand she was the sun in the sky to him.

He had choices to make. He couldn't help Ginny. She was too busy destroying everything she touched, just like her father, ignorant to the beauty she could have if only she would open her heart.

The shanty was small but it was home. He prepared for bed to the music of coyote song. He stretched out on soft sheets and listened to the symphony of night—of owls hooting, the wind always blowing, and the galloping horses charging across the plains.

What had Linnea called it? Racing the wind.

The mustangs were back. He'd have to tell her.

He drifted off to sleep in his lonely bed, dreaming of her.

Always dreaming of her.

"We should take the leftover ham and bread up to Ginny," Mama suggested from her bench in the shade of the orchard. "She is all alone and has not cooked for hayers before."

"I'm sure she doesn't need our help." Or want it, Linnea figured, but didn't say it as she plucked the last pin from her mouth and gouged it into the fabric. "There, the seam is pinned. Are you sure you want to do this?"

"Yes. I wish to sew a dress for my beautiful girl." Mama took the pieces of the skirt with care and laid them on her lap. "I only need a little help, but I can still make myself useful."

"You are indispensable and you know it." Linnea pressed a kiss to her mother's cheek, unable to say what troubled her. Without knowing it, Mama had once again provided a comforting haven. A soft place to fall.

"I think we must take the food up to Ginny. We have so much of it left over! We cannot eat it all."

"No, Mama. You know I don't like Ginny."

"Forgiveness, child. Life has not been easy for her. And think of the goodness we can do for our neighbor."

"I don't want to think about it."

Mama chuckled as she felt with her fingers the

edge of the fabric and started her needle there. "We cannot let good food go to waste. Maybe the men who were so kind to mow our fields will appreciate good food."

"You're implying Ginny is a bad cook."

"It is possible, so we must do what we can for our neighbors."

Mama was only teasing, trying to change her mind, and it worked. "Fine. I'll wrap the leftovers. You stay here in the shade."

"That's my good girl."

"I'm not five years old, Mama." Laughing, Linnea retreated to the kitchen. If she hurried, then she could deliver the food well before noon and there would be no danger of seeing Seth.

Thinking of his name made her break a little more. She told herself it didn't matter. She'd lost much more in her life. And this heartache was her fault, believing in love when she knew better.

When the basket was ready, she told her mother goodbye, but Mama insisted on coming.

"It's too hot, Mama."

"Yes, but if Ginny needs help, then there are two of us."

The midsummer sun blazed with unrelenting force on the dry land. Prairie grasses crackled and rustled with the wind's force, and against the crest of a rise she could see the men in the field. The mowing machine pulled by Seth's oxen and the men forking the mowed grass into tall wagons.

"I can hear them working hard." Mama cocked her head, turning to catch the faint *whir* of the machine and the low murmur of men's voices. "I miss running the ranch, miss the seasons of life. That's when you feel them, when you farm. The harrowing and planting in spring. The summer of growth and the autumn of harvest. The winter where we rest and prepare for our next spring, whatever that may be.''

''Having the hayers again made you miss Papa more.''

''Yes. How I miss him.''

Me, too. Sorrow gathered into a hard ball in her throat, and she couldn't speak. So she said nothing, listening to the rhythm of their shoes padding against the chalk-dry earth and the snap of their skirts.

Her mother swayed and missed a step.

''Mama!'' Linnea held the older woman steady. ''Are you all right?''

''Goodness, I should hope so. It is so hot is all.''

''I should have made you stay home.''

''It is only dizziness and it shall pass.''

''*Only* dizziness?'' Linnea couldn't stop the sense of foreboding that skidded down her spine as cold as ice. ''We need to get you out of this sun.''

''We must be nearly there. All I need is a cold glass of water. Do not worry so, my *flicka*.''

Ginny's house soon came into view, and the basket felt as if it were suddenly made of stone.

''This way, Mama.'' Their arms looped, Linnea guided her mother off the road and across the uneven stone path around the side of the house. ''We'll try the back door since Ginny will be in the kitchen. Careful. We're almost there.''

Her mother didn't answer and seemed feeble as she hobbled through the yard toward the shade trees.

Worry magnified with each step. She never should have let Mama have her own way.

"Here's a bench. You sit here." Linnea set the basket aside and took her mother by both arms.

How frail she felt. She looked pale slumped against the armrest.

"I am so very thirsty."

"I'll get some water." She ran as fast as she could into the backyard.

Ginny turned from the table set up in the shade of the house. Contempt pinched her face as Linnea approached. "Don't tell me you've come to see my brother."

"It's my mother. She's not well. She needs water."

"What were you two doing? Walking in this heat?" Ginny snatched a tin cup from the table. "Here. The trough is there."

"In the field?"

"It's clean and it's cool." Ginny's eyes narrowed.

Linnea snatched the cup from her. There was no time to argue. She hurried to the fence line, where fresh water spilled into a deep trough, and filled the tin.

"*Dotter,* you need not have hurried!" Mama scolded. "You should not run in this heat. You will feel dizzy next!"

"Drink all of it." Linnea pressed the cup into her mother's hands.

She complied, sipping the last drop. "I feel better."

"Don't you dare move." Linnea kissed her mother's cheek, took the cup and the heavy basket and hurried through the unkempt flower garden.

"Linnea." There was Seth blocking the path, looking hot and tired from his work in the fields. Men clustered behind him, and he sent them around to the other side of the house.

Looking at him made her want him. Want all her dreams to come true with him—*this* man, the one who gazed at her with sweet, tender longing.

"I didn't expect to see you today." His gaze was a question, an intimate one she could not answer.

She'd spied on him this morning as he'd left fresh flowers beside the faded ones. How could she pretend she wasn't falling in love with him?

"Mama wanted to help Ginny."

"Hello, Major." Mama limped down the path. "We've come to see if you could use extra loaves of bread and ham. It has been so long since we have cooked for hayers I could not remember how much they ate. We made too much! And too much for us to eat if we worked at it for a week."

"Mama, you promised to stay sitting down." Linnea set the basket and cup on the ground and rushed to her mother's side. "Come with me."

"My *dotter* fusses," Mama explained to Seth.

"She's not feeling well." Linnea led the way to the bench. "Mama, let me take care of you. Please. You are the only mother I have."

"Now, how can I argue?" Tenderly Mama brushed her hand over Linnea's cheek, smoothing back wayward curls. "I shall stay."

"Good." Linnea stood to find Seth at her side. "Excuse me. I need to get more water. Would you mind taking the basket in to Ginny?"

He followed her. "We need to talk."

"No. My mother can hear you." She lowered her voice and shoved the basket at him. "Besides, there is nothing to say."

"Whatever Ginny said to you, I want you to forget. Wipe it away like dust from a blackboard—"

"Excuse me." She stepped off the path, pushed against a stout lilac branch and shouldered past him.

Ginny stood in the way. "What are you still doing here? I thought you were going to get some water and leave?"

"Ginny—" Seth's voice rang in warning.

"My mother isn't strong enough to head home." Linnea gripped the cup so tightly the handle cut into her fingers. "We'll leave as soon as she can."

Ginny's gaze fastened on the basket Seth carried. There was no mistaking the displeasure on her face, and then she looked at the ground. A muscle strained beneath the smooth skin of her jaw.

"Mrs. Holmstrom brought bread and ham to go with the meal." Seth held the basket to his sister. He quirked one brow.

"I am quite capable of providing a meal." Ginny's chin lowered. "But I'm sure the men will appreciate your thoughtfulness. Thank you. Seth, will you take the basket to the table?"

"No. I'd best look after Mrs. Holmstrom." His brow furrowed. "Ginny, the men are waiting."

Although it was clear she didn't like it, Ginny took the basket and marched out of sight.

Seth took the cup out of her hands. "I'll fill this for your mother. You go keep her company. She looks like she needs it."

She couldn't thank him. If he did one more thing to become more noble in her eyes, then she'd never be able to let him go.

He only acts like this now because he doesn't know about the baby. The truth splashed over her like cold water, and she didn't thank him. Just turned away.

"So much fuss!" Mama fretted.

"Don't worry." Linnea knelt in front of her. "Seth is fetching more water, and you're going to be fine."

Mama covered her face with her hands, ashamed of her weakness.

"Here." Seth returned with a full cup. "You stay here as long as your mother needs to. When you're ready to leave, I want you to drive. I'll hitch General to my buggy and leave him in the yard. When you get home, unhitch him and put him in the shade with some water. I'll be over to fetch him tonight when I'm done here."

"How can I repay you?"

"I'll think on it and let you know." He winked, but his brow remained furrowed. His gaze shot to Mama.

She didn't look any better.

"Here. Sip this slowly." Linnea held the cup until her mother grew stubborn and took it herself. "Fine, then I'll go fetch a washcloth and basin. Will you be all right alone?"

"Go. I am fine."

"Liar." She hurried down the path, knowing Seth was near if Mama needed him.

The sounds of men's laughter and the clink of flatware carried from the yard. Dread filled her. She cornered the house and Oscar Hansson stared right at her.

Linnea stared hard at the ground in front of her as she hurried toward the back steps.

"Hey, look who's come to serve us," Oscar called just loud enough to carry above the other men's voices.

"Sit down, boy!" a man ordered.

Linnea dashed up the steps and into the house.

"You're never going to be respectable enough for

him, anyway.'' Ginny was at the counter, filling a plate with bread. ''Anytime he's not around, that's how other men are going to treat you.''

''I need to borrow a basin and a washcloth.''

Ginny reached with one hand into a drawer and tossed a ragged dishcloth onto the table. ''You didn't come here because you wanted to help me. You wanted Seth to think well of you. But it won't work. Nothing can change what you are.''

Linnea snatched the cloth. ''Are you going to tell him?''

''If you don't leave now. Your mother is well enough to climb into the buggy. I heard every word Seth said to you through the window. How he cares.''

''Goodbye, Ginny.'' Linnea grabbed her empty basket from the table, taking that, too.

''He won't care for you when he finds out the truth. His wife was a beautiful girl. Decent. Innocent. As pure as could be.''

Linnea tripped down the step, blind with hurt and fury. She heard Oscar call out, ''I've got a dollar, Miss Linnea,'' and then fall silent when Seth strode into the yard.

She couldn't look at him as she wet the cloth beneath the running water. The men silenced, and not even the scrap of a fork on a plate broke the awful tension as she headed down the path. The lilacs closed around her, hiding her from their sight.

What else had Oscar said? What if one of the men pulled Seth aside and told him the basis of the joke? How could she stand having him know the truth?

''Here, Mama. This will cool your face.'' Linnea pressed the cloth against her mother's papery cheek.

''Feels good. Oh, you have the basket.''

"Yes. You heard Seth say he'd let us drive his beautiful stallion home. How would you like to try out his fancy buggy?"

"What a delight." She stood, trembling and weak.

Linnea wrapped her arm around the older woman's tiny waist. "Lean on me, Mama."

"Always, my precious girl."

The worry over her mother remained through the day and into the night. She read Mama to sleep and tucked her in gently, grateful that this woman was the one who'd given her life.

Linnea retreated with her sewing into the parlor where the calico kept her company. Listening to the cat's contented purr, she pieced her squares with pins, then stitched them.

A faint off-rhythm beat whispered in through the open windows. Could it be? She dropped her sewing and ran to the door. Through the screen door she could see the dark mystery of the night, the flickering brilliance of stars, and the prairies bathed in moonlight.

The drumming beat continued, growing until the entire plains seemed alive with it. They moved like shadows, evading the full blaze of the moon as it shone on a gleaming mane or a velvety shoulder. Then they became darkness again.

Linnea pushed open the screen door and raced down the steps. They were galloping so far away.

"I wondered if I'd catch you out here."

"Seth!" She laid her hand over her chest. "You've got to stop sneaking up on me like that."

"You don't seem to notice when I'm around. That can't be a good sign."

She took a step into the shadows.

"A woman ought to be glad to see the man court-ing her."

"I suppose that's true." She wanted to hold on to the slightest hope. To dream that he would accept her even if he knew the truth.

He stood tall with the honor he'd earned over a lifetime as a major and as a man. Other men tossed silver coins and made jokes about her. Seth Gatlin wouldn't take that kind of a woman as his wife. Ginny was right.

The beauty of the night broke like crystal shattering on dirt and rock. A thousand shards that could never be repaired and made whole again.

Just say it, Linnea. She owed that kindness to Seth, the kindness of turning him away. He deserved an innocent woman who would bring him happiness, not someone with mistakes and flaws and lines on her face.

She gathered her courage and turned her back on him, staring hard at the horses in her cow field. "Mama's health is growing worse, and so I have to make some difficult decisions."

"What do you mean?"

"She needs me more than ever right now. She's my first responsibility."

"Of course she is. She's your mother. Does this have to do with why you're pushing me away? After our Sunday drive, I thought you understood. I'm courting you. With hopes of marrying you."

"No." She covered her face with her hands. "Don't say any more—"

"I'm going slow," he cut in. "Trying to do it the

right way. Showing you my intentions. This is for the rest of our lives, Linnea. Do you want me?''

''Yes. Once.'' How could she find the strength to tell him now? ''I can't—''

''What does that mean? You either do or you don't.''

''I told you. I have other responsibilities.''

''To your mother.'' He sounded skeptical. He sounded angry. Lost in the night. ''Does Ginny have anything to do with this? She doesn't seem to like you. I wouldn't put it past her to say something to drive us apart.''

''Ginny isn't at fault.''

''I don't believe you. Whatever Ginny's said, she's wrong. I have faith in you, Linnea. Let me court you the right way.''

''I have my mother to take care of. I can't be riding through the countryside with my beau.''

''We'll take her with us next time. If we marry, she can live with us. I have no problem with that.''

Why did he have to be so good-hearted? He made it impossible to break off with him.

''I don't want to be with you.'' It wasn't the truth. It would never be the truth.

''I see.'' He paused, and the world stilled as if waiting for his verdict. ''This has nothing to do with Ginny?''

''No.'' She'd made her own mistakes.

He took a step away. Then another. Until the width of the road separated them. ''I'll just hitch up General and be on my way then.''

''Good.''

She wanted to crumple to the ground and cry until

there were no feelings left. Nothing had ever hurt like this loss, this lost second chance at love.

She stared with unseeing eyes at the faint shadow of the mustangs against the horizon. Coyote song rang sad and lonely, and the who-who of the owl hunting near the barn seemed as desolate as she felt.

Steeled horseshoes echoed in the barnyard. Buggy wheels whirred and a harness jingled as Seth drove close.

She couldn't look at him.

He drew General to a stop. The night seemed cold and she couldn't stop shaking.

He said nothing at all. Not one word.

He drove away into the darkness. Leaving her alone.

Just like that, their courtship was over.

Chapter Thirteen

"**M**ajor? Is that you?" a frail, sweet voice called out over the rattle of harnesses as he drove into the yard.

"It sure is, ma'am."

"What a treat to have you visit again." Mrs. Holmstrom's face wreathed a smile. "I still cannot get over the kitchen pump. What a luxury! I praise you every time I use it."

"Then I reckon you might be glad I stopped by today." He set the brake.

"Another surprise?"

"Yes, ma'am." He climbed down. "I've got nothing much to do while the wheat's ripening in the fields. So I figured I'd come over here and put on a new roof. If that's all right with you."

"Oh, yes! You did not forgot your promise!"

"I never break my word to a pretty lady." He circled around to the back of the wagon. "As long as you're feeling all right?"

"I am fine as can be! Too much fuss over a little dizziness that was soon gone."

"I heard the doctor was out to visit the other day."

He unloaded his tools and a bucket of nails. "I saw his buggy parked in your yard."

"I am old is all. Linnea made me *tosca* cake yesterday and there is plenty. Please, come have a little treat before you start."

"Is Linnea in the house?"

"Does it matter?" She waited, a sly look on her face.

"No, ma'am. I just wanted to check with her. Maybe it's not a good day to work on your roof."

The sly, slightly hopeful look faded from the older woman's face. "Of course. Polite as always. I assure you, Linnea will not mind. She is in the orchard picking peaches by the bucketful."

Mrs. Holmstrom led the way into her cozy house. Seth noticed the quilt pieces piled on the corner table in the parlor. The flowery scent of lilacs lingered in the air, and everywhere he looked he saw the grace of a woman's touch—lace, ruffles, soft handmade cushions.

All of it reminded him of Linnea, who said she didn't want him. He gritted his teeth and ignored the pain deep in his soul. Mrs. Holmstrom offered him a chair at the table as she worked at the counter.

An ill mother. That wasn't enough of a reason to refuse a man's love. It was an excuse, plain and simple. Linnea was too damn kind to say it. She didn't want him.

Sitting in her house wasn't the easiest thing he'd ever done, but he survived it. He complimented Mrs. Holmstrom on her mother's recipe and on her daughter's baking.

He noticed as he finished the last piece of the cake

that the old woman looked extremely delicate. She rubbed her brow on and off as if she had a headache.

An icy chill skidded down his spine, and he had to admit that maybe Linnea was telling the truth. Maybe Mrs. Holmstrom didn't feel as well as she pretended.

"I'm going to be making a whole lot of noise," he told her. "Maybe it would be best if I only worked until noon. That way you'd have some peace and quiet later in the day."

"What? Will you be fussing after me, too? Nonsense. I do not mind the sound of a man at work."

"As long as you promise to tell me if it's too loud. Promise?"

"I suppose, but it will do my heart good to see a new roof on this place."

Mrs. Holmstrom's happiness warmed his hurting heart just a little. He couldn't help worrying about her, seeing up close the delicate bruises beneath her eyes and her pale skin.

He took her arm. "Let me escort you outside and make sure you're comfortable."

"Why, that would be an honor. How I have missed you, Major. You have not been by for me to bake for you. The fruit is falling off the trees, there is so much! I have plenty to make a fresh pie. Cherries? Or peaches?"

"Cherries with extra sugar, and I'd be forever in your debt, ma'am."

She patted his arm. "Perfect. I must keep my landlord happy. I hear the McIntyres have offered you the land."

"I may take it. I haven't decided."

"It would be a fine thing to have you for our neighbor permanently. I would not worry then about losing the house my dear Olaf built for me. The only other house I could bear to live in would be one I shared with my dear sister. She is in Oregon, so far away.''

"Here's the bench. Sit and enjoy the day."

"Thank you, my dear man." She found the edge of the seat with her fingertips and settled onto it. "You are as bad as Linnea, always looking after me. She thinks there is trouble when it is only old age. One day may you have a daughter who loves you so."

He'd had a daughter, and Mrs. Holmstrom's well-meaning words were like a blade through his heart. "Maybe one day, ma'am. A man never knows. Tell me the truth, now. How many dizzy spells have you had?''

"I am fine, and you must not tell Linnea otherwise. She has enough on her hands providing for the two of us.''

Linnea was right. There was serious cause for concern. Seth patted the woman's frail hand, wishing he knew what to do.

"Mr. Gatlin." Linnea marched into sight, flushed from the heat, a leaf caught on her sunbonnet. She smelled of ripe peaches as she crooked her finger.

Simply looking at her made his loneliness double. She'd told him, "I don't want to be with you." Her words had hurt like nothing had since he'd lost his family.

Words she'd said for her mother's sake.

He glanced at the old woman drowsing and remembered how ill she'd been at Ginny's house. The icy feeling returned. What else had Linnea said? *She needs me more than ever.*

Linnea gestured again. He obliged by following her

into the sun-dappled orchard, where bees buzzed lazily and boughs hung heavy with ripening fruit.

He studied the buckets heaped with velvety peaches. "Want me to carry those in for you?"

"I can manage." She looked at him with a cool gaze. "Why are you here?"

"I promised your mother the first day I met her that I'd replace the roof for her this summer. I have time now."

"She's not well. All the hammering will upset her."

"She says different. She wants a new roof on her house. I won't have time again until after harvest. It could be raining by then."

Linnea sighed, a frustrated sound, and peered through the trees to where her mother sat, chin bobbing forward as she napped. Linnea's face softened with unmistakable affection.

There was no missing the daughter's tenderness or her devotion.

Renewed love for Linnea surged to life in his heart. Did she think she had to choose between him and her Mama?

"I'll stop if it's too much for her. Work only mornings or something. Whatever it takes."

"Truly?" She faced him, her eyes luminous, more beautiful because of the depth of her heart. "That would be fine."

"She did offer to bake me a cherry pie, but I can talk her out of it if she gets the notion."

He was rewarded with a smile.

"I'll bake you that pie myself if you want. Out of thanks, nothing else." Linnea emphasized with a reserved politeness that set his teeth on edge.

"I told you the other night, but I want to say it again," he said. "Your mother might be the reason other men haven't courted you, but I like her. I understand she's your responsibility. I'm ready to make her mine, too."

For a brief instant her eyes darkened, the sorrow in them hopeless and stark. Then she blinked and it was gone.

"I told you. That's not the problem." Her lower lip trembled once. She walked away from him as if he'd never mattered to her at all.

The earsplitting sound of a hammer driving nails into wood seemed endless. Linnea hurried as quickly as she could, gathering the bowls and paring knife she needed, then headed for the door.

"Drove you out into the open, did I?" Seth's shadow fell across the back steps, elongated by the morning sun. "Sorry about that."

"You don't look sorry."

"That's because I'm done."

She'd put up with him for the better part of three days while he crouched on their roof and watched every move she made. Whether she was plucking fruit from the trees or pitting peaches in the shade, he'd been peering at her from beneath the brim of his Stetson.

"What a marvelous job you have done, Major!" Mama praised, setting her sewing aside and rising from the bench.

"I'll take what praise I can, ma'am, but the truth is you won't know if I did a good job or not until it rains."

"I have faith in you."

''No need to frown, Linnea. It won't leak.'' The light faded from his voice when he spoke to her. ''I'll just pack up and be on my way.''

''Good.''

''Can't wait to be rid of me?''

''Exactly.'' She drove a knife into a succulent peach. With a twist of the knife's sharp tip, she carved out the dark pit and flicked it into a waste pail.

She felt his gaze on her, as bold as a lover's touch, and she refused to look at him. Ginny's threat and Oscar Hansson's contempt remained between them.

She groped for a peach in the bucket. The fruit was bruised, just as she was, and she set it in the preserves pail to be made into jam.

''Goodness. Now look what I've done!'' Mama fretted as she searched the front of her dress and along the bench seat with her fingers. ''I have dropped my needle.''

''Don't worry so. I'll find it.'' Linnea wasn't used to seeing her mother like this, growing more fragile by the day. ''You know I drop my needle all the time. Remember last week when it slipped from my fingers and fell through the floorboards? I had to crawl under the house to find it.''

''I will never finish your dress if I keep this up.'' Mama sounded so unlike herself.

Linnea covered her mother's frantic hands. ''Listen to me. The dress will be done in its own time, and it will be a dress I treasure because you chose the fabric and sewed it just for me.''

''Oh, my girl. I want this so much.''

''You are what matters to me. You are my life, Mama, you know that. Please, don't be upset.''

"Oh, my *flicka*, I do not know what is wrong with me. I do not think I am feeling well."

Seth's step tapped behind them. He'd returned. "Mrs. Holmstrom, I'm disappointed. You swore to me that my hammering wasn't bothering you."

"It was not! I am so happy to have a new roof. Olaf would never have let it go so long if he'd lived."

"I'm sure he wouldn't."

If he'd lived. Those words shamed Linnea now. She watched Seth take Mama's hand with kindness and press a kiss to her knuckles.

Mama wouldn't be alone, they wouldn't be without Papa, if she'd been the sensible girl her parents had raised her to be.

Linnea dropped to her knees and searched through the grass, her vision blurring so that she couldn't see the bench. How was she going to find the needle?

Look how she'd almost made the same mistake again, because she was always wishing for, always dreaming of the same kind of love her parents had shared. One of beauty and respect and undying affection.

"Here it is." Seth's words rumbled through her, warm and intimate, reminding her of all the times his touch had cast desire through her. Reminding her of the velvet heat of his kiss and the joy of his flowers waiting for her on the doorstep.

"You are a wonder!" Mama praised weakly.

Linnea climbed to her feet. Her pain didn't matter. What mattered was the fragile woman seated in front of her, hands trembling so badly she couldn't thread the needle.

"Mama, let's get you to rest for a bit." She took the needle and thread and set it in the nearby basket.

"But I want to finish this seam."

"Later." Linnea closed the basket and set it aside.

"How on earth do you sew?" Seth settled onto the bench, his voice light but his face lined with sorrow.

"I have my Linnea to cut the pieces and match them up for me. I have not seen for years, but my fingers know what they are doing. I have sewed since I was a little girl."

"Mama taught me," Linnea added as she lifted the basted bodice from her mother's lap. "I'm not as good as she is, even now."

"I had a way with a needle, when I could see. It is true." Mama smiled fondly, falling silent for a moment, as if lost in the past.

"I'm going to run inside and fetch a pillow," Linnea told Seth. "You'll stay with her?"

"Count on it."

He was the kind of man she wanted to rely on for the rest of her life.

She couldn't help wishing, just a little, as she carried Mama's basket into the house, grabbed her pillow and filled a glass with cool water.

After they had Mama lying down, Linnea accompanied Seth to his wagon. "I can't thank you enough for being so good to her."

"She's a nice lady. I'd like to think my mother would have been like that if my father hadn't died when I was young."

"How old were you?"

"Seven." He lifted the bucket of nails into the wagon bed. "My mother remarried right away, she had no choice. He was cruel to her and she died young. Of a broken heart, I always figured."

His sadness touched her, this man who'd lost so much. "I didn't know."

"I admire how you take care of her, Linnea. A lot of daughters wouldn't be so devoted."

"It's not me, it's Mama. She's been an amazing mother. She's loved me through what I didn't think I could survive, and I owe her my life."

"I'll say it again. I'm going to say it until you believe me. You can take care of your mother in my house, as my wife."

"And I'll answer the same way every time. Mama isn't the reason I will never be your wife." She lifted her chin, letting go of her dreams. "I'll be along in a few days with the rent money. Tell Ginny I won't be late."

"Forget the rent money this month. The property's being sold."

"What?" She clutched the wagon box for support. "Someone's buying this property? Mama said that you might—"

"Might what?" He fitted the tailgate into place.

"Then your obligations to your sister are done. You'll be leaving." Sadness filled her. She knew he would probably leave after the harvest. But the thought of never seeing him again—

"Oh, I'll be staying around. I'm the buyer." He swung onto the seat. "Should I head to town and fetch the doctor?"

"He's scheduled to come tomorrow. Mama will be fine after a nap. This isn't the first time this has happened."

"Let me know if there's anything I can do." Sincere and steadfast, he was the man she loved.

It wasn't easy to let him go. "You've been a good

landlord to us. I'm glad you're buying the land. You said you wanted to ranch.''

"Yes." He seemed to look past her, as if she'd disappointed him, and gathered the reins. He nodded formally and drove away.

Her sadness felt as thick as the dust fogging the air in his wake. He'd bought the land. He was going to stay. Somehow that was worse than if he'd left.

As the years passed, she saw a future that weighed down her soul. She would have to hold her head high as he drove by on the road to town. One day, when he married a deserving woman from town, she'd sew him a wedding gift. And later, knit a baby blanket as each child arrived.

His buggy would be filled with a family, with Seth's warmth and laughter.

She would not let her heart grow sad. She had love in her life. She had beauty. She had more than she deserved.

Linnea blinked against the harsh sun's glare. The dust in the road had settled, and Seth was gone from her sight.

From her life.

From her dreams.

The days blurred together after that. Work kept her tired enough so that she couldn't think about Seth. The apples came ripe and, with Mama feeling poorly, she did all the work herself. The drying, the canning. Making applesauce, apple butter, apple preserves and cider. Then there was the garden.

She tumbled into bed well after midnight only to rise before dawn. Exhaustion turned out to be a good way to keep Seth Gatlin off her mind.

"I feel better today," Mama insisted. "I can help."

"You will do as the doctor orders and rest." Linnea swiped a wisp of hair out of her eyes and continued cutting the kernels from the cob. "I'm almost done with the corn. After I set this last bit out to dry, I'll get supper ready. Do you want corn tonight or green beans?"

"Both are always a treat. They taste so good fresh from the garden." Mama stumbled, then pressed the heel of her hand to her forehead. "Goodness, I need to sit a spell, I guess."

"Are you all right?" Linnea dropped the knife and raced around the table.

Mama was wobbling, reaching out blindly for something to hold on to. Linnea caught her elbow and wrapped her arms around her mother's frail body.

How little she felt, like a fallen bird, trembling and weak.

Mama mumbled, her words slurring together, and lost consciousness.

"Ginny, this is for the best." Seth's week had been hard enough and the last thing he wanted was for his sister to break down over what couldn't be helped.

He laid the signed paperwork on the kitchen table. "You're free of the second mortgage Jimmy took out before he skipped town. I own the land."

"I suppose you'll be collecting the rent money from now on." She bowed her head but looked through her lashes at him. "And rent from me, too?"

"I'll let you live in the house for as long as you need. I won't charge you a cent. I promised I'd help you, and I will. But you have to help yourself. You'll have to take a job in town."

"A job. How can I do that? I have Jamie to raise. He's so sickly in the winters with his weak lungs."

"You can work while he's in school."

"And when he's sick?" Her mouth pursed into a thin line and she launched out of the chair, hands fisted, skirts snapping. She halted at the window, breathing hard, staring out at the apples falling from the trees. "I won't live like this. With a house tumbling down around my ears and my son wearing secondhand clothes."

"We've had a dry summer and you know it. I put in two wells to irrigate and the wheat crop is half what it should be. We won't see the profit we had hoped for."

"It's not fair. I don't deserve this."

"I didn't see you out there digging a well and I didn't see you pounding timbers for a windmill."

"I had Jamie to take care of."

"Then you wasted your time because you're doing a damn poor job of it." He was tired and his temper flared. "I've worked nonstop since I've been here, and I haven't asked for a dime. I've put in wells, planted your fields, fixed your fences, buildings and rental house and bought you a cow. This land sale is a good deal for me, not for you, but it's still better than your alternatives."

"You mean you'd put me out? Just like that. You said you'd help me. Isn't that just like a man?"

"I'm giving you a house rent-free. You make your own opportunities from here. For better or worse. That's it. Get a job. Take care of your son. Put up beets and apples and make jam. Fix up your house."

"Why are you doing this?" Rage burned inside her and she tried to contain it. She didn't want to make

Seth any angrier. "I thought you were going to help me sell the grain and hay. Even find a buyer for the land. I would have money for a nice little house in town. It wouldn't be fancy, but at least it wouldn't be here in the country—"

"Seth!" A woman shouted from the backyard. "Seth!"

Linnea Holmstrom ran into sight, her sunbonnet hanging down her back, her face red from exertion.

Seth took one look at the terror in her eyes and his heart stopped. He knew why she was here.

"It's Mama. She lost consciousness for a few minutes. Will you ride for the doctor?"

He was already running full bore. "Get back to her, Linnea. I'll have the doc there as fast as I can. Trust me."

"I do."

Whatever had happened between them, her words lit his hope. She depended on him. She needed him. She'd come to him.

He whistled and General lifted his head, pricking his ears. Like old times, the stallion loped toward him. He didn't take time for a bit or saddle. Just hopped on the horse's back and took off through the fields.

"Seth is bringing the doctor, Mama." Linnea wrung water from the cloth and folded it in thirds. "He's riding that fast stallion of his, so he should be back in no time."

"S-Seth," Mama slurred, smiling slightly with only one half of her mouth.

"We can count on him." It had been a long time since she'd had a neighbor to rely on. Whatever happened, she was over her heartache. From this moment on, she'd be grateful—not sad—that Seth was their neighbor and their landlord.

She laid the cool cloth on her mother's brow. "Is that better?"

Mama could only nod. Her eyes drifted shut. She lay so still she didn't look as if she were breathing. There seemed so little of her left beneath the sheet.

Was she going to die?

"Don't leave me, Mama. Please." She laid her hand on her mother's. "Don't go to Papa yet."

Silence filled the room. Linnea slid her fingertips to the inside of Mama's wrist so she could feel the faint pulse, slow and irregular.

Horse hooves drummed outside. She raced through the house, but Seth had already opened the door, standing aside to let the doctor through.

"She's in the bedroom." Linnea pointed to where Mama lay so still.

"What happened?" Seth's hand curled around her nape, his touch comforting. Infinitely comforting.

It was a comfort she didn't deserve and she stepped away. "Mama was dizzy and had a terrible headache. I need to see if the doctor needs anything."

"I'll help. I'll stay by your side."

His honor touched her, arrowing past the fear she felt for her mother. Why was he being so good to her? She'd treated him harshly and hurt him, and still he would help her.

"I've been keeping cold presses on her forehead," she told the doctor.

Grim faced, the medical man nodded his head. "That brought her comfort, I'm sure. Seth, take Linnea outside and calm her down."

"I am calm!"

"No, you're not." The doctor said it kindly as he brushed past her. "The last thing your mother needs is to sense how upset you are. You can help her best by staying out of the way and getting hold of your emotions."

"But she's my mother. I can't leave—"

"It would be best." The doctor pumped water into the basin and reached for the soap. "Seth, take her outside."

"No." They weren't going to send her away, not when Mama needed her. Mama was confused and in pain and maybe dying. "She can't be alone."

"I'll be with her. If there's a serious change, I'll let you know."

"Come, Linnea." Seth's touch was heaven's comfort as he drew his arm around her waist. His touch, the contact of his body to hers, made her feel as if she wasn't alone. "We'll wait outside for a few minutes. Let the doctor do his work."

"I'm the one who takes care of her." Linnea glanced at the open doorway. She could see her mother's gray curls on the pillow. "It doesn't look as if she's breathing."

"The doctor knows what to do, Linnea. He has a medical degree." Wise words, tenderly spoken.

How could she resist? He made her weak when she should fight. He made her melt until there was only her true self, afraid and alone and vulnerable.

"I can't bear to leave her." She pressed her face into his chest.

"I know. We'll let the doc do his work, and then we'll sneak back in. Doesn't matter if he likes it or not."

Light was bleeding from the sky in the long, slow

dance of a late summer's sunset. The world went on as it always did, the calves and yearlings meandering out from the shade of the barn to graze. The family of goldfinches in the tree trilled happily as the fat babies practiced their flying.

"It feels like any other day. Except my mother could be dying."

Seth's arm tightened around her waist. He said nothing. There was nothing to say. No words could comfort her. The sweet prairie breezes fanned her face as they did every night, and the swallows argued in the barnyard as they bathed in the dust.

Like any other day.

"Maybe she'll be all right. Maybe it's just a spell. She gets smaller ones now and then. She recovers from them."

"It's possible."

They both knew it was more serious than that. More serious than even the doctor had let on.

"You might as well go home." She lifted her chin, refusing to be weak when she had to be strong. "I appreciate your riding to town."

"I'm glad you came to me." His arm tightened around her waist. His free hand covered hers. "I like knowing that you need me."

"I don't need you." It was a lie, and it was the truth. She wasn't going to lean on a man who wasn't hers.

"Too bad, because I'm staying. A man doesn't leave when the going gets tough. Especially when it involves the woman he loves."

"You can't love me."

"It's not something you get a voice in. It's something my heart decided all on its own."

"I don't love you."

"Now that's something I don't believe."

He held her, simply held her, as the blue of the sky faded and the sun turned to flame at the western horizon. Streaks of fire raked through the clouds, turning them crimson and purple.

A beautiful sunset on this day unlike all others.

"I can't wait any longer." She tried to get up.

Seth held her firm. "Give the doc a little more time. He seems like a smart man to me."

"Mama could be afraid. She might need me."

"I'm sure she does."

"She's alone and it's my fault." She hated the truth that felt as dark as the shadows creeping across the prairie. "It's my fault that my father isn't here for her. I took care of her the best I could, but it can never make up for what I did."

"Shh." He pressed his lips to her temple. "Your mother's going to be all right. We'll keep believing that until we know otherwise."

How could he be like this? So wonderful and stubborn and true? He couldn't love her, she wouldn't let him.

"I have to go." She ripped away from his side. "Excuse me."

"Linnea." He caught her on the porch, his hand at her elbow, his strength greater than hers. "Don't go in there like that. The doc wanted you calm. For your mother's sake."

"I can't help her sitting out here."

"You can't help her like this."

"Then what do I do? Sit idle? I'm responsible for her. I'm the reason she's alone and I live with that every day of my life. Let me go, because you wouldn't be holding on to me if you knew the truth.''

"I'd always want to hold you." He seemed so certain of it, this man and his unfailing love.

What did it take? She twisted away from him, but she slammed into something equally solid in the shadowed threshold.

The doctor.

Fear iced her veins. She stumbled back, grabbing the rail for support. "How is she?"

"She's had a stroke. We'll need a few days to know how extensive it's been. She needs complete rest. I mean, complete. No upset."

"I can be calm," she promised. "I'm going to be calm."

"I know she's all you have, Linnea." The doctor's kindness hurt worse and made her feel weak against his strength.

She took a deep breath. Night came quietly as the light drained from the sky. "I'm calm."

"All right. Come sit by her side." The doctor disappeared into the shadows.

"Figure I'll stay, too. Just in case you need a shoulder to lean on."

"I've done enough leaning." She longed for the shelter of his arms, but she could stand on her own two feet. Her mother had taught her that. "Good night, Seth."

She slipped away before he could reach for her, leaving him alone in the dark.

Chapter Fourteen

Linnea had never seen a more beautiful sight than her mother awakening the next morning. "Mama, it's me."

"D-dotter." She slurred a little and her smile was still one sided. Tears traced down her cheeks.

"I don't want you to worry." She brushed the tears away with her thumb. "The doctor says you're going to be fine. You need complete rest, so don't *think* about trying to get out of this bed to bake him a pie."

More tears trailed down her face.

"That's right. No pie baking for a few days at least." The doctor approached, his face marked with weariness. "Linnea, why don't you go boil some tea water for your mother? I'd like some time alone to examine her."

"I'll be right back, Mama." Linnea hated leaving. Hated the frightened look in her mother's eyes. It was tough leaving the room, but the doctor was kind and competent.

How bad was the stroke? She burned her finger on the match and spilled water twice, dreading what the doctor would say.

A rap at the door shot through the quiet house, and she dropped the measuring spoon. It clanked against the counter, spilling tea leaves.

"Sorry about that." Seth ambled in. His face was lined with exhaustion, but he stood tall and straight, as strong as ever. "I suppose you didn't expect me so early."

Seeing him made her feel more brave. "I'm glad you're here."

"I saw smoke from the stovepipe and figured it wasn't too early to see how your mother's doing."

"She's awake. Better." Linnea swept the loose tea into her hand. "The doctor's with her."

"I brought over my horse and buggy. Put them in the barn for you. They're yours to use as long as you need them."

"No. That's not right." Linnea tapped the spilled tea into the ball and snapped the lid. "Your stallion alone is worth more than I make in a year. I can't accept. It's not right."

"Is it right to expect your mother to walk to town? Even if she recovers, she won't be strong for a long while."

"My mother is my responsibility."

"I want her to be mine."

"It doesn't matter what you want." Linnea lowered the ball into the teapot, temper flaring.

He was tenderness and caring and the kind of unyielding strength she needed. Everything she couldn't have. Fueled by fear and exhaustion, she poured steaming water into the pot and slammed the kettle back on the stove. "Outside. Now."

He hesitated at the door. "Linnea, push me away

all you want. I'm not going to budge. I'm here for good. There's nothing you can do to change that.''

"Not one thing? Are you sure about that?'' She rushed onto the porch and skidded to a stop. "Come out and stay out. I'll lock the door if I have to.''

"Pushing harder won't send me away either. Look.'' He gestured to the top step. Soft blue blossoms lifted slightly with the breeze. "Looks like your secret admirer has returned.''

"He's no admirer. He's a thickheaded, overbearing mule.''

"Maybe, but he's a man in love with you. Forever, Linnea. For better or worse.'' His hand lighted on her shoulder.

"You say that because you don't know. I thought your sister might have told you before now. Or any of the neighbors.'' She slipped away from his touch, his wonderful touch she didn't deserve, and scooped the flowers into her arms.

"Told me what?''

"That I had a baby outside of marriage.'' She couldn't look at him. The kindness and respect would fade from his face, the love from his eyes.

"What baby?''

"The one buried on the rise behind the house, next to my father. They died within a month of each other. Papa from a broken heart, and my baby from an early birth.'' She squared her shoulders, prepared for his disdain. "That's how I cost my family nearly everything. My father died, my son died, and we had to sell the homestead. So now that you know, you might as well take your horse and leave.''

She turned her back so she couldn't see him walk away. Couldn't see the tenderness in his eyes fade.

This is the way it has to be, she told herself, staring hard at the flowers he'd brought her. She ran her fingertips over the delicate blossoms, the last of the summer's bluebonnets. A reminder that everything had its season.

Everything came to an end.

Seth didn't leave. "You thought I knew about the baby. When I came calling, you thought I already knew."

"Everyone knows how I was dumb enough to believe a *boy,* not a man, when he said he loved me. He was the McIntyres' son—"

"Not Jimmy?"

"Yes, Jimmy. He'd broken up with Ginny and took an interest in me. I felt so honored when he paid attention to me. He was from one of the finest families in town. He was handsome and dashing and bold. He charmed me so thoroughly, a foolish country girl, that I saw forever when I looked at him."

She shook her head, bitterness sour on her tongue. "I know what I did wrong. Believe me. I was always dreaming and that led me to the biggest mistake of my life." She marched toward the steps, overwhelmed by pain and embarrassment. "The tea's steeped by now. I have to get back to my mother."

"Linnea."

She closed the door behind her, shutting him out.

"Linnea!" he called through the wood.

She turned her back, filled a bud vase and arranged the pretty blossoms.

"Linnea." He peered in at her through the open window.

She marched around the table, closed the window

and untied the curtains. Ruffled fabric tumbled free, covering him from her sight.

He knew the truth. What more did he want from her? A complete confession? The memories were too painful. The cups rattled on the tray as she crossed the room and the bluebonnets swayed in their vase. Bluebonnets that were hard to find this late in the summer.

He'd searched out these flowers for her, because he loved her. But he didn't love her now. There was no way. No possibility.

"The major picked you some flowers, Mama. Wasn't that thoughtful of him? He came by to see how you were doing."

Mama's smile remained lopsided, but not quite as bad as before.

"Your mother is a remarkable woman, Miss Holmstrom," the doctor commented as he put away his stethoscope. "She's already improving and has some strength in her hand. I predict a full recovery."

The tray slipped from her fingers and clattered to a rest on the bureau. The worst of her fears vanished. "Thank you, Doctor."

Grateful beyond words, she dropped to her knees and took Mama's hand.

An illegitimate baby. That explained a lot. From the threshold, Seth watched Linnea hold the teacup for her mother. Her words were soothing, her touch gentle, her love as bright as the sunshine streaming into the room.

Yes, it explained a lot. He rubbed his brow. She thought that this painful time in her past would change the way he felt about her. Well, she thought wrong.

The doctor strolled into the room, sipping a cup of tea. "Morning, Major. I'm ready to head home. There's nothing more I can do here. It looks as if Mrs. Holmstrom got lucky. A very minor stroke. She should recover well enough, but she'll be frail for a long time."

"She'll need care, is what you're telling me."

"Yes." The doctor set the empty cup on the table. "I've got rounds to make. I'll be back in the afternoon to check on her."

"Send me the bill." Seth read the surprise in the man's eyes. "I'll be responsible for Mrs. Holmstrom from now on."

"So, it's like that, is it?" The doctor nodded once with quiet approval. "Linnea's a nice woman. I'll be glad to see her happy."

"He'll not send you the bill." Linnea closed the door behind her, fire sparking in her eyes. "Seth, I don't understand why you're doing this."

"Isn't it obvious?"

"Time to go." The doctor grabbed his medical bag and showed himself out.

"You came in the back door. You had no right." Linnea looked brittle and the hurt that drove her was evident, even though she was waving a fist at him. "And what you offered the doctor was just plain wrong. I don't need charity. I won't have you pitying me like some of those women in town."

"This isn't about pity." He caught hold of her fist before she could hit him. "I love you. It's that simple."

"You can't love me."

"Why not?"

She didn't answer.

He knew what that loss felt like. He recognized the bleak grief in Linnea's eyes, felt it in the sobs that wrenched through her.

"The past is gone," he told her. "We don't have to dig it up, bring it back and carry it around with us forever. I'm sorry your baby died. I'm sorry a man lied to you. But I'm standing in front of you with the truth. This is a second chance for both of us. Will you take it with me?"

"I want to more than anything. But I can't." Her lower lip wobbled and he felt her defenses crumbling. He held out his arms and she came to him, with needs and fears and flaws.

No different than he was.

"Life takes a toll on all of us. But together we can make those hardships easier to take." He pressed a kiss into her silken curls. "Believe in my love for you. Don't ever doubt it again."

She was crying, tiny trembles that ran deep. They'd both been lonely and hurting. Now that was over.

He'd make damn sure to cushion every blow life gave her. Love for her flared in his heart, brighter and stronger than any he'd known. Love for this woman he would love for the rest of his life.

"Let me take care of you and your mother." It felt right to provide for her. To be the man she needed.

"Don't leave me," she whispered.

"Not on my life." He held her, breathing in her delicate scent, drinking in her warmth, loving the feel of her feminine curves and softness.

This was the way he wanted to hold her. Forever. "Tell me what to do to help."

She gazed up at him, true love lighting her up. How glad he was to see it.

"I love you, Seth Gatlin." She smiled and, without a word, he knew.

Everything was going to be all right.

"There. Your bath is done." Linnea set the towel and washcloth in the basin. "You rest now."

"Thank you, my *dotter*." Her speech was a touch slurred, but she sounded like herself.

She laid her hand to her mother's face and kissed her brow. "The doctor says you may get out of bed tomorrow, if you continue to strengthen. I bet you'll like that."

"Yes. Did you have the major take my letter?"

"He posted it yesterday." She gathered the basin, towels and soap. "And yes, I added a note about your stroke."

"You should not have done that."

"She needs to know, Mama. But I also wrote down every word of the doctor's prognosis so Aunt Eva wouldn't worry. You get some sleep."

She left the room, leaving the door ajar. The afternoon was dark and the curtains whipped in front of the open windows.

Dark clouds marched across the sky from the western horizon. A storm would hit by nightfall.

Too weary to even think about all the work that would bring, added to her already unending list, Linnea tossed the towels and cloth onto the pile of laundry. She'd been working day and night with little sleep for a week. Somehow she'd have to find time to do the laundry. Mama needed clean sheets.

Wagon wheels rattled in the yard. She pulled back

the curtains to watch Seth drive up. There was a young woman at his side, someone Linnea didn't know. Seth caught sight of her at the window and grinned, tipping his hat.

"I want you to believe in my love for you," he'd told her, even after he'd learned the truth about her. How could he be so forgiving?

"Linnea, this is Claire Rhodes." Seth helped the young woman, hardly more than a girl, from the wagon seat. "I've hired Claire to help you with your mother and the housework. She assures me she's a hard worker."

"I'm grateful for the work, ma'am." The quiet girl offered a shy grin, then stared hard at her shoes.

They were patched, Linnea noticed, even more than her own pair. Her dress was threadbare in spots, but clean and pressed. How could she say no to either the girl needing to work or the man?

"Claire, I'm pleased to have you. Why don't you go inside and put on wash water to boil?"

"Oh, yes! Thank you." Claire hurried to the house, her eagerness unmistakable.

Seth crooked one brow, his smile slow and sure. "What? No protest? I can't believe it."

"I know what it's like to need work."

"Claire lives with relatives, so she needs an income more than most. See how easy it is to accept my help? Maybe you could get used to it."

"You do too much, and you know it."

"This is just the beginning. I plan on spoiling you all I can." He pulled her into his arms, his love for her in his touch, in the velvet caress of his kiss, in the way he closed his eyes as if to savor her.

Desire swirled through her like warm molasses,

thick, rich and tempting. He splayed his hands on her back, caressing in slow circles as he deepened the kiss. She opened to him, lost in the tantalizing swirl of his tongue on hers. Being in his arms felt right.

This time, with this man, she could believe in love.

He broke the kiss but didn't move away. He leaned his forehead to hers so they were eye to eye and she was lost in him.

"How is your mother?"

"Mama's napping. She's stronger. She can walk on her own with the cane the doctor left, but I'm not letting her out of bed yet. Tomorrow, maybe."

"I want you to come with me tonight after she's asleep. Claire will stay with her."

He swept his hands down Linnea's back to rest in the dip of her spine. He pressed her more firmly against him so she could feel the strong wall of his chest and abdomen, the powerful contour of his thighs and his unmistakable arousal. "There's something I want to show you."

"I bet there is." She laughed, knowing she shouldn't encourage him. "I can't leave Mama for that. And besides, I—"

"*That's* not what I want to show you. Well, that's not true." His laughter rumbled through her, as if he were part of her.

She blushed. She didn't know what to say.

"I love you, Linnea. You. Come with me tonight. There's something I want to ask you."

He kissed her again, slow this time. A tender brush of his lips that left her senses spinning.

This was his land. His very own. Seth liked the feel of walking on his own piece of the Montana prairie. It had cost him dearly—nearly every penny of his savings, but it was a fair trade. The wind rustling through the dry grasses seemed to welcome him.

Here's where he planned on putting the house, if it was all right with Linnea. The knoll where she'd be able to gaze out over the flower-dotted plains in the summer. On the other side of the house, she could sew in the winter's sunshine with a view of the snow-covered mountains.

He'd make it roomy, with a bedroom on the main floor for her mother. He could already see it in his imagination, with a wraparound porch and plenty of rooms upstairs for the children they would have.

Children. Now there was a thought. He'd give anything to have the privilege of marrying Linnea. He'd give even more to be the father of her children. Little girls with golden curls like their mother. Maybe a son to teach to ride.

Bittersweetness filled him. He ached for the children he'd lost. And for the children he might have one day soon.

It felt good to have a life again.

And it was because of Linnea. She'd done this. No other woman had awakened his heart. But she had. Her love had saved him. Chased away the unbearable loneliness. Given him a future.

Maybe he'd build a large corral here, a good distance from the house, but close enough to watch the horses from the front porch. If he raised the fence to eight feet, it'd be too high to jump. Even for a wild stallion.

He took the ring from his pocket, the one he'd picked up in town today. The small diamond winked merrily.

Second chances were rare in this life. He was a damn lucky man.

Now it was all up to Linnea.

"Mama?" Linnea pushed open the door. "I've been waiting for you to awaken. Seth brought you another surprise."

"Oh, that man." The nap had done her good. The color had returned to her cheeks. "What did he do now?"

"He hired someone to help us out. Her name is Claire and she lives on the other side of the river near town."

"Oh, the orphan girl come to stay with the Burgains." Mama sat up, determined to adjust her own pillows. "Now I will not worry so. I have made so much work. And the canning cannot wait."

"You're all that matters, Mama." Linnea hurried to snatch the pillow from her mother's hand and plumped it. "There, sit back. Do you want anything to eat? I have soup heating on the stove. And the last of the cucumbers and tomatoes from the garden."

"Yes, that would be fine."

"Good. You wait right here." Linnea turned up the wick so light tumbled across the bed, turning her mother's curls platinum.

"*Dotter?* Bring me my crocheting. I feel restless lying here. I must do something."

"I have just the thing." Linnea lifted the lid of her cedar chest. Of the three balls of silk thread she'd bought, two had been ruined when Oscar Hansson had accosted her. One ball of thread was like new.

She hadn't been able to look at it without remembering. But maybe now was the time to turn the sadness into something beautiful.

"Look at what I've been saving for a surprise." Linnea placed the thread in her mother's hand. "The finest in Mrs. Jance's shop."

"Why, it must be beautiful." Mama shone, showing more strength in her new project. "Quick, my needles. My hand is not as good as I would like it, but I will manage."

Linnea fetched the little basket that held all of her mother's crochet needles. Mama unwound a length of thread from the thick ball.

She looks like her old self. Grateful, Linnea didn't mind the exhaustion weighing her down as she headed to the kitchen. Claire was in the yard, scrubbing towels on the washboard.

"Here's some cider, cool from the cellar." Linnea handed her the cup. "Why don't you come in and eat? You've worked far too hard today."

"I'm pleased to have the work, ma'am." With the back of her hand, Claire brushed away the dark wisps that had escaped from her braids.

"Leave the towels. It won't hurt them to soak."

Claire smiled, and tiny lines dug into the corners of her eyes. In the half-light of dusk, she looked older than Linnea had first thought.

Claire filled her plate with bread, leftover bacon from the morning meal and thick slices of tomatoes. She retreated outside. As Linnea ladled soup into a bowl, she heard the splash of wash water through the open windows.

Claire was a good worker and would be a big help. She owed Seth dearly. What a good man he was. What a good husband he would make.

Did she dare hope that he really planned to marry her?

Mama would hardly stop crocheting long enough to eat her supper, and then continued to work into the evening. Darkness fell, and the hour grew late. Linnea had to pry the needles from her mother's fingers. She laid the perfect start to what would be exquisite lace in the basket and set it on the bureau.

As she did every night, she opened one of Papa's books and began to read. Slowly Mama drifted off to sleep.

"I'll sit with her," Claire whispered as she stepped into the tiny room. "Major Gatlin asked me to do so. I'll take good care of her, don't worry."

"I'm not worried at all." There was a kindness in Claire that Linnea recognized, and she doubted Seth could have found a gentler caretaker in all of Iron County.

Even so, it was hard to leave her mother's side. Harder still to walk away from the room and out onto the porch. Seth rose from the shadowed steps.

When he smiled at her, she felt like the most desired woman in the world. He took her hand and she never wanted to let go.

"Looks like there's going to be a storm tonight. Hope you don't mind being out in it."

"I love a good storm. I should close the windows before I leave."

"Claire can handle it." He twined his fingers through hers. "How are you holding up?"

"Better because of all you've done."

He liked knowing that. "I haven't seen the mustangs in a while."

"They'll be here to stay when snow comes to the mountains. Probably in a month or so."

"Good. I figure they could use a permanent home." He watched her out of the corner of his eye. She had a tender heart, that was for sure. He wasn't sure how she'd take the news. "Neilson's not the only rancher who's tired of fighting wild animals. It's a hard life for the mustangs. I could give them better."

"You'd take their freedom."

"Not entirely." He considered his words as the wind gusted around them, whipping through the dried stalks and tangling Linnea's skirts.

They stopped while she untwisted her petticoats, then gathered her hem in her free hand.

"This is where I'm thinking of building a corral. One big enough for them to run."

"How big?"

"I'll start with an acre and add on over time. Figure I have all winter with nothing to do. It'll keep me busy." He could see his dream so clearly he could almost touch it. "I was thinking that I'd build it there, where the plains stretch out. I'll tame only the mustangs that adjust to it. The mares who stay wild will give me foals every year, and I'll train those."

She didn't say anything, and was so still she didn't seem to be breathing. The wind tore at her knot until it tumbled loose. Silken curls twisted free. "I hate to think of the plains without the wild mustangs."

"All things change. It was a dry summer. There isn't going to be the food there was for them last year. The ranchers sold their extra hay for income. They're going to protect what they have to keep their own livestock healthy through the winter."

She closed her eyes. "The anger at the horses has been getting worse over the years."

"I can offer them a safe home. They'll never be hungry or mistreated. They'll have their own piece of the prairie to run on."

She nodded. "This is what you've always wanted, isn't it?"

"Always hoped one day I'd own a piece of Montana. It takes time to build a herd. If I capture the mustangs, I have one ready-made."

Her fingers tightened around his, and her unspoken approval gave him courage. He led her to the edge of the rise at the end of the field. From here, they could see the far reaches of the prairie and the mountains that made the horizon. They sat down together, shoulder to shoulder.

"Like it here?" he asked. "I thought it might be a good spot to build a house."

"A house?" She tucked her bottom lip between her teeth. "I thought you were living in the claim shanty near Ginny's house."

"It's good enough for a bachelor, but it's no place to bring a wife."

"A wife?"

"She's the kindest lady I've ever met. I want her to have the best of me. And the best of what I can give her." He reached into his pocket, shaking like a leaf. "This is the biggest risk I've ever taken in my life, Linnea. Nothing has ever mattered to me more than what your answer is going to be."

"I see." Her eyes were round and luminous, deep and full of longing. "What answer are you looking for?"

"I want you to say yes." He took her left hand

and slipped the ring over her finger. "I would be honored if you'd agree to be my wife."

"You want to marry me?" Her voice wobbled.

"Yes. I want you with all that I am." He felt her hand tremble in his, felt the sob shake her.

"You want to marry *me*."

"Well, the Widow Johanson turned me down first, and since I had the ring and the lumber bought for the house—"

"Don't tease me." Linnea laughed and cried, flying into his arms. Holding him was heaven, pure heaven. "Yes, Seth Gatlin, I'll marry you."

She couldn't believe it. This was really happening. She was going to be Seth's wife.

His lips claimed her like a sizzling brand. Leaving her breathless, leaving her weak. He was heat and passion, and she couldn't resist him.

Like the thunder booming across the sky, desire crashed through her. She sucked playfully on his bottom lip, and he chuckled. She breathed in his smile as he pulled her onto his lap.

"That's better," he murmured against her lips.

Wrapping her arms around his neck was a fantasy come true. She boldly met his kiss with a sweep of her tongue and a gentle suction on his upper lip. His fingers wound deep into her hair, cradling her head. His other hand slid slowly up and down her back. Her spine tingled.

To think that she had the right to kiss him like this for every night to come. For the rest of their lives together. The ring felt strange on her finger as she brushed her fingertips across his nape and into the silken locks at his collar. She loved the way he felt, iron solid beneath warm skin.

"It's starting to rain," he told her.

"I didn't notice." Only then did she realize the earth smelled sharp and heavy. The warm rain tapped in lazy drops, spotting her forehead and then her cheek.

His mouth grazed hers, broke away, returned to nibble and sip. She sighed, drinking in the sweetness of being with him. Wished they could do this all night long—and much, much more than kiss.

"I figure we can get married as soon as your mother is a little stronger." He leaned in the crackling grass, taking her with him.

"I'd like that, but it would be nice to have time to make a new dress. After all, a girl doesn't get married every day."

"True." He traced his finger down the curve of her nose, slowly, and then he kissed the tip of her nose. "You have no idea how much I want to make love with you right now."

Desire fluttered low in her abdomen at the thought. "I might have some idea."

"Is that so?"

She blushed, grateful for the dark so he couldn't tell. "A man isn't alone in the need to be loved. A woman wants that, too."

"I'm glad to hear that." He kissed her deeply and passionately, with enough heat to leave her dazed. "We don't have to wait. Not if we planned to get married in a week. Two at the most."

"I should make you wait." Her pulse soared as he traced a finger across her bottom lip. She caught his fingertip with his tongue and laved it.

"Don't make me wait." His fingers lingered at her

collar. "I feel as if I've already waited a lifetime for you."

"I know just what you mean."

Seth trailed kisses across her chin and down her throat. The years of loneliness vanished like fog to sun as he closed the space between them. The skies opened up, the wind blustered over them, but all she could feel was Seth and the wild beat of her heart.

He tugged at the buttons at her throat but not fast enough, and it frustrated her. She wanted to feel the heat of his palm on her, so she helped him with the buttons. Their fingers kept bumping and their knuckles kept knocking.

Seth's chuckle breezed against her throat. "You are beauty and passion. No need to be shy, okay?"

"Okay." She lay back in anticipation.

Rain-damp fabric clung to her skin and she moaned when he peeled the cotton away. Cool rain tapped across her bared breasts. Then his hands covered her with warmth. Sweet, kneading warmth that made her bones melt.

"You are like silk," he whispered, his breath hot against her rain-dotted skin.

His palms were calloused. As he kneaded and caressed her breasts, his rough skin grated deliciously across her nipples. She closed her eyes, and a moan was torn from her throat.

Such exquisite sensation. Heat swirled in her midsection, and she arched her back more. His mouth closed over her and suckled. Pleasure twisted deep in her stomach. She curled her hands around his neck and held him, pressing kisses to his brow.

He lifted his mouth from her. "You're shivering."

"Trembling."

"You're getting cold." He covered her breasts with clear regret. "It's really starting to rain."

"I don't mind." She caught his wrist so he couldn't move away from her. "Please don't stop."

He brushed her lips with reverence, with tenderness that could not be measured. "I can't believe I'm here with you like this."

"Lucky me." She pressed her hand to his jaw. Fine stubble rasped against her palm. The ring on her hand caught her attention, a faint circle of smooth gold with a stone that shimmered even in the near darkness. "I made a mistake before, believing a man's words of love."

"This is no mistake." He kissed her palm, sending delicious pleasure tickling up her arm. "I want you for my wife. I want to make a family with you. Only with you, Linnea."

Her heart opened, just like that. When he touched her, he touched more than her skin, more than the pebbled tips of her breasts swollen from his kisses. He touched the deepest part of her.

Loving him seemed natural. As if she'd been made to be with this man and in this place. The rain tapped down, warm trickles that made her dress buttons slick and made them laugh.

"I never noticed it took so many buttons to get a woman out of her clothes," Seth teased against her bare skin. "It takes more than sweet talk to get a woman out of her drawers. It takes dexterity."

She laughed as she tugged off his shirt. The garment fell away. The night shadows worshiped his sculptured form. He looked like marble but felt like warm steel. She splayed her hands across his chest.

"Here. Lie back." He lay down with her on a bed

of their clothing. His solid knee rested against her thigh. "I'd better cover you up so you don't get cold."

"Good idea."

His knee parted her thighs and he settled over her. She shivered harder, but she wasn't cold. She was hot from his touch and trembling with need. Rain dappled her forehead as she wrapped her arms around his shoulders, pulling her to him.

He covered her with his heat and strength. His arousal lay against the curve of her stomach, proof that he desired her. His kiss was tender, proof that he loved her.

He touched her and made sensation streak through her raw nerve endings. He kissed her breasts, her stomach and grazed his hands down her thighs, all the while murmuring soft loving words. Praises that made her feel beautiful and wanted. Wanted by this man.

He entered her slowly. It felt as if he were melting into her, his unyielding hardness into her aching heat. She tipped her hips, needing more of him, taking him as deep as she could.

Breathless, she met his gaze. Love burned there, unmistakable and bright. She wanted to hold him like this forever. To treasure the feel of his weight, the hardness of his body and the length of his shaft heavy and thrumming inside her.

But desire drove her. She moved and so did he, withdrawing and thrusting with a slow, steady rhythm. Sharp pleasure spiraled through her, so intense it made her cry out. Made her lock her thighs around his hips. The beautiful pleasure wasn't enough—she wanted more. Much more.

She rocked against him, meeting him stroke for

stroke. Sensation and heat gathered there, where they met, and then exploded in a pulsing wave of pleasure and light.

He cried out, stiffening over her, driving deep. She felt him pulse and the wet rush of his seed. With a shaky sigh, he rested on top of her, keeping his weight on his elbows. He caught her hands and twined their fingers together. He kissed her, simply kissed her.

His silence said everything.

She'd never known love before this night. She'd never felt this intense pleasure or a bond so deep. Her body pulsed with a pleasant exhilaration.

She twined her legs around his and returned his kisses. Until he loved her all over again.

Chapter Fifteen

From the front step of his shanty, Seth watched the storm as the hours passed. The thunderheads glowed faintly purple against the ebony night. Dry lightning rippled across the sky, accompanied by a deafening thunderclap.

All he could think about was Linnea. She'd said yes. To his ring and to making love. Being with her had been paradise. Tenderness grew in his heart with every beat. The love he felt for her was so fierce, if it were light it would blot out the sun.

First thing in the morning, he'd purchase lumber for the house. He'd order enough fence posts to make the corral to hold the mustangs. Judging by the change of weather, the horses would be returning to the plains soon.

Another spear of lightning stabbed across the sky. It didn't touch down, but it was too close for comfort. He'd rather be in bed right now, dreaming of Linnea, but the brief sprinkle earlier in the night hadn't been enough. The prairie was still tinder dry. It wouldn't take but a spark to start a wildfire.

He'd stay up until dawn if he had to. He'd do whatever it took to make sure his land stayed safe. He had a future to protect. A future with Linnea.

He took another sip of coffee and waited. Dreaming of her. Always.

The ring felt like a promise on her finger as she lit the fire in the kitchen stove. The diamond glittered pure white as if it had been plucked from the heavens just for her.

"Morning, Linnea." Claire carried in a load of wood. "Let me get that. I planned to do the ironing this morning."

"Let's get breakfast cooking first. Mama is still sleeping. We'll keep hers warm for when she awakens."

Linnea snapped the match tin shut and opened the damper wide. The gold band chinked softly against the iron door.

"That's an awfully pretty ring." Claire filled the wood tin one piece at a time. "Is it from the major?"

Linnea blushed, remembering last night and the intimacy they'd shared. "We're going to be married."

"I'm so happy for you." Claire's smile was genuine. "You haven't told your mother yet, have you?"

"She's been asleep." Linnea plunked the fry pan on the burner. "I can't decide if I should tell her outright or wait for her to discover the ring on my finger."

"She'll be excited. It will lift her spirits." Claire brushed the bark from her sleeves into the bin. "What can I do to help?"

"You can fetch the bacon from the cellar. And a new jar of preserves."

Claire washed her hands, then found the ring handle in the floor. The hinges squeaked as she pulled, and her shoes echoed in the room below.

Think of how happy Mama would be! This was exactly what her mother had hoped for with all that baking and cooking. Linnea nearly laughed out loud imagining it.

Who would have thought *she* would be his bride?

Joy made her work easy. Claire returned with the bacon and soon the meat was sizzling in the pan. The sweet scent of strawberry jelly filled the kitchen and the yeasty goodness of bread.

"That's the last of it," Claire announced as she cut the loaf into slices. "I wouldn't mind baking a new batch of bread."

"You were hired to help out, not to do all my work. You iron and I'll bake."

It was a good plan. After they ate, Claire set up the ironing board on the table and began tackling the large stack of sheets, towels and nightgowns. Linnea melted butter, warmed water and buttermilk and spooned out flour.

After measuring her ingredients, Linnea checked on Mama. She was still sleeping. She looked frail beneath the quilt, but her chest lifted with regular breathing and her color remained good.

Although Linnea was bubbling with her good news, it would keep. She was going to marry Seth Gatlin, and nothing in the world could change it. She closed the door, leaving her mother to sleep.

The yeast water was hot enough, so she hurried to the stove.

"Uncle Seth?" His nephew lurched to a stop in the shanty's doorway. A lunch pail dangled from one hand and he clutched a slate in the other. "It's time for school."

"It's that late already?"

The boy nodded. "Don't want to be tardy. Tommy Wheeler got late last week and he had to sit in the corner for an hour."

"We'd best get going, then." Seth grabbed his hat from the wall peg, feeling happier than he'd been in years.

With the flat-footed stomp of a little boy, Jamie marched out into the sunshine, where a nippy wind chased them all the way to the barn.

He hitched the oxen to the wagon and waited while the child climbed into the seat. He ruffled Jamie's hair and then sent the oxen walking at a fast pace.

They passed Linnea's house, and he remembered last night. How he remembered the sweet passion she'd shown him. He would never be able to get enough of her.

He could see her through the window, intent at her kitchen work. Pride filled him. That beautiful, gentle woman was going to be his wife.

"Thanks for the ride, Uncle Seth!" Jamie called at the schoolyard. He ran to join other little boys, throwing his lunch pail and slate onto the grass. The whooping delight of the children at play filled the air with a happy sound.

Seth drove away, trying to concentrate on his driving, but thought of Linnea instead. Maybe they could be alone together today. Maybe she'd come to see him in the field.

"Morning, Major." The sheriff called as he unlocked his office door.

Seth returned the greeting, tipped his hat and kept driving. Yes, it was a fine morning.

He stopped the wagon in the lumberyard and hopped down. The earth vibrated beneath his boots. Looked like a train was coming in earlier than usual. That was a first.

Seth told the lumberyard owner what he needed.

"Why don't you take the good cured lumber over there." Mr. Randall pointed to two tall stacks of cut wood. "I'll send out an order for more fence rails on this morning's train."

"Appreciate it. I'll help you load."

The train arrived with a squealing of iron on iron and a loud whistle. Seth helped Randall fill the wagon with honeyed wood, in spite of the choking smoke from the engine drifting their way.

His back was aching when the sheriff rode into sight. "Major, there you are. Figured I could find you here. I need you to help me out."

"Morning, Sheriff." Seth signed the bill Randall presented him with and handed it back. "What can I do you for?"

"Got some folks just off the train. They're elderly and not from around here. I hate to trust them with Griswold down at the livery. He'd do about anything to make an extra buck."

"You want me to drive them somewhere? I've got a full load."

"Don't you worry about that. These folks say they're looking for the Holmstrom place. With the news of that ring you bought traveling like greased lightning around town, I figured you might want to be responsible for them."

"You heard about that, did you?"

''There are a lot of sad women in this town this morning. No mistaking that. My sister-in-law is one of them.'' The sheriff rolled his eyes. ''Her and my wife were jawing about it over breakfast. Now, if you want to do me a favor, you can take my wife's sister off my hands.''

''I can't help you with that.'' Seth grabbed his hat from the seat and released the brake.

The sheriff chuckled. ''Didn't hurt to ask. They're waiting on the platform. Look like real nice folks.'' He rode on.

Elderly people looking for the Holmstrom place? Had to be relatives, he figured, remembering the letter he'd mailed for Linnea late last week. Curiosity got the best of him and he hurried the team.

Sure enough, there was an elderly man and woman waiting on the platform, a small clothes case on the floor between them. The man was dressed in finely tailored clothes and stood pole-straight. He looked powerful, even for his age.

The woman at his side was the spitting image of Mrs. Holmstrom, right down to her violet-blue eyes and brilliant smile. She could see. Her eyes lit at the sight of him. ''Oh, have you come for us, young man? The sheriff promised he'd find someone to help us.''

''I'm Seth Gatlin.'' He tipped his hat.

''The major.'' The man held out his hand and they shook. ''I've read about you in Linnea's letters. I'm Fred Hudson, and this is my wife, Eva.''

''Have you been by to see my twin sister, Elsa? How is she?'' Eva's face was wreathed with worry. ''When we received Linnea's letter, I feared the worst. The mail takes too long! So my dear Frederick was good enough to buy tickets on the very next train and bring me here to see for myself how she is.''

Seth grabbed the case and tucked it behind the seat. He had other errands, but they could wait. ''Your sister is better, ma'am. She's weak, but other than that she's getting stronger with every passing day.''

''I am so glad. When I read she'd had a stroke, I feared the worst. Although Linnea wrote quite plainly that Elsa was expected to be fine.''

Such a dear lady. Seth offered her his hand, but Fred Hudson was faster.

''She's my wife. We are newly married.'' He smiled, a contented man. ''It's my job to help her.''

''He spoils me.'' Eva beamed, settling her pretty skirts on the seat. ''Oh, hurry, young man. I have not seen my Elsa since baby Linnea was two months old. You cannot drive these oxen fast enough.''

Fred laughed. ''Such is my Eva. We'll get there in good time, love. And then you'll never be apart from your sister again.''

Seth gathered the reins, ordering the oxen forward. The wagon bucked and groaned with the heavy load in back. He considered Fred's comment. ''Are you moving here?''

''Us? Goodness, no.'' Eva clasped her hands. ''Frederick has his business in Oregon. We cannot move.''

Foreboding snaked down Seth's spine.

''We will be moving my Elsa and her Linnea back with us. All these years we have not had the money to visit, and Elsa could not return to us after her Olaf died. Now after all these years, I have Frederick, who gives me the gift of my sister.''

Seth didn't know what to say. Surely Linnea

wouldn't be going. He liked Mrs. Holmstrom. He'd consider it an honor to provide for her. But if she wanted to go to live with her sister, then he'd make sure Linnea could visit as often as she liked.

The cold shiver down his spine remained.

"Mama, there's a chill in the air." Linnea hovered at her mother's elbow in case she tripped. "Stay in the house until it warms up."

"I love autumn." Her cane tip thumped against the wood floor. "I will sit here and cause you no trouble."

"You're no trouble, Mama, but I want you to stay inside."

"I have been in the house for so long. I cannot bear it a moment longer. Please. I wish to feel the prairie breezes and imagine where they've been."

"All right." Linnea pushed open the door. "I'm going to check on you. If you seem cold, then I'm ordering you in."

"You do not need to fuss over me, my *flicka*."

"What fuss? I'm only taking care of my lovely Mama. Sit here." She pulled two chairs onto the porch and led her mother to one of them.

"I can hear the leaves rattling along the ground. Where did summer go?" Mama sank into the cushioned seat still dressed in her nightgown. "Oh, too much time has passed without me. Time. It is slipping away from me."

"Don't fret so, Mama." Linnea fetched the blue shawl and settled it around Mama's fragile shoulders. "Let me pour tea and we'll talk."

"Go back to your work. I am burden enough."

"You are no burden, Mama."

"I wish to be alone."

The stroke had brought about a melancholy that worried Linnea.

She returned to the kitchen and filled enamel cups with steaming tea. The dough had a little more rising to do, so she grabbed *Jane Eyre* from the shelf, set the book on the wooden tray, and headed out into the bright sunshine.

"Here comes the major." Mama perked up, turned toward the road. "He has his wagon loaded heavy. He is always keeping busy, that one. A sign of an industrious man."

Seth. She turned to greet him, her spirits lifting at the sight of his familiar smile. But he wasn't alone. A man and a woman sat beside him on the seat. A woman who looked like— The tray slipped from her fingers and clattered to the empty chair seat. The book thudded to the floor.

"Goodness, child, are you all right?"

Linnea blinked, but the woman seated beside Seth was still there and still looked exactly like her mother. It had to be—no, it *couldn't be*. "Aunt Eva?"

Mama stiffened. "What did you say, *dotter?*"

"It's Aunt Eva." Linnea took Mama's arm. "Come, let's greet them."

"You jest. Surely my sister could not come all this way. The expense!" Mama rose shakily, searching for her cane. "Major, is that you? Linnea says you are not alone—"

"Elsa!" The frail gray-haired woman practically leaped from the wagon the instant it stopped. "Elsa! You *are* well."

"Eva?" Mama clutched the rail. "Eva. How can it be—?"

"I was so worried—" Aunt Eva flew up the steps. "But now I can see for myself. The fears I had!"

Mama opened her arms and her sister ran into them. Like two peas in a pod, they hugged tearfully.

Tears streamed down Mama's face. "I cannot believe you have come. After all this time."

"Over twenty-five years, my sister. And my babies are grown, too. Look at your Linnea." Aunt Eva swiped the tears from her eyes with her daintily gloved fingers. "Oh, she is a beauty. Just like her mother."

"I'm so glad you've come to visit." Linnea hugged her mother's sister for the first time.

"And this is my new husband, Frederick. He brought me here just to see you, Elsa. To take care of you."

"I cannot believe this good fortune." Mama collapsed into her chair, still crying, shining with happiness. "Welcome, Frederick. I am so very pleased to meet you."

Linnea felt Seth's fingers on her sleeve. He touched her secretly as the sisters talked.

"I plan to start building today," he whispered.

"I'll bring you a lunch."

His eyes twinkled with a devilish glint. "I'd like that. A man can get mighty hungry." He wiggled his brows.

"You are a naughty man, Seth Gatlin," she scolded him in a whisper. But her body melted as if he'd kissed her a thousand times.

"I'll bring in the chairs," he told her. "They're going inside. I expect they have news to share."

"We do, too." She snatched the tray and the fallen book.

Seth grabbed the chairs and followed her into the house. Claire was scrambling to clear the table of the ironing board and the stack of sheets. Frederick helped her with quiet courtesy. Aunt Elsa aided Mama across the room and to her place at the table.

How amazing to see them together, identical faces shedding identical tears. And smiling identical smiles. They sat side by side, chatting as if they'd never been apart. Mama radiated pure joy, something Linnea hadn't seen since her father died.

"I'll pour the tea," Claire offered, lending a hand. "Look, the bread is ready."

"If I pop that in the oven, we'll have fresh bread for lunch." Linnea thanked Claire for her help and then lifted the cloth over the bread bowl.

The soft yeasty dough ballooned over the rim, and she fisted her hand and plunged it into the center.

Her ring! Dough was stuck to it like glue. She pulled the golden band off her finger and set it on the windowsill. The diamond winked at her.

Using flour to coat the breadboard, she divided the dough into fourths and rolled each into balls. The merry chatter of the sisters filled the house like music. Sweet and uplifting. Frederick sat at the table, simply watching them.

"I've got to get working." Seth headed for the door. He said his goodbyes, and the sisters stopped talking long enough to wish him well, then went right on chatting.

Seth chuckled, his gaze finding her. Linnea longed to blurt out her news right there, but she'd wait until the room was a little quieter. Tenderness shone in Seth's eyes, and then he tipped his hat to her and was gone.

She'd pack him a lunch today and meet him in the field. On their knoll. She would definitely remember to bring a blanket this time. The ground wasn't the most comfortable place to make love, but she wasn't about to complain. Soon she would spend every night in his bed.

After rolling the first bread loaf, she took care to pinch the ends into a tight seam, happy to be working, half-listening to the sisters talk.

Aunt Eva's voice lifted and fell. "...beautiful land. With two houses."

"Two houses! What wealth he must have."

Linnea placed the loaf into a bread pan and reached for the second section of sticky dough.

"The second house is a darling little cottage, as homey as can be."

Linnea spread more flour across the board and reached for the rolling pin.

Aunt Eva thanked Claire for the tea and continued on. "The cottage has two ample bedrooms. There are big windows in every room to let in the sunlight. There is a porch to sit on and soak up the summer sun, and a rose garden like you cannot imagine. The house smells of roses from May to September."

Linnea's rolling pin faltered.

"To think that is only the smallest house!" Mama marveled. "I am so glad your life will be better now, my Eva."

Linnea ran her hand over the curve of the rolling pin, brushing off bits of flour and dough. But she wasn't paying attention to her work.

A spoon grated against enamel as Aunt Eva stirred sugar into her tea. "The cottage is just a few steps

from my house. A little brick path goes from door to
door.''

"Imagine that,'' Mama marveled.

"Fred has offered the cottage to you and your
daughter.''

"What?"

Linnea's fingers slipped and the rolling pin crashed
into the wall.

"Think of it, Elsa. We can be together again.''

"You mean for me to live in Oregon with you?''

"We have dreamed of being together again since
you lost your Olaf.'' Aunt Elsa took Mama's hand.
"Think of it. Your health is poor. You have never
complained, but I can see how difficult it is for you
here. You have had a stroke and are here without
more family to help. We will take you home to
Oregon and settle you into the cottage.''

"What about Linnea?''

"Linnea will come. How can you make do without
your sweet girl? We can be together and talk all we
like. We can sit on your porch and crochet together.
Oh, Elsa, we are old and growing older every day.
Come home with me, and let me care for you. Spend
the days with me like we did when we were young.''

Fred cleared his throat. "Please come, Elsa. You'll
have a housekeeper so your daughter will never scrub
another floor. You will want for nothing.''

"Charity, although kindly offered, I cannot accept.''

"But my Elsa! What is Frederick's is mine, and
what is mine I choose to share with my sister. Now
make me happy by saying yes.''

Tears streaked down Mama's pale cheeks. "How
can I say no to my dear sister? How can I say yes? I
need to speak to my Linnea.''

Chapter Sixteen

Linnea felt as hollow as a wooden toy. She took a shaky breath and waited while Aunt Eva and her husband excused themselves and headed out back to sit in the shade.

Linnea waited until the door closed. "Mama, you aren't going to say yes to them."

"It is so sudden. Frederick must be back to his work in a few days. I must decide now, Eva said. I believe I am strong enough to travel, and I will have you to help me. The question is, do I go with them?"

"Tell me what's in your heart." Linnea spoke past the pressure in her chest, a growing pressure that began to hurt. "What do you want, Mama?"

"I want both. I want to stay here in my beloved house Olaf built me. I want to go with my sister. I cannot have both."

"No, you can't." Linnea knelt at her mother's side and took her small hand.

"There are so many memories here. If I look hard enough, I can see the past. With you as a little girl dashing through the house and Olaf hitching the horses in the yard." Her eyes gleamed with warm memories from the past. "But my sister is here and alive. I was afraid, *dotter,* when I had the stroke. Afraid not of dying, but of never saying goodbye to my twin sister. We are so close, even after all these years apart."

Tears burned Linnea's throat. "You want to go?"

"How can I stay? I do not know how much time I have left on this earth."

Linnea thought of Seth. "Then you've decided."

"I do not wish to leave here, but to be with my sister again!" Mama's eyes filled with tears. "A door has closed on my life, but a window has opened. What do you think I should do?"

"What will make you happy?"

"Being with Eva." Mama's smile was young, so very young. "If we go to Oregon and live in Frederick's second house, there will be a housekeeper. Imagine! My *dotter* will not have to work so hard to take care of me. Eva talks of a woman she employs who does nothing but cook! She will cook for us, too. Life will be easier for my girl."

"Oh, Mama." Linnea glanced at her ring on the windowsill. "Maybe I can see you settled in Oregon, but that is all. You won't need me around if you have Aunt Eva and her housekeeper."

"Not need you? My dear, I would wither without my sweet girl to take care of me. I need you more than anything."

Her dreams shattered. Linnea collapsed into the closest chair. Did she tell Mama about Seth's ring? How could she? Aunt Eva had offered Mama a house. She hadn't offered to tend to her night and day.

Linnea thought of Seth. All he meant to her. All he offered her. "Are you sure you want to leave the house Papa built for you? You said before that you couldn't leave. There are too many memories here. It would be like leaving him behind.''

''Your papa will come for me one day, and he will find me just as well in Oregon as he will here. You will come with me and we will find happiness in Eva's little cottage.''

Linnea felt Seth, even though she hadn't heard him approach. She saw him through the open door, standing in the yard in front of the steps, larger than life, her very own champion.

He didn't say a word. He didn't have to. She knew by the shock on his face and the sadness in his eyes. He'd heard every word.

He set Frederick's traveling case on the porch, turned his back and walked away.

A cool wind whipped through the dry grasses. Linnea patted the oxen grazing near the wagon. ''Seth?''

''Look in the wagon.''

She turned toward the sound of his voice, as cool as the wind. There he was, sitting on the ground, his forearms on his knees. The sunlight bronzed him as he stared out over the golden-brown plains. He looked so alone.

''Just look.''

She approached the shadowed vehicle, noticing the milled wood protruding from the wagon bed. The smell of freshly sawed lumber tickled her nose. So much expensive lumber.

''For our new house.'' He stood, bracing his feet apart, planting his fists on his hips. ''Figured if I got started right away, I'd have enough time to get a roof and walls up before the snow falls.''

The wind gusted, driving a tumbleweed between them. The weed clacked and rattled as it rolled away.

"I don't know what to say, Seth." She set the lunch pail on the lip of the wagon bed. "You overhead what Mama said. She wants to go live with her sister more than anything."

"Then let her go. Travel with her. Get her settled. Then come back to me."

"She doesn't want me to leave her." She took a breath that rattled as much as the tumbleweed.

"You promised to marry me." How lost he sounded, as if he'd misplaced his heart. "You lay with me right here and gave me the right to love you."

"I want to be with you more than anything." She ran her fingers over the rough texture of the thick timber, one that might make the floor or the corner post of Seth's house.

"Then tell me you aren't going to leave. Say anything but that."

"I wish I could, but I can't lie to you." She turned toward the spot on the prairie where Seth would build his house. "The love I feel for you is greater than anything I've ever known."

"I'll travel with you to Oregon. Help you get your mother settled. We could even get married there if you wanted. We'll come back here and start our life together."

She closed her mind against the pictures in her mind. Images she had no right to. Making curtains for the windows in his pretty new house. Waking up in bed together. Anticipating a baby on the way.

Those are only dreams, she reminded herself. Like the thousand she'd had over the years. Fantasies without substance, easily blown away like dust on the wind.

"I have a duty to Mama. I can't leave her. If she wants to go to Oregon, I have to go with her." She said the words because she had to. "Why don't you come with me? We can still be together."

"I just sank nearly every penny I've ever saved into this land. Into your land." He pulled her to him and kissed her temple, kissed the crown of her head, holding her tight. "I don't have the money to start again."

"I don't care about marrying a wealthy man. We don't need money to be happy."

He grimaced. He tensed as hard as stone. "I can't leave. I'd throw away everything for you. Except for my word. I have responsibilities, too."

She closed her eyes. "Ginny."

"I can't leave her destitute. Even if I gave her the land, it's not worth what I paid for it. She can't sell it and she'll never be able to farm it. She couldn't support herself and her boy entirely on the income from any job she'd get in town."

"You can't leave. I can't stay. What do we do?"

"You have your responsibility. I knew that from the beginning, but now your mother has her sister, Linnea." He said it as gently as he could, but he couldn't help the stubborn ball of pain wedging its way into his chest. "Why can't you stay with me? Don't you want to marry me?"

She buried her face in his shoulder. "I thought of that, too. Of leaving her with Aunt Eva. But she needs me. You heard her."

"I did." Truth was, he cared for Mrs. Holmstrom. He wouldn't want to see her alone.

"She needs me. How can I turn away from her now? She could have died from that stroke. It could have been much worse. What if there's a next time? I need to be there for her. To return to her all the love she's given me."

"I can't let you go, Linnea. I've lost my heart once. Don't make me go through that again."

"She stood by me when I was pregnant. When Jimmy McIntyre walked away from me because he wouldn't marry an immigrant's daughter." Tears wet her cheeks. "I was broken by the humiliation and the shame. And for feeling so stupid for thinking he was like a prince from a fairy tale when he was just a selfish boy."

Linnea stepped out of his arms and wiped her tears with the back of her sleeve. No more fell as she faced him, chin up, nothing but courage. "She held me when I cried. Saw me through morning sickness. My father died, and even in her grief she never blamed me.

"When my baby came, she stayed with me. And even when the doctor said the infant had died and I was bleeding badly, she didn't let me go. She willed me to live and in the end I couldn't leave her. I owe her my life."

Seth heard all she didn't say—how many families disowned an unmarried pregnant daughter. He hated to think of Linnea hurting and alone. Pregnant and afraid. Giving birth to a baby that did not live. "She saw you through an unbearable time."

"She loves me unconditionally and without end." Sadness twisted Linnea's face. "How many daughters can say that about their mothers? She needs me, Seth. After all she's done for me, it would be wrong to leave her now. I want to be with you more than anything.''

"I know." He felt pain. Anger. Loss. He was furious at the injustice of finding love. Only to lose it again. ''Maybe you should speak with your mother. Tell her about the plans we made.''

"Then she would feel guilty. She's been so worried about being a burden. As if she could ever be that for me.'' Linnea dipped her head and the brim of her sunbonnet hid the sorrow in her eyes. ''This isn't forever. Maybe you could wait for me.''

Her lower lip trembled. She looked vulnerable and hurt. He knew just how that felt. He pulled her into his arms, kissing her tear-damp cheeks.

"Forever is a long time," he said quietly.

She twisted away and fled, her skirts trailing behind her, taking all that mattered in his life.

His world was ending, and he felt the darkness wrap around his heart. He couldn't do this again. Couldn't face sorrow again.

He wanted to run after her and make her stay. Yet he wouldn't be a man if he did. She had her duty.

He had his.

Linnea couldn't think of anything but the look on Seth's face before she ran away from him as she tucked the diamond ring into the velvet pocket inside her cedar chest.

"Linnea, dear," Aunt Eva called from the front door. "We are leaving now to take your mother to the doctor. We must have his approval to travel so far with her. Do you need anything from town?''

"I'll run errands when you return." There was Mrs. Jance to thank and her fabric bill to pay.

"That's fine, dear. How nice of the major to lend his horse and buggy. Elsa said that she had hopes for you and Mr. Gatlin."

"She actually admitted it?"

"A mother never stops hoping for her daughter. You will keep packing while we are away?"

"Yes." Pain tore through her like a hooked claw, but she didn't let it show. She tucked the sewing kit Seth had given her into the middle of the chest, for safe traveling.

She didn't want to leave. Her hands felt cold and clumsy as she began emptying Mama's bureau drawers. The new trunks Uncle Frederick had brought shone like polished silver in the bright autumn sunshine.

This is good for Mama. For all that she has done for me, this is my chance to pay her back.

Linnea tried to find joy in that but failed. The truth was that she wanted to be with Seth more than anything.

The house was in disarray. Claire had gone to town in the buggy too, her work here done. Alone, Linnea's footsteps echoed in the parlor. The shelves that had held Papa's books were empty. The tapestries were gone from the walls. The lace stripped from the tables and the curtains from the windows.

Tomorrow, assuming the doctor said Mama could travel, this room would be empty. They would be on their way to Oregon.

A knock tapped on the open door and she jumped. "Seth."

"I was in the fields building my corral when I saw the buggy leave." He stood awkwardly, as if her porch was the last place he wanted to be. "Thought I'd take a chance on finding you alone."

"I am." She couldn't help noticing the quilt he carried over one arm. "Don't tell me you're giving me back the quilt."

"The one I bought for the woman I intended to marry."

Intended. Linnea gripped the back of the sofa for support. It really was over between them. "I don't want it back."

He laid the delicate quilt over the rocking chair. "Maybe one day you'll return it to me. When you're free to marry me."

"You'd wait for me?"

"I would wait forever."

Her bottom lip wobbled. "If I could find a way, I'd stay. I'd never leave you. *Never.*"

"I know." It made him angry but he understood. If she could walk away from her mother, who'd just had a stroke, then she wouldn't be the woman he honored above all else.

"I want to make love with you one last time." Desire pounded through his blood, but it wasn't sex he needed.

It was Linnea. He wanted to cling to her one last time. To be a part of her once again. So that throughout the lonely nights to come, he would remember.

"I don't want to risk becoming pregnant, since we won't be getting married." Her bottom lip trembled. So vulnerable. "Once is all it takes. I learned that before."

"I don't want to leave you pregnant. It wouldn't be right."

Love for him burned greater than all the stars in

the sky. Making love to him once wasn't enough. Would never be enough. She craved him like the air she breathed.

How was she going to be all right without him? To never again feel his kiss, his touch or the amazing thrill of him inside her?

"I'll drive you to the depot in the morning." He sounded dead inside, tired and hurting.

She longed to reach out for him, but she was afraid she'd never let go. "It would be best if you didn't. It will only make it harder to get on the train. Uncle Frederick is hiring a wagon for our luggage."

"Then I guess this is goodbye." He kissed her cheek, a brief brush of his lips. "We made love, and I'm going to worry about you. You'll write me if you find out you're pregnant?"

"If I am, I'll let you know." Not that it would change her decision.

It was time to leave him. She wanted to shrug off the responsibilities that tugged at her now and run into Seth's arms.

But a part of her, the sensible part that never wished or yearned, knew the truth. She'd chosen her path long ago, when she'd been young and loved foolishly. Her own choices had led her here, to this path she had to follow.

She had Mama. Nothing could change that. Not even love.

He tipped his hat, always a gentleman, and walked away from her for the last time.

She didn't sleep that night while she lay in the trundle bed next to her mother. But neither did she dream.

* * *

Dawn came quickly and Linnea forced herself out of bed. She washed and changed, shivering in the cool morning air.

"*Dotter,* this is the day." Mama pushed off the covers and sat up. "I cannot wait to get started. I dreamed all night that we missed the train!"

"We have hours yet before we have to be at the depot." Linnea shivered into her clothes. "Let's get you dressed since you're in such a hurry. I know this will make you happy, Mama."

"I thought you and the major might find romance, but I guess I was too eager, pushing you two together." She shrugged her frail shoulders. "Maybe there will be a nice man in Oregon for you to marry. Eva says there is a good man who works in Frederick's office who might be perfect."

"Promise me, no matchmaking." Linnea knelt to unbutton her Mama's nightgown, tucking away her heartache. She helped her mother dress and escorted her to the table.

Aunt Eva was busy in the kitchen and had tea already steeping. Frederick stacked the trunks by the front door, his step echoing in the nearly empty room.

Only the furniture remained, pieces Claire's uncle's family had paid for.

Linnea grabbed the milk pail and headed for the door. There would be one more milking before Claire's family took the livestock, too. One more morning in this place where she'd spent her entire life. This place where she would leave her heart.

She stepped out into the cool morning. A light frost glittered across the blades of grass and the fallen leaves. She closed the door and took two steps.

A splash of color on the worn porch board caught

her eye. Sprigs of bluebonnets, perfect and fragile. Made of cloth and silk. From Mrs. Jance's shop, she guessed.

Seth. She gazed down the road and through the grasses, but he was already gone. She gathered this last token and knew she would treasure it always.

In remembrance of the man who'd loved her.

"Uncle Seth, you're goin' the wrong way." Jamie saw fit to inform him in the middle of town. "I gotta go to the mercantile. I lost my slate stylus and I hafta buy a new one."

The train rumbled at the platform, westbound this morning, spewing a thick river of black smoke into the crisp air. Seth couldn't look away from it. He didn't see Linnea on the platform, so she had to be sitting in one of the cars. Maybe near a window, thinking of him.

He wanted to hop on that train more than anything. But the boy at his side needed him. He couldn't go.

"Uncle Seth! I'm gonna be late."

He snapped the reins, sending General into the traffic on Front Street. A whistle blasted and the train chugged forward on the tracks.

Taking Linnea from him. Taking everything that mattered.

"More rain! I had forgotten how much it can rain here at the end of January." Mama chuckled from her rocking chair in the roomy parlor of their Oregon home, the calico curled up at her feet. "Look, my *flicka*. I have finished your dress. It only took me most of the winter!"

"It took you so long because you can't see. That

you can sew at all is a wonder." Linnea left the quilt
she was finishing as a thank-you gift for Mrs. Jance,
and knelt at her mother's side. "You do fine work,
Mama."

"Do you like it?"

"I love it." The stitches were so fine she could
barely see them. Even the bits of ribbon and lace, the
buttons and the buttonholes were perfect. "I'll wear
it to church on Sunday."

"You put as much work into that dress as I did.
Marking the seams. Cutting for me. Checking my
basting. That was too much work! Now I will make
the sunbonnet to match."

"I will sew if you need it," Aunt Eva volunteered
from the sofa, her knitting needles clacking merrily.
"Linnea, I have invited a young man to Sunday dinner. You might like him."

"Not again."

"This one has good table manners. Or, I think he
does. Well, we can always hope he will not give us
an embarrassing display of his digestive problems
while we are enjoying dessert."

Mama and Aunt Eva burst into endless giggles, like
young schoolgirls. How good it was that they were
together.

Linnea picked up her needle and knelt beside her
quilting frame. Her thoughts wondered to Montana. It
would be snowing. During the day, the prairie would
sparkle beneath a bright winter sun. At night, the
plains would glow black beneath a brooding sky and
the mustangs would race the wind.

Had Seth managed to capture them? Her dreams
turned to him as they always did. As they always
would.

* * *

"Getting used to me, are you, girls?" Seth spoke low and charming to the mustangs that were brave enough to approach the corral fence. He pulled quartered apples from his coat pocket and tossed them through the rails.

The mares snatched the treats from the snow while the rest of the herd whinnied in protest.

"You'll have to come closer if you want a treat," he told the others.

The golden mare he and Linnea had saved from the barbed wire pushed close, demanding more apples with a shake of her head.

"Come closer and I'll give it to you."

The mare wasn't sure about that and held her ground. It was a standoff Seth knew he'd win in time.

He'd captured over half the herd—the thirty-three mares and almost as many colts. It wasn't a bad way to spend his time working with horses on the high Montana plains.

Except his life was nothing without Linnea.

Dusk fell early this time of year, when the winds howled from the north, driving snow. The cold cut through his clothes, chilling him to the bone. He finished forking hay for the horses and broke the ice on their water trough.

He headed for home, the claim shanty behind Ginny's orchard. It looked as cold and lonely as he felt. He kicked off his boots on the front step.

"Seth?" Ginny appeared on the path. "Are you busy?"

"Just finished up with the horses. Come on in while I build up the fire."

He grabbed his boots and walked through the dark

shanty. At the stove, he dropped his boots to warm on the hearthstones and lit a match. Light from the wall lantern filled the room.

"What do you need me to do now?" He knelt in front of the stove and opened the door.

"I just thought you should know I secured a job in town today. I'll be working at the front desk at the Bluebonnet Inn."

"Good for you, Ginny." He hid his surprise the best he could by stuffing wood onto the dying flames.

"I'll be taking Jamie to school from now on since I'll need to start work at eight." She wrapped her arms around her waist, standing in the corner. "You look so sad. You could come have supper with us if you'd like. I made chicken and dumplings for Jamie. I know that's your favorite, too."

"Not tonight." He appreciated the invitation, but nothing could fill the emptiness he felt. It would do no good to try. "I'll have your mare hitched to the sleigh come morning."

"All right." She nodded, lingering. "You miss her."

"I *more* than miss her." He opened the damper and shut the door. "I don't want to talk about her."

"You were going to marry her. You were in love with her."

"I still am." He turned his back and took the coffee mill from the top shelf.

"I've never seen you this sad."

"I'll have your sleigh ready in the morning, Ginny," he said sharply. "Goodbye."

"I kept you two apart. She didn't tell you that, did she?" Ginny came closer, the shame in her words as dark as the shadowed corners where no light shone.

"When I found out that you were serious about her, I threatened her. I told her if she didn't break off with you, I'd tell you about her past. I said you wouldn't want a woman who'd had an illegitimate baby."

"Ginny." He slammed his fist on the table, pain slicing through him. "She had to bury that baby. You don't know how it hurts to hold your lifeless child in your arms. It's a pain that never leaves. Nothing can change it or ease it. What you did to her was cruel."

"As cruel as what I did to you. I hate that you chose her, but she made you happy. I could see that in you, the brother I remember from long ago. I'm sorry, Seth."

He nodded, holding back his anger and he shook with the force of it. "If I knew that at the time, I would have left. I'd have made sure you didn't starve, but I wouldn't have harvested your crop for you."

"I know. That's how I knew Linnea didn't tell you. I said more things that weren't true. She didn't break up my marriage. I only said that because I wanted to be angry at someone."

"Who are you angry with now?"

"Myself. I got a good look at Jamie today when I went to visit Sidney and stopped to watch him play in the schoolyard. His clothes are secondhand and his coat is patched."

"There's nothing wrong with handed-down clothes, Ginny."

"I know, but I could do better for him. His father won't, and that made me realize I'm taking my anger out on everyone and I'm neglecting my child."

"That's what I've been telling you."

"I know." She touched the doorknob, ready to go, then hesitated. "Maybe you'll find someone else to love one day. There are a lot of nice women in this town.''

She meant well, he figured, but she didn't understand. Because she'd never been truly in love, never had her life changed by its beauty.

''They'll be no other woman for me, Ginny. I intend to love Linnea for the rest of my life. Whether she's here or not.''

Ginny opened the door and left him alone.

Chapter Seventeen

Bright spring sunshine tumbled in through the curtained windows of her roomy bedroom, making the room cheery. Linnea folded the supply of winter shawls and sweaters—freshly washed and dried and no longer needed in May.

"Linnea, I have one more." Mama stepped into the room with a shawl in one hand. The pretty blue shawl she'd made with the yarn last spring remained around her shoulders. "This is my favorite, so I shall not be storing it. Let me help."

"I'm here to help you, Mama. Sit and enjoy the sunshine. Heaven knows it's been so long since we've seen it."

Mama laughed. "I loved the prairie, but I missed this place. It was always green and fresh. Eva has invited us for lunch at her house. She spoils us. Let me help."

"No." Mama may have fully recovered from the stroke's effects, but she appeared more frail than ever.

Linnea pulled a chair from the corner and dragged it over to the window. "Sit here and talk with me while I fold these things."

"Nonsense. I shall sit right here and put them away for you. Here, in your trunk?" Mama knelt to lift the lid.

"No!" That was her hope chest, tucked with secrets not even her mother knew. "The trunk is against the wall next to the wardrobe."

The brightness faded from Mama's face. She didn't move. When Linnea stepped closer, she could see what her mother was touching with fingers sensitive enough to know the tiny stitches by feel.

"This is the quilt you sold Mrs. Jance." Mama slipped to her knees, her hands brushing over the cloth appliquéd roses. "I am right. This is the one. What is it doing in your trunk?"

"Mama, let's put the sweaters over here." She grabbed her mother's hand and clasped it gently. "Come help me."

"But *dotter,* let me think. Let me remember what that kind Mrs. Jance said."

"She asked for more quilts that day, remember?" Linnea tried to help her mother to her feet, but the frail woman wouldn't budge. "Mama, leave it alone. Please."

"She said a young man had bought this quilt for his bride. His bride." Mama ran her fingers over the alternating squares of appliquéd flowers and stitched blocks. "Why do you have it? Were you to be the bride? That cannot be. My own *dotter* would tell me if she was to marry."

Linnea didn't know how to answer. "We should put away the sweaters—"

"You did not lie to me!" Mama's eyes filled with tears, her face wreathed in distress. "My own *dotter.*"

"I didn't lie, Mama. I promise."

"You did not tell me the truth. Did the major give this to you?"

"It doesn't matter now. Come sit in the sunshine and I'll read to you until it's time to visit Aunt Eva—"

"Linnea Anna Holmstrom, you will answer your mother." Fierce, she stood, not so frail after all. "You were to marry the major?"

"He did propose to me."

"And you did not tell me?"

"How could I? Aunt Eva came the very next day. I couldn't break your heart."

"So you would break yours." Mama sank onto the bed. "All my life I have dreamed you would find the happiness I shared with your papa. To know the depth of a love that shelters and strengthens. Glad would I give my life so that you would know the greatest of all gifts, and you did not tell me."

"You come first, Mama. Always you."

"No, my sweet girl. You are wrong. What a good *dotter* I have, one who would do this for me. But I cannot allow it." She traced the scalloped stitches along the quilt's edge. "I am well now. You must not stay. You must hurry back to the major and marry him."

"Who will take care of you?" Linnea sat next to her mother and brushed the tears from her cheeks. "Your love has sheltered me my entire life. How could I do less for you?"

"Do you know what you can do? To repay this love you think you owe me? You marry the major and you love him the way your father and I taught you. You cherish him, and make me lots of grand-babies. That is what I truly want.''

''You'll be alone, Mama.''

''I carry your love inside my heart, *dotter*. I will never be alone.''

''I do love him, Mama.'' At last she felt the tears come, hot and aching with all the loneliness of the past months. Winter had come and gone without him.

But she would not let one more season pass without being at his side.

''We will tell Eva,'' Mama announced, beaming with happiness. ''To think this lunch would be a cel-ebration. A goodbye celebration for my *dotter*. She is to be married!''

Married. Linnea knelt and took the ring from the velvet pocket in her trunk. The ring Seth had given her. He'd said he'd wait. That he would love her for-ever.

He was a man of his word. He would be waiting.

Seth leaned his shovel against the fence and snared the water jug from the grass. He uncorked the lid and drank deeply. Cool water slid down his throat. Gen-eral nickered, probably wanting some, too.

Seth cupped one hand to pour water into his palm, but General turned tail and neighed. The stallion saw something. It wasn't unusual to have coyotes hunt in the daylight, especially when there were new foals in the fields.

Seth set the jug aside and scanned the wild grasses undulating in the wind. A movement of blue and gold caught his eye. He blinked, and she was still there.

Linnea. Real and not a dream.

She was carrying his quilt over her arm. The quilt

he'd given back to her. The quilt for their wedding bed.

"Seth!" She flew into his arms as if she belonged there. As if she'd never left. "I knew I'd find you here."

"You're here to stay?"

He kissed her before she could answer. She was sweet silk and warm woman and he buried his face in her hair and breathed deeply. Lilacs. He'd awakened more nights than he could count, still smelling lilacs from his dreams.

"I'm here to marry you." The ring sparkled on her finger and the question lurked in her eyes. "If you still want me."

"I told you I'd wait forever." He kissed her again, joy rising in his heart like daybreak. Then he stilled. If Linnea was here, did that mean Mrs. Holmstrom had passed away? "What happened to your mother?"

"She's probably sitting on the porch with her sister right now, speculating on whether or not she'll have a grandbaby in exactly nine months."

Linnea blushed but her smile was coy. He kissed her again and felt the longing in her kiss. The way she surrendered herself to him as the prairie did to the sky.

"You have to wait to marry me," he told her between breathless kisses. "Seeing as the pastor's out of town. But we can get started on that baby right away."

"I've thought of nothing else but loving you." She buried her face in the hollow of his throat, holding him tight. "I missed you so much. I didn't feel alive without you."

Tender love filled him. He curled his hand around

her nape, holding her to his heart. "You are my greatest love, Linnea. You always will be."

She smiled up at him through her tears. He kissed them away, just as he vowed to do for the rest of her life. She made his heart live. For all the nights he'd dreamed about her, all the days he longed to love her, he couldn't wait. Not one more minute.

He took the quilt still hooked around her arm. "Come with me. I know a private place right over here. We've been there before."

"I remember." She helped him spread out the quilt amid the grasses and wildflowers. She didn't say a word, working quietly, smoothing the wrinkles with her gentle hands.

How could he be this lucky? He plucked a single bluebonnet and brushed it along her face. Slowly, because this was important, this moment. "Let me love you. Really love you."

"This is truly happening. I've done nothing but dream about this moment. I'm never going to leave you."

"Good. Because I'm never going to let you."

Sweet joy filled her. Linnea lay back on the quilt and welcomed Seth into her arms.

Mama was right. Loving a man, and being truly loved by him, was the greatest of gifts.

Epilogue

The prairie winds rustled the pages of the Bible the pastor held and sent the bluebonnets dancing against the hem of her dress, the blue one her mother had worked so hard to make for her.

"You look beautiful," Seth whispered in her ear.

"I've never seen you in a suit. You're so handsome. I'm proud to be marrying you." She looked down at their hands, clasped together. "I'm nervous."

"There's nothing to worry about. The pastor is only going to unite us until death do us part and for better or worse."

"Why does it remind me of a jail sentence?"

"They wrote it that way on purpose to scare couples." Seth leaned his forehead to hers and they smiled together.

"Enough of this," the pastor complained, trying to stand so the sun wasn't in his eyes. "Let us move to the shade of the cottonwoods over there."

"I'm afraid we have to say our vows here. This is a sentimental place," Seth told him, but didn't mention why it was special.

Linnea blushed. She wasn't going to point out what they'd been doing at this exact place only a few hours ago. And many times before that.

"I'd better get the house built quick, because summer's going to be here soon and we're going to get sunburned," Seth quipped.

And so she was laughing as their wedding began, with Seth at her side. Where he'd be for always and forever. The man who had changed her life with his love.

*   *   *   *   *

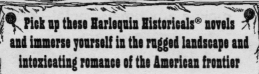

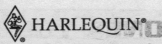

CALL THE ONES YOU LOVE OVER THE HOLIDAYS!

Save $25 off future book purchases when you buy any four Harlequin® or Silhouette® books in October, November and December 2001,

PLUS

receive a phone card good for 15 minutes of long-distance calls to anyone you want in North America!

WHAT AN INCREDIBLE DEAL!

Just fill out this form and attach 4 proofs of purchase (cash register receipts) from October, November and December 2001 books, and Harlequin Books will send you a coupon booklet worth a total savings of $25 off future purchases of Harlequin® and Silhouette® books, AND a 15-minute phone card to call the ones you love, anywhere in North America.

Please send this form, along with your cash register receipts as proofs of purchase, to:
In the USA: Harlequin Books, P.O. Box 9057, Buffalo, NY 14269-9057
In Canada: Harlequin Books, P.O. Box 622, Fort Erie, Ontario L2A 5X3
Cash register receipts must be dated no later than December 31, 2001.
Limit of 1 coupon booklet and phone card per household.
Please allow 4-6 weeks for delivery.

**I accept your offer! Enclosed are 4 proofs of purchase.
Please send me my coupon booklet
and a 15-minute phone card:**

Name: _____

Address: _____ City: _____

State/Prov.: _____ Zip/Postal Code: _____

Account Number (if available): _____

---

097 KJB DAGL
PHQ4013

*H*ugh Blake,
soon to become stepfather to
the Maitland clan, has produced three
high-performing offspring of his own. But
at the rate they're going, they're never going to
make him a grandpa!

There's *Suzanne*, a work-obsessed CEO whose Christmas spirit
could use a little topping up....

And *Thomas*, a lawyer whose ability to hold on to the woman
he loves is evaporating by the minute....

And *Diane*, a teacher so dedicated to her teenage students she
hasn't noticed she's put her own life on hold.

But there's a Christmas wake-up call in store
for the Blake siblings. Love *and* Christmas miracles
are in store for all three!

Maitland Maternity Christmas

A collection from three of Harlequin's favorite authors

Muriel Jensen
Judy Christenberry
&Tina Leonard

Look for it in November 2001.

*Together for the first time
in one Collector's Edition!*

New York Times bestselling authors

Barbara Delinsky

Catherine Coulter   Linda Howard

Forever Yours

**A special trade-size volume containing three
complete novels that showcase the passion,
imagination and stunning power that these
talented authors are famous for.**

Coming to your favorite retail outlet in December 2001.

HARLEQUIN®
Makes any time special®